THE LOVE OF OLD EGYPT

'If you're about to suck me, don't.'

Jeremy came away from Graham's body and leant on one elbow. 'I'm sorry. I didn't mean . . .'

Graham laughed. 'Hey! Hey! I don't mean to hurt your feelings. It's just that, let's face it, the women are good at that sort of thing. I would prefer it, now I have the opportunity, if we did something I can only get from a man. You follow my meaning?'

He didn't wait for an answer, but rolled over on to his front and pulled down his pants.

Dearest Otto,

I thought this would be right up your (back-)street.

Love you lots,

Mom x

Not giving it you would have been snus hurty

x x x

THE LOVE OF OLD EGYPT

Philip Markham

First published in Great Britain in 1999 by
Idol
an imprint of Virgin Publishing Ltd
Thames Wharf Studios,
Rainville Road, London W6 9HT

ISBN 0 352 33354 5

Cover photograph by Colin Clarke Photography

Typeset by SetSystems Ltd, Saffron Walden, Essex
Printed and bound in Great Britain by
Mackays of Chatham PLC

The Terrence Higgins Trust

SAFER SEX GUIDELINES

These books are sexual fantasies – in real life, everyone needs to think about safe sex.

While there have been major advances in the drug treatments for people with HIV and AIDS, there is still no cure for AIDS or a vaccine against HIV. Safe sex is still the only way of being sure of avoiding HIV sexually.

HIV can only be transmitted through blood, come and vaginal fluids (but no other body fluids) passing from one person (with HIV) into another person's bloodstream. It cannot get through healthy, undamaged skin. The only real risk of HIV is through anal sex without a condom – this accounts for almost all HIV transmissions between men.

Being safe
Even if you don't come inside someone, there is still a risk to both partners from blood (tiny cuts in the arse) and pre-come. Using strong condoms and water-based lubricant greatly reduces the risk of HIV. However, condoms can break or slip off, so:
* Make sure that condoms are stored away from hot or damp places.
* Check the expiry date – condoms have a limited life.
* Gently squeeze the air out of the tip.
* Check the condom is put on the right way up and unroll it down the erect cock.
* Use plenty of water-based lubricant (lube), up the arse and on the condom.
* While fucking, check occasionally to see the condom is still in one piece (you could also add more lube).

* When you withdraw, hold the condom tight to your cock as you pull out.
* Never re-use a condom or use the same condom with more than one person.
* If you're not used to condoms you might practise putting them on.
* Sex toys like dildos and plugs are safe. But if you're sharing them use a new condom each time or wash the toys well.

For the safest sex, make sure you use the strongest condoms, such as Durex Ultra Strong, Mates Super Strong, HT Specials and Rubberstuffers packs. Condoms are free in many STD (Sexually Transmitted Disease) clinics (sometimes called GUM clinics) and from many gay bars. It's also essential to use lots of water-based lube such as KY, Wet Stuff, Slik or Liquid Silk. Never use come as a lubricant.

Oral sex
Compared with fucking, sucking someone's cock is far safer. Swallowing come does not necessarily mean that HIV gets absorbed into the bloodstream. While a tiny fraction of cases of HIV infection have been linked to sucking, we know the risk is minimal. But certain factors increase the risk:
* Letting someone come in your mouth
* Throat infections such as gonorrhoea
* If you have cuts, sores or infections in your mouth and throat

So what is safe?
There are so many things you can do which are absolutely safe: wanking each other; rubbing your cocks against one another; kissing, sucking and licking all over the body; rimming – to name but a few.

If you're finding safe sex difficult, call a helpline or speak to someone you feel you can trust for support. The Terrence Higgins Trust Helpline, which is open from noon to 10pm every day, can be reached on 0171 242 1010.

Or, if you're in the United States, you can ring the Center for Disease Control toll free on 1 800 458 5231.

One

———

It is said those who are born during the summer months will always seek the sun. Jeremy Oakland was born on 3 July 1900 and, during his 25 years, not only had sought the sun, but had successfully avoided cold weather of any kind.

During the period in which Europe was torn by war, Jeremy had been in India. As soon as the Armistice was signed, his CO, General Garratt, had retired; Jeremy had resigned his commission as a staff officer and had spent the ensuing years touring sun-drenched places and trying his hardest to become a 'bad lot'. Now he was back in Egypt for his second visit. With the injured leg which had been his means of escaping the carnage of the trenches stretched out before him, he was gazing at the clear sky in utter contentment. He was contemplating how much nicer a male leg looks when it is a rich, brown colour.

It was a leg that was pleasing to look upon. It was maybe a little stiff sometimes, but, as he always joked, 'I have another one which works perfectly.' Both these limbs were dusted in light, curly hair and were shaped to perfection. Jeremy had always avoided exercise of any sort and it was something of a mystery to him how he had come to be blessed with the body

1

of a healthy outdoor type. He was tall – nearly six foot – and, although his preference was for men who were shorter than this, he was quite happy with his height and always managed to be graceful rather than gangly.

He unbuttoned his shirt and let his old friend, the searing Egyptian sun, do its work on his chest. His skin was going just a little red, but he knew this would soon be remedied. By morning, when they had docked and had their first night in Luxor, it would have changed to a lovely golden brown and he would feel quite safe in taking off his shirt by the pool and showing his body. The older guests would think him Bohemian, but he cared for their opinion not a jot.

He had saved the business of getting a tan until now and he had done so quite deliberately. He had a silly notion of being able to boast that his colour had been given to him by the Pharaohs. These Pharaohs were here in Luxor: here they had built their great temples and here they lay waiting for their gods to transport them to the afterlife.

Because of his fanciful idea, during his stay in Cairo, Jeremy had kept himself covered: played the Englishman abroad. Now the *Jewel of the Nile* had reached Luxor, he was going to change his act to that of 'the old colonial'. He was determined to use the two or three words he knew of Arabic as often as possible. He was not going to look like a tourist. He was certainly not going to buy any of the trinkets or ornaments that the other Europeans on the boat would be plagued with as soon as it landed.

He passed his large, strong hands over his skin and rubbed the heat of Egypt into his flesh. The pleasant smell of unguents drifted up to him and he gave a deep, contented sigh. His shirt, which was a dazzling white, was undone completely and he sneaked a satisfying tweak of his left nipple, making his cock stir in his shorts. Soon, very soon, he would be in some café negotiating the price of an hour or so with a beautiful dusky man. Sex was always on offer here if one knew where to go for it. Jeremy had spent his last visit making damn sure he had exactly that information. Most of the young Egyptian men of his age were quite relaxed about indulging in male-to-male lovemaking; they were so much more sensible than their English counterparts.

The west bank of the Nile was now recognisable to him and the line of buildings to the east was also familiar.

The west: where lay those dwelling places of the ancient dead, the Valley of the Kings and the Valley of the Queens. They were now being plundered to fill the rooms of museums in America, France and England. Howard Carter, under the patronage of Lord Carnarvon, had opened the sarcophagus of the boy-king, Tutankhamun, in 1922. Egyptian styles were fashionable throughout the world.

The east: where the ancient city of Thebes had once stood. Here the temples of Karnak and Luxor had been built, thousands of years before. Their architectural brilliance could still be discerned, now they had been rescued from the desert sands. Here also was the present-day city of Luxor with its French-colonial buildings proudly rising over the mud huts and crude brick buildings of the modern inhabitants. The Winter Palace Hotel beckoned the approaching vessel and the crowds of excited locals were already swarming down to the landing stage in front of it.

Jeremy pushed his Panama hat over his eyes and lay back in his deckchair. The other tourists were gathering at the sides of the boat, eager for their first glimpse of this sand-blown, smelly, dusty, delectable place. He was above such exertion. He was feigning boredom: seen all, done all.

This jaded pretence, he supposed, made him enigmatic, and was so much more attractive than if he had emulated other young Englishmen and bounded about the deck as though he'd never been out of Surrey in his life before. To give him some excuse, it has to be said that Jeremy did rather rely on creating an impression of some sort. For, though his clothes were beautifully tailored and his wristwatch was expensive, he had little or no money of his own.

Still, what use money? It was always available to him when he needed it. That's what people like Percy and Mrs Dryden were for.

'Your hair is getting far too long. I don't wonder you want to cover it with that ridiculous hat, but I fail to see why you insist on denying me a view of your face.'

Jeremy poked the offending headgear upward and squinted at the silhouetted figure which blocked his sunlight. 'Do move your parasol, my dear. I can't possibly describe how cold it is when I'm forced into shadow.'

'Naughty boy!' Mrs Dryden scolded. She clicked her fingers to summon one of the deck attendants. The boy brought her a chair and bowed several times, grinning at her, clearly expectant of remuneration.

'He wants baksheesh,' Jeremy murmured. 'Twenty-five piastres will be far too much, but I don't expect he'll protest.'

Mrs Dryden fished in her bag and produced the money with more than a little fuss. She was always complaining that nothing came to hand when one required it and her purse was always the most elusive thing. This had caused Jeremy himself embarrassment on several occasions. Why the woman couldn't be discreet about paying he had no idea. Even when she was surreptitiously (she thought) handing Jeremy cash, she made a song and dance out of it. By the time the notes were in his hand, everybody in the room was well aware he was being looked after by a woman twice his age. He tried not to let this bother him. They probably assumed she was his mother.

Percy was very different and a much better prospect altogether. Had Percy not been stupidly afraid of water and therefore taken the train from Cairo, Jeremy would have had no need of Mrs Dryden and wouldn't have had to invent a recently deceased girlfriend and a sob story about having all his things stolen by a wicked hotel porter.

'My hair used to be black,' she mused. She arranged Jeremy's hat (which was extremely smart and not ridiculous at all) and tucked a wayward lock neatly back under it. 'I suppose yours will never grey. Blond men go bald instead, which is always such a shame.'

'I'm twenty-five!' Jeremy protested. 'I don't want to contemplate being in my dotage until I absolutely have to.'

'That is indeed what you must think of me,' she affirmed sadly. 'And I suppose you're correct. Anyway, at least your looks are the sort that will last. You're so smooth and symmetrical and those eyes . . . Blue eyes will still twinkle when you're sixty. Whereas mine . . .' She shuddered. 'Piggy little pale pins in the middle of a saggy cushion of a face!'

This was intended to provoke a denial of its being the truth, but it *was* the truth and Jeremy hadn't the energy to bother to lie about it. He smiled weakly and she immediately began communicating her frustration by gabbling self-deprecating nonsense.

'I can understand why a young thing like you should find me dull. I am *so* dull! I thank the good Lord I've been given this small opportunity to travel now. Before my husband died, the only country of which I had any knowledge, apart from England, was America – and America is so vulgar, don't you think? Make the most of your youth, Jeremy my dear. One grows old so quickly, so quickly . . .'

He'd heard it all before and didn't grace her speech with a response of any kind. Thwarted in her quest for sympathy or compliments, she resorted to flirtatious simpering.

Jeremy was canny enough not to allow his patron any indulgences. He excused himself and took his lithe young body away from her possessive gaze.

Jeremy's actions were often dictated by his libido and now was such an instance. He had a hard-on and he was not the type to ignore it until it subsided of its own accord.

His cabin was small, but comfortable enough and cool. He

flopped on to his bed and searched through his mind for a suitably sexual scenario to drift into as a prelude. He wanted to make the most of the pleasant yearnings which were building in his breast.

He had about five minutes before the boat docked and, as nearly everybody was up on deck, he could assume he wouldn't be disturbed. He didn't bother to lock the door.

Egypt: was he the only person aboard who appreciated it for what it really was? What use wandering around the treasures of the past when the past was not alive to you? When Jeremy looked upon a statue, he could see the man, not a block of stone.

During his last visit to Luxor, he had wandered around the temples with a group of twittering women and a couple of old professors. They had gaped and gawped, as they were no doubt supposed to, but Jeremy had been transported back over the centuries. He had been taken back to when those brown pillars had been vibrant with colour, and small, perfectly formed, olive-skinned men had walked beneath them.

There was a framed papyrus on the wall of his cabin. In it, Tuthmosis the Third stood triumphant over the captive enemy. They crawled beneath him in chains and he accepted the praise of his subjects and the blessings of his gods.

Jeremy closed his eyes and let the image take substance. The flat profile of the Pharaoh bulged into life. His tiny waist gained the extra few inches it needed to make it real, but his torso retained its impressive shape. The man was a compact parcel of muscle and power. His face was almost girlish: straight nose; full lips; haunting, slightly slanted, eyes. His chest glistened with sweat and exotic oils, rising and falling as he breathed; at the same time, his stomach tightened. This took Jeremy's mind's eye down, beyond that flat abdominal beauty, to the Pharaoh's loins, which were wound about with luscious material. Over his genitals was a richly decorated flap of sparkling gold and blue. It drew the eyes of onlookers to the place where his cock lay hidden from view.

Then prisoners came into Jeremy's picture. They were scantily clad, in loincloths, and were weighed down with heavy chains. Jeremy took time to look at the cumbersome metal encircling their strong wrists and ankles. He felt the same iron restricting his own limbs. He pictured himself with nothing but a piece of rough cloth to cover his nakedness, and the exquisite bite of the lash on his back as he was forced to worship before the conquering hero.

He was chained to a line of men now. They had been forced to crawl across the cool flags of some great palace. Tomorrow they would be sold as slaves and, unlike his fellow captives, Jeremy was glad of it. Here, in his secret Egypt of long ago, the men of Thebes used their prisoners as whores. He would be taken away and shaved of his body hair – totally. Then he would be painted in gold from head to foot. He would be transformed into a living sculpture: his chest, his legs, his buttocks, even his cock, would be gilded. His face would be given a mythical quality under its mask of make-up. His masters would want their slave to be a thing, not a man.

He broke out of his daydream long enough to tear his modern clothing from his body. He threw it on the floor of his cabin in a heap. Then he reclined once more and let his hand wander very gently over his twitching shaft. He was uncircumcised and a light pull on his foreskin exposed the sensitive head of his cock. He spat on his finger and smoothed the saliva over the throbbing bulb as he drifted back into his imagination.

The slaves were being paraded in the centre of Thebes. Those who were manacled nearest to him were people he knew. His best friend from home was on his right. No longer the champion of the village cricket team, he was now all the more manly for having been stripped, shaved of his dark-brown hair, decorated and chained. He hung his head in shame. Probably, Jeremy considered, he will be bought by some nobleman's bored wife and made to service her before being fucked by their handsome son.

On his other side was a man whom Jeremy had known in India during the war. He was a suave, upper-class officer from Kent, but now, as he had done before, Jeremy could mentally strip him of his dignity and his clothes. He had been muzzled as an extra punishment. His face was raining bitter tears of self-pity. His strong, square jaw was encased in leather straps. The bit he was forced to hold between his teeth lowered him to the status of a human horse. He would be bought by a landowner who would yolk him to a plough and make him pull through the soil all day before taking him back to his bed in the evening.

Jeremy knew who his own master would be: he was there in the crowd in front of them. He had already come close and taken Jeremy's cock in his hand to test the length and weight of it. He had seemed pleased and had already handed over a purse of money to the slavetrader. He was younger than Jeremy: maybe about 22. He had great wealth and kept a large household where orgies went on every night of the week. His slaves were kept in large cages where guests could come and take their pick of which they wanted to fuck. When one had been chosen, that slave would be made to walk in front of the guest who had favoured him. His head would be bowed and any slight stumbling would be rewarded with a strap across his naked buttocks.

The great hall of his master's house, now lit by flaming torches, was a mass of handsome men. On this occasion, the master had decided to have Jeremy to himself while others looked on. Jeremy couldn't understand what they called out, for their language was not his own. He knew enough from their tones to know his physical attributes were being assessed.

Two servants took him and laid him down on a low bed in the middle of the hall. His manacled hands were forcibly stretched above his head and the links of his fetters were fastened to a metal loop in the floor. Then cushions were placed under the small of his back so his arse was raised to the required height. Each man took hold of one of his ankles and spread his legs wide, holding them up to give maximum exposure to his sphincter.

His master then whipped away the clothing that Jeremy's mind's eye had given himself. He knelt close to Jeremy, in between his legs. His master's cock was small and nearly hairless, with just a tight bush of black pubes, shaved to a perfect triangle over the organ. His abdomen was tight and rippled with every intake of breath. His shoulders and arms were where his years of physical combat displayed their effect. He had very short, black hair on his dome-shaped head. It came to a widow's peak on his wide forehead. The shape it created was mirrored by his arched brows, under which were hooded, mysterious eyes; a long, thin nose and the same full lips he had seen on the Pharaoh.

The master gave some command to the two servants, who pulled Jeremy's legs still further apart. Men around them were now fondling each other, but absent-mindedly, for they were saving themselves for the show that was about to be given them.

The penetration was easy enough for Jeremy to take. It went in in one short stab and the pain was over in a moment. Then Jeremy's master stretched himself full length over his slave and, supporting himself on his strong arms each side of Jeremy's body, he fucked him brutally.

All this while, Jeremy's cock had continued to be gently stimulated to keep it hard. He had not been aware of it before, but there was another young man kneeling by the side of them and it was evidently his task to masturbate the slave while he was being fucked. The intrusive hand felt like a hard ball in between the colliding bellies, but he was skilled at his job. A combination of squeezes and pulls was having its effect. Jeremy allowed the twin sensations, one deep inside him and the other at the most external point of his body, to carry him to bliss. What had been a glow around his cock-head became a fire, and then a fire that could not possibly burn any longer. His penis spewed its juice over his belly and splattered it on to his master's chest. At the same time, he was aware of the corresponding eruption filling his bowels.

And so the scene faded from his mind and he was back in the cabin. He felt the boat begin to turn towards the landing stage. He looked at his hand: it was covered in spunk. As he always did, he licked some of it from his fingers and wiped the rest on a towel. Maybe one day he would meet a man who would be willing to indulge this fantasy. Yes, it was an impractical one: it necessitated being shaved for a start. That would mean hiding away until his hair grew back again, but it would be worth it. Being put in chains was perhaps not so difficult, but how on earth do you suggest this to a man you're about to bed? He'd never before met anybody who found it stimulating, but maybe, like him, they just never mentioned it for fear of being thought perverted.

Perhaps he might get Khalid to do it to him. Khalid never seemed to be worried about anything sexual. He was quite happy to screw men or women – but he preferred men. They had met last time Jeremy was in Luxor. Jeremy had walked past Khalid five or six times before summoning up the courage to speak to him. Khalid had made it more and more obvious that he would be glad of Jeremy's company. His white teeth had flashed in a beaming smile every time Jeremy had looked at him, and his coal-black eyes had spoken volumes.

Then, Jeremy had been new to this country and had not dared speak to any of the native people for fear of being robbed or assaulted. He was aware of the English being very popular in Egypt, but xenophobia was ingrained into every white man's brain and he was convinced no Arab could be his friend.

Then Khalid had taken the initiative and told Jeremy that his cousin had a felucca in which perhaps Jeremy might like a sunset trip to the west bank and back? It would be very cheap. Jeremy's stay in Luxor could not possibly be called complete until he'd sailed over the waters of the Nile in one of these swanlike craft with their billowing white sails.

The cousin had vacated the boat as soon as Khalid arrived. It seemed there was an agreement made: Khalid had found the customer so therefore Khalid was to be his guide. The Arabs were like this: everything was shared and one man could provide a European friend with taxis, boats, carriages, camels – anything – but there was always a cousin who happened to own what was asked for.

Once he had negotiated the plank that served as a means of boarding, Jeremy was settled down in pride of place on a cushioned bench at the side of the boat. Khalid (and a host of other people who had appeared as if from nowhere) had launched *Evening Mist*. One of the teenagers who had helped in pushing the boat out on to the river jumped in and, with precocious skill, began the business of adjusting the sail.

On this occasion however, Khalid wanted to sail the boat by himself and a heated argument followed. Both seemed unnecessarily outraged by the other's stubborn refusal to compromise and Jeremy had been on the point of intervening when the offending boy jumped into the shallow water and, with one last curse, half-swam, half-waded back to the bank. Khalid grinned and the face that so shortly before had been screwed in anger was suddenly open and quite lovely.

His skin was young enough not to have been affected by the harsh climate. It was smooth, dark, chocolate brown. His body was curved and almost plump. That is not to say he carried any excess weight; he didn't. Rather, all his amorphous parts appeared to have been cushioned underneath to give a perfect, rounded quality to the bulges of his cheeks, his arms, his chest. He had little body hair: the merest suggestion on his chest and a satisfying sprouting under his arms.

Despite the agreeable sight the rest of him presented, his greatest feature had to be his face. True, Jeremy was to find out how it could fall into a very effective pout when he decided to

11

sulk. (It was something Khalid was very good at indeed.) Or, as he had just witnessed, how it could be transformed by sudden rages which would flare and then vanish as suddenly and as completely as an extinguished flame. But when he was serene (as he seemed to be for a far greater proportion of his waking day than he had reason to be, given the stresses of his life) he was like a dark god. Jeremy was always put in mind of an Arab prince who had lost his kingdom but retained his wisdom and dignity amid the hardships he then had to endure. Dark, flashing, amused eyes; the open quality of youth, with the burgeoning form of the man apparent in his bone structure and his sturdy neck; exquisitely shaped brows and a snub button of a nose. (Jeremy had made fun of his nose and Khalid had immediately sulked until he was quite persuaded that Europeans found such things attractive and not childish.)

He would produce his lightning smile readily and easily and everything about him would appear to be ridiculously pleased with the slightest thing: a flower, a sunset, a friend on the street. Khalid was truly animated in everything he did. His whole body would display the mood he was in. When he was happy he would be unable to resist jigging about from foot to foot and giving Jeremy an involuntary hug or a squeeze. When he was cross, he would wave his arms like windmills and shake his fist at the object of his anger. When he was asleep, everything would completely relax as though he had been drained of energy and he would never be able to bring rigidity to his body ever again.

Some of this had been apparent to Jeremy on that first meeting, for Khalid was not difficult to get to know well. He hid nothing of his personality from anybody and cared nothing for Jeremy's English reserve.

'I make tea,' he said proudly.

Jeremy had been told not to drink the water unless it had been boiled ferociously at least twice. He tried to politely decline the offer until he discovered to do so would offend greatly.

12

'I'm not used to drinking Egyptian water,' he said. 'It will make me ill – sick.'

Khalid waved this objection away and began the preparations. He had a small oil-lamp and had already placed a tiny pan upon a wire frame over the top of it.

This done, he pulled on a few ropes, set the sail to the required position, tied it off and sat himself down far too close to Jeremy for there to be any mistaking his intention.

'You like Egyptian banana?' he asked suggestively.

Jeremy pretended not to understand.

'I've never had one,' he replied. 'Are they nice?'

Khalid threw back his head and guffawed as though this was the most witty thing he'd heard in ages. Then his face fell back to the serious look he had adopted before. He placed his hand on Jeremy's knee, rubbing the flannel of his trousers up and down firmly against the skin underneath. Jeremy gave a nervous smile and placed his own hand on top of Khalid's to check the movement before it went further.

'OK, OK,' Khalid said, nodding vehemently. 'I understand. You want me for free. You my friend. We talk price later.'

Jeremy had a twinge of fear. He had, after all, been foolish enough to allow himself to be alone with this man, in a boat, in the middle of the River Nile. No one would know if he were thrown overboard or stabbed and dumped somewhere on the west bank. He tried to be reassured, telling himself this was a truly ridiculous thought. Khalid must have read what was in his mind.

'You safe here with me. Felucca very safe vessel. We don't sink. We float and watch the sun go down. We drink tea.'

This last was said in response to the water beginning to boil. In one leap, Khalid was at the other end of the boat and very soon produced two cups of black liquid which, to Jeremy's surprise, tasted sweet and rather pleasant.

'You will not have "pharaohs' revenge"', Khalid assured him. 'Quite safe.'

13

Jeremy was familiar with the euphemism and with the condition, having suffered terrible stomach cramps after eating a badly washed salad a few days before. He smiled and nodded. Khalid seemed content for the moment to sip his tea and smile every once in a while. Jeremy produced his cigarettes and offered one. This was readily accepted. (In fact, Khalid took three, sticking the other two behind his ears.) Khalid drained his cup of tea and placed his hand where it had been before. He was studying Jeremy's face for any reaction and seemed disappointed that it remained impassive.

His face might not have betrayed any response, but Jeremy's cock was growing hard and he was thinking how he might shift his position so this wasn't quite so obvious. He was still nervous and, though part of his mind was telling him to give in to this attention and see where it might lead, another part was telling him to be careful of his safety and not to do anything so stupid.

At that point he had been in Egypt precisely three days, and had not till then left the hotel alone. Percy, who had come with him from Alexandria, where they had first met, was waiting for him back at the hotel and had warned him against going anywhere with the natives. According to the older man, they were all out for money and not to be trusted on any account.

Somehow, when he looked into Khalid's expectant face, he knew what Percy had told him was not true. Khalid was presumably not averse to being paid for all this, but he appeared to be just as interested in physical pleasure as was Jeremy.

Khalid took the cup from Jeremy and placed it on the floor. Then he took Jeremy's hand and put it on his own thigh, moving it in a stroking motion so as to indicate what he wanted. Jeremy gave Khalid's leg a pathetic and rather patronising little pat and returned his hand to his own lap. Khalid looked hurt.

'You don't like me? I think you did.'

'Yes, I like you very much. It's just rather open here. Somebody might see what we're doing.'

This too was treated as a huge joke. Jeremy had to admit it

was blatantly not true. There was no other boat within sight of them and they were by now right in the middle of the river, far away from the intrusive gaze of anybody on the eastern bank.

'I mean it,' he protested. 'I mustn't get into trouble – and I don't want you to either.'

'OK, OK,' said Khalid. 'We don't do anything here. Here there are too many people to watch.'

The sarcasm was not lost on Jeremy and it soon became clear that Khalid had not given up on the idea of sex. He changed the sweep of the sail and sat himself by the rudder, guiding the felucca further west, towards a deserted part of the bank where palm trees shaded reedlike plants which stretched out into the river where the water was shallow.

Within five minutes or so, Jeremy was able to see the riverbed and make out fish swimming lazily about. Strange birds swept down from the sky and called to each other before swooping down further and floating close to the boat.

'Birds don't mind what we do,' Khalid explained wickedly. 'They seen this before and they pretend not notice.'

The boat came into ground and bobbed about among the reeds. They were quite hidden – unless, as Jeremy's paranoia suggested to him, there were police officers on the far bank with trained telescopes to find them out.

Khalid knelt in front of him and gently undid his flannels. Jeremy's underwear was more difficult to negotiate, but Khalid managed it expertly without making the action seem crude or awkward.

'Banana time!' Khalid said, pleased at the sight of Jeremy's erection, which undoubtedly spoke for itself. He took his head down to Jeremy's penis and enveloped it in his lovely mouth. Jeremy lay back against the side of the boat and looked up at the sky, which was now a deep red. Apart from the sounds of nature and the far-distant noise of the city, there was silence around them. Khalid brought his hand into play and gently massaged Jeremy's cock while he licked and sucked on it. Jeremy felt the cool breeze around his genitals and the enveloping warmth of Khalid's mouth. The stimulation was elusive, now rising and causing his body to tense, now vanishing, leaving only the physical pleasure of wet warmth around his cock. Khalid let go of him and stripped himself of his jellaba.

This being the first time Jeremy had seen his body, Khalid took some time to show it off proudly. Khalid knew himself to be handsome and he evidently knew he was appreciated as such by this uptight Englishman. He was wearing snow-white trunks under which was a promising bulge. He slowly moved until he was standing in between Jeremy's open legs. Whereupon he pushed his groin forward to make his penis accessible to Jeremy's mouth.

Jeremy didn't want to take off Khalid's underwear just yet. It looked incredibly beautiful, accentuating the power of the man's chest and legs with its tightness. He kissed the material, a mere pressing of his lips against it at first, then with his mouth open, leaving a wet patch were he had made contact. Khalid was impatient. He took Jeremy's head in both of his hands and brought it firmly on to himself. Jeremy responded, using his tongue, gently biting around the encased monster with his teeth. He slid off the bench and knelt, fisting his own penis as he worked on Khalid's.

Khalid pulled his underpants down with one hand, keeping his grip on the back of Jeremy's head to prevent him pulling away. The cotton grazed against Jeremy's face, giving way to hot, musky skin. Jeremy pressed his nose into the tight, black curls which surrounded Khalid's dick and tried to get his lips round the back of the base of his organ, forcing it downward so a strand of Khalid's pre-come attached itself to his chin. He licked along its length: along the back, on to the knob. His tongue probed into the tiny slit. He drew back for air and Khalid's penis, released temporarily, bobbed back against his belly. Khalid grinned and knelt also. He brought his face close to Jeremy's and, hesitatingly, offered his lips to be kissed.

Then they abandoned the foreplay, for both of them needed release. They plunged their tongues into each other's mouth while attending to their own cocks with rapid friction of their fists. Urgent grunts from Jeremy showed his climax was about to happen. Khalid increased his own speed and was soon making the same sounds in perfect unison with Jeremy. They sighed deeply – together – and pulled apart.

Hitherto, Jeremy had always found the aftermath of love-making rather distasteful. Towels had to be produced, sometimes the other man had to bring himself off and took longer about it than Jeremy was prepared to indulge him for. Not so that time: Khalid grinned again and took Jeremy's sticky hand.

'We swim,' he announced.

Not stopping to worry about the propriety of diving into the River Nile, Jeremy allowed himself to be stripped of his shirt, sandals and the rest and jumped into the wonderfully cool water.

They splashed about like two children for well over half an hour. Back on the boat, having allowed the breeze to dry their bodies, they dressed and kissed once more.

The moon was now full in the sky. It had arrived within only twenty minutes of the red glow which heralded it. The city was a blaze of lights. Jeremy had had his first taste of what Egypt had to offer.

That same bank was now before them. It loomed close as the *Jewel of the Nile* prepared to dock. The eager chatter and shouts of pedlars and guides, calash drivers, and excited children reached the ears of the travellers. All these locals were gathered around the landing stage hoping for business from the wealthy Europeans which the cruiser was bringing to them.

The Winter Palace Hotel stood resplendent on the dusty road behind the landing stage. Red carpets lined the symmetrically curved steps which swept up to the grand entrance, one floor up from the ground level. Its pillars and porticos set it apart from the grubby vitality of the city around it. To the left of the building, some few hundred yards down the road, lay the temple of Luxor, dedicated to the glory of the god Amon. It was broken and sun-blistered, but still wonderfully evocative of the world of Jeremy's long-dead pharaohs.

Behind it lay the bazaar where all the traders seemed to be selling the same sort of ornaments to gullible tourists. Visitors strolled about, some of them wearing their souvenirs, which were incongruous with their western clothes and their light skin: an American wearing a jellaba (much to the amusement of the children who followed him asking for baksheesh); a French woman about whose head some tradesman had expertly wound a turban; a young man struggling with a hookah which every two minutes his chattering wife told him was too expensive – she would have arranged the purchase for only half the price had it been left to her.

Up and down the road went the horse-drawn calashes, many of them empty of passengers. They trotted on their dusty way, always on the lookout for trade, even when occupied. The smell of horse manure and camel dung pervaded the air. Strangely, this smell was not unpleasant to Jeremy, though some of his fellow passengers were already holding handkerchiefs to their noses to block it out.

Jeremy pushed through the throng until he was standing next to Mrs Dryden. Needless to say, she was one of the ones who found the entire experience somewhat intimidating.

'How on earth is one to get through all those people? They look like they're ready to eat us alive. I hope we can find a respectable-looking porter from the hotel. At least it's close enough to escape into before we're kidnapped and spirited away into the desert.'

'The desert is on the other bank,' Jeremy said. 'They'd have to spirit you away to the cattle market. That's just behind the town.'

'Wicked youth.' She smiled. 'I keep forgetting you've been here before. I'm so looking forward to being shown around.

You say your friend is here already? I presume he's waiting for you? I hope you'll introduce us.'

This was not part of Jeremy's plan. He didn't quite know how he would keep Percy and Mrs Dryden separate, but he appreciated he would be wise to attempt it. Years before, when he'd first visited this country, he'd managed to attach himself to Percy. Then he'd used a slightly different story from the one he'd told Mrs Dryden. (He'd told the truth, in fact.) This time, hard up and finding himself in that lady's company, he'd thought he'd been astute in recognising the need for a more romantic ploy which would appeal to the female heart. Now he wished he'd been consistent. It would have made life so much easier. He should have known his two sponsors were bound to meet.

Of course he could resort to being disarmingly honest with the old lady and admit to having no money of his own and that he was simply trading off his good-looks. Neither she nor Percy had any claim on his affections. He was simply a companion: a handsome blond Englishman they could wear on their arm when they walked into the restaurant in the evening. Such transactions were entirely respectable. Had he been a frumpy spinster, nobody would have thought twice about his living off the lady; had he been a middle-aged secretary with a bald head and three chins, the gentleman needn't have worried about gossip either.

'We'll get you settled in the hotel easily enough,' he told Mrs Dryden. 'My friend suffers from appalling shyness, so you must excuse me if I keep him to myself for a few days at least. I have to prepare him for you.'

'He sounds most intriguing,' she cooed. 'You say he's my age. Perhaps you might play Cupid for us.'

Jeremy smiled. He was thinking, If only she knew, but she took this to be an affirmative answer to her proposal. He left her with her fantasies and went up to the other deck, where, he explained, he could see things better.

★

'I'm terribly sorry.'

Jeremy removed his foot from the other man's shoe and shifted to allow him space at the rail.

The cruiser was beginning to disgorge its passengers down below, but some were taking their time to view Luxor before disembarking. Jeremy had seen Mrs Dryden disappear to her cabin for one last check around before leaving the boat. He had about ten minutes.

The man to whom the shoe belonged smiled at him, and he smiled back.

'You're with that nice old lady, aren't you?' the man said. 'My fiancée and I were talking to her at dinner some time ago. She says you're a seasoned traveller.'

'I've been here before,' Jeremy answered. 'I really love this place. Is this your first time?'

Jeremy had a safety valve when it came to good-looking males. He was able to put aside any burgeoning attraction he felt for them. He might use them to populate his dreams, but he never bothered to run after the unobtainable. The word 'fiancée' had therefore put this man outside his remit and he took only a passing interest in his exterior charms.

But there was something about him that was instantly likeable. He had an educated voice which was deep enough to thrill and casual enough not to sound off-putting. He had a ready smile and a boyish, sporty relaxation about his movements which at least stopped him from being a stuffed shirt or a twit, as so many other British men had turned out to be.

'I'm Graham Etherington,' he volunteered. 'You're Oakland, I know.'

He smiled again and Jeremy became aware that his green eyes were speckled with flecks of brown. This was most becoming against his black curly hair and bronzed skin. He wore a light-blue blazer and a white shirt with a cravat. Jeremy found himself wondering, fleetingly, if the material round his neck covered that tantalising tuft of chest hair which so often made him want

20

to see such men without their shirts. Graham's flannels were immaculately creased and everything about him said 'money'. Jeremy's imagination immediately placed him on a cricket field: he would be the one who scored all the runs and, afterwards, charmed all the old ladies in the pavilion.

It was no good. Graham was so evidently heterosexual there was really no point in bothering. In fact, his all-round maleness was an integral part of what was attractive about him. He was the sort one had a crush on at school. I bet his fiancée is a pretty little flighty thing with a whining voice, thought Jeremy.

'I expect we'd better attend to the ladies,' Jeremy said. 'I suppose yours is easier to deal with than mine.'

'Hey! Hey!' Graham scolded jokingly. 'You make them sound like excess baggage. I'll have you know, Maria can quite well attend to herself. She's a darned sight better at this travelling thing than I'll ever be.'

'That might be true for Maria. I have Mrs Dryden to contend with and she's quite sure that a dark skin and broken English are the marks of the latent cannibal.'

Graham laughed. He clapped Jeremy on the back and, with his arm around the other's shoulder, accompanied him down below to join the queue.

Percy had left a message for Jeremy, telling him that he was out sightseeing and they should meet that evening in the bar of the hotel. When the time came, Mrs Dryden was safely ensconced in her room with her headache, pills for the same and a romantic novel that she had been reading ever since Cairo and that, she claimed, was unspeakably vulgar.

Percy hadn't yet arrived, but Graham was there again, this time with Maria in tow. He waved cheerily across the bar and indicated a vacant armchair. Jeremy went over to join them.

'So you're the famous Jeremy Oakland,' Maria said in greeting. 'I've been dying to meet you. Graham says you're amusing.'

21

'Am I? Perhaps I am. But I need at least a double G and T before I can perform. It's deserved and I mean to have it.'

This was apparently proof enough that what Graham had said was the truth. Maria clicked her fingers to summon the waiter. She ordered the drinks using what sounded like flawless Arabic. Then she settled herself back into the armchair as though what she had just achieved was only what the others would have done had they been quick enough. Jeremy was impressed but tried not to show it.

She was not flighty and she did not have a whiny voice. She was small, elegant and sparkling. It was entirely evident that she would be a dangerous person to be on the wrong side of, and she treated Graham as though he were a pet dog. Every so often she would pat him on the knee or frown at him severely when he said something of which she disapproved. He responded obediently to her every nuance. She was quite happy to admit that she had him under her thumb.

'Men should be trained,' she declared. 'Otherwise they just go off and be naughty boys all over the place. I think it's good for them to know where they stand and how far they can go.'

'Does that include me?' Jeremy asked. 'I'm a man.'

'Yes, it includes you,' she replied.

She looked at him over her glass and gave him a meaningful smile. 'I know you,' that smile seemed to say. 'You're a rival for the attentions of my future husband. I accept the challenge and I mean to win.'

Two

To Percy Gilbert, the very smell of this country suggested sex. He had been here on several occasions before and had each time been gratified to find there were plenty of agreeable young men who, far from seeing his (very slightly overweight) frame as a problem, actually preferred the amorous advances of older men.

Egypt had become a familiar place to him over the years. He had made friends in Luxor and in Cairo and now was just as much at home here as he might have been in Hammersmith. He had one special friend: Ahmed, who drove a calash for a living (the same one in which Percy was travelling now, in fact). Ahmed was thirty-something and extremely jealous of his position as an Englishman's favourite. He was quite aware of the interest the other drivers showed in his friend. In fact, each time Percy visited, a whole litany of does and don'ts had to be gone through to reassure Ahmed of his claim on Percy's time.

'Always, you ask for my carriage. The others only want you for money. They don't love you. I love you. You ask for Ahmed. You no speak to guide unless you talk with me. They are bad people. They, too, want your money.'

23

And so on: What cafés were frequented by these predatory monsters. What translators were friendly to Ahmed and therefore to be trusted. What shops were owned by wicked money-grubbers selling nothing but rubbish and which had quality goods. Where one could eat without being poisoned. Percy always assured him he would do nothing that hadn't been sanctioned, and, in any case, he was quite happy to spend most of his time in Ahmed's company and eschew all other charmers.

Percy knew he would not be disappointed in any way by narrowing his field down. After they had driven round for the requisite amount of time to satisfy Ahmed's sense of propriety, they would always, as now, take a turn off the main road, eventually pulling up in some dingy Egyptian hotel where the manager, surprisingly, always turned out to be a cousin of Ahmed's. Once inside, Percy would remove his hat and casually let it hover over the enormous bulge in his trousers.

He still found sex to be far more palatable when it was not talked about too much beforehand. On this occasion, the manager of the hotel, with his broken teeth and suggestive smile, must have known what they were about, but he refrained from letting on. They had been to this establishment before, many times. The hotelier knew Ahmed would never have brought Percy unless it was to be fucked, but he knew nothing of this must be spoken lest Percy accuse him of being sordid.

Up the dark staircase – the walls with their blistered light-blue paint and gaudy pictures purloined from magazines. A small windchime above them on this floor; on the stairs leading to the next, a young boy with a dirty ball. Up then to the very top room, where their business together would not be disturbed and they might stay all night should they wish it.

'You like some tea?'

Percy fanned himself with his straw hat. He wasn't bothering to cover his erection now for they were alone. He knew Ahmed would not be so vulgar as to refer to it before the polite preliminaries were done.

'Oh, gin, gin!' Percy said. 'It must be about time for it. We seem to have been all over the town and back again.'

Ahmed looked offended. 'You don't like our ride together?'

Percy smiled at him and the smile was immediately returned with a beam which lit up the whole room. Ahmed was incredibly good-looking, he thought. There was a degree of subjectivity in Percy's assessment of his friend's looks. He had once noticed how Ahmed's nose was slightly crooked where it had been broken in a fight when he was a child. He had confessed to another friend that Ahmed had a gap in his teeth, but he had *not* confessed that he found that particular imperfection to be enormously attractive. He saw the rough, heavy hands and the unshaven chin; he saw the crooked nose and the dental gap and he found it all irresistible.

Ahmed had wonderful eyes. (Percy had to admit that most of Ahmed's countrymen could boast of similar.) Ahmed was a working man with a thick frame and strong arms, but he was capable of being so gentle and caring. The combination of these two opposites was Percy's idea of heaven.

When he had passed the age of fifty, three years ago now, Percy had assumed any chance of meaningful relationships with other men was now over. He had contented himself with befriending attractive, idle 'young things' whose love life he could dip into vicariously and whose problems – usually of a financial nature – were sufficient to mean Percy's presence would always be required.

Which is not to say he was a man who could be easily used. He was quite aware of the nature of the arrangements he entered into. Even if they were not spoken of, they were understood by both parties. The young man required to be witty and charming and make a fuss of him; Percy was required to pay the bill. It worked out very well.

He had expected a variation on this scenario with Ahmed – at first.

'It is hot,' Ahmed said. 'I take off my clothes.'

Suiting action to word, he stripped off his dusty gown and hung it on a peg behind the door. He stood just a little too close to Percy and let the older man's eyes wander over his dark skin. Percy ventured to touch Ahmed's stomach, like a person who, upon being presented with a WET PAINT notice, cannot resist checking to see.

The light brush of his friend's hand was not enough for Ahmed. He grabbed Percy's wrist before it had a chance to withdraw properly and he held it hard against his stomach. Percy began to fluster. He was still not used to this sort of thing. In his dreams he was always a voyeur, watching two younger men making love and not taking any part in it himself. He was aware this might be because, before his meeting Ahmed, nature had denied him the wherewithal to find a partner and this fantasy was his way of compensating for it.

Or it might be that he found such a thing appealing and there was nothing wrong in it. He had only once dared to suggest a voyeuristic fantasy to Ahmed. His lover hadn't seemed very keen at the time but, since then, he had referred to the proposal slyly on more than one occasion. Percy had been nonchalant about it – it was up to Ahmed – but he continued to hope. Ahmed liked to think of himself as Percy's only lover. Percy had at least explained about meeting Jeremy and this, surprisingly, had gone down reasonably well, though Ahmed needed some little persuading that the two of them weren't sleeping together.

'I lie down now,' he said. 'You must have drink and then come and lie with me. We then make love.'

Percy mopped his face with his handkerchief and suddenly became very coy.

'Really, my dear,' he said. 'We don't have to have a schedule. Just let things happen naturally.'

He poured himself a drink from the bottle on the table next to him and sat back in his chair. He allowed himself a good hard stare at Ahmed's near-naked body. Ahmed, used to this, managed to shift himself until he was in a satisfactorily suggestive pose. He brought one of his hands down to his own stomach and pushed three fingers into the band of his underpants. Like a lot of the Arabs, he wore white cotton which gleamed against his brown skin as though it were a source of light itself.

'You like to see me without these?' He pulled at the cloth and his penis moved discernibly within it. Percy swallowed the gin in two mouthfuls and nodded slowly.

'You take them off my body. It is your task.'

He bounced on to his back and lay there happily waiting. Percy took some time to get up, for his joints were stiff.

'I'm getting far too old for this.'

Ahmed gave him a playful punch.

'I like old men. I don't have young people. They are too . . . I don't know English word, but they are too much of it.'

'Flighty?' suggested Percy. He was now kneeling down by Ahmed's bed.

Ahmed looked puzzled. 'Flighty?' he said. Then the light dawned: 'Ah! You mean like a bird?'

The adjective amused him and he declared he would make a point of bringing it into the conversations he had with his customers to test it out.

Percy laughed with him. It was so nice just to spend time with someone who treated him as an equal and didn't mind the fact that he had no hair on top and was inclined to go bright red as soon as he was exposed to the sun. What if Ahmed was looking for a substitute father? Or if he, Percy, was attempting to recapture his lost youth? They had fun together for God's sake! And they fancied each other.

This last statement was the one that made Percy almost burst with pride. He had found a man who did actually fancy him. There was no doubt about it. It certainly wasn't his money Ahmed was after. When anything other than the going rate for the calash rides was offered, Ahmed would instantly refuse it and sometimes be offended it had even been suggested. When Percy pointed out younger, more conventionally attractive men, Ahmed pooh-poohed them and declared he wasn't interested.

'I want to be naked,' he said. 'I not take my pants off. You have to do this for me.'

Percy eased the covering down, taking time to appreciate Ahmed's sturdy legs as the white cotton slid over them. Ahmed's cock sprang forward hungrily. It was not particularly long, but it was thicker than any other Percy had ever seen. He kissed the tip of it lovingly.

'Let me say hello to my friend,' Percy said.

Ahmed laughed and lay back, enjoying the pull of the older man's mouth around his genitals. Percy, for his part, was happy to indulge his friend for as long as he wanted it. He was slightly apprehensive, but not as much as he would have been had Ahmed's mood suggested he was spoiling for a fight. On these occasions, more often than not there would be a row. The argument would be prompted by Ahmed wanting Percy to fuck him and Percy refusing. Percy had tried to explain he was not particularly sexually active, but he well understood the physical needs of a young man in the prime of his sexual life. It was a problem they were always going to have to deal with. It shouldn't get in the way of their affection.

'I know what you think,' Ahmed said. 'You think I go shout at you very soon.'

How he'd managed to work this out was a mystery. Percy wondered if his own feelings were really so transparent. Maybe Ahmed was more intuitive than most, or maybe they knew each other so well there was no longer any need of words. Whatever the case it was fruitless to deny it.

'Is OK,' Ahmed declared, putting Percy's head back to its task. 'I have surprise for you.'

Percy pulled away again. 'I'm not sure I like surprises.'

'You like this one.'

Ahmed rose and went to the door. On the way, he discarded his trunks completely. He stood naked, grinning suggestively.

Then he opened the door a little and gave a low whistle as a signal to somebody further down the stairs.

Seemingly enjoying Percy's puzzled expression, he then came back to the bed and lay down with his hands behind his head. His cock twitched invitingly and his face was creased in a broad grin.

After a few moments, the door opened a couple of inches. Ahmed looked up and smiled again. There was a hesitant little knock.

'Is your surprise. Tell him to come in.'

Percy's heart leapt, but the pleasant feeling was suddenly overtaken by fear. This was not a careful thing for Ahmed to have done. Percy still thought of the dangers of being a white man, alone in the company of so many strangers. Still, he reasoned, Ahmed was there and, should there be any trouble, Ahmed would be able to cope with it. He was strong enough to protect them both.

Percy told the visitor to enter. He wished, as he often wished, he could remember the few words of Arabic he had been taught, but English always seemed to be acceptable with these people. The door opened fully to reveal a man who was about as near to physical perfection as it was possible to get.

He was about 22 or 23. He had skin of Ahmed's colour, or maybe slightly lighter. His hair was cut close to his head and this was a superb compliment to his muscular neck and broad shoulders. He was dressed in shorts and a white shirt which was open to reveal a powerful chest covered in a white vest. His breast was showing over the top, broad and gently moving up and down as he breathed heavily. Unlike his torso (or what could be seen of it), his legs were hairy – black, black hairs that lay flat to his skin and invited stroking. Up near where his shorts covered his thighs, the hair became denser. Percy wanted immediately to trail his hand up there and bury his fingers in the furlike growth. He was already imagining a forest surrounding enormous genitals. Oh, if he could kneel before this youth and kiss him from his feet upward, before burying his face in that wonderful hair.

Instead, he sat back and smiled politely. The man nodded to him pleasantly and, seeming only the smallest bit nervous, he came into the room and sat cross-legged on the floor at the foot of the bed. Percy allowed his eyes to wander towards the gap in his shorts. Sure enough, the sight was exactly as he had imagined it a few seconds earlier. The young man was not wearing underclothes and Percy was able to catch the merest glimpse of heavy, dark balls amid a profusion of pubic growth.

'He is René,' Ahmed said. 'He has French mother and Arab father. He likes me. He does not want to marry, but he must soon. He does not mind if you watch us together.'

After this concise history, he put his hand on René's shoulder. René responded by nuzzling up to Ahmed's palm and licking it lasciviously. All the time, René's eyes were fixed on Percy, waiting for approval or censure. Percy gave his assent.

'It is nice to see you, René. I would like to watch you and Ahmed together. I will watch you from here. Take your time and enjoy yourselves.'

Ahmed translated this to René in a mixture of French and Arabic. René smiled and his smooth face became a mass of dimples and delight. He had the same coal-black eyes his countrymen all had, but his brows were thin and delicate and there was something quite artistic about his cheekbones. Percy realised, almost unconsciously, that his burly physique was manufactured. This was a delicate lad who had learnt he must build himself up in order to be accepted among his peers.

René pulled off his shirt, revealing respectably strong biceps which tapered to his thin wrists. He put his arms up in the air and allowed Ahmed to strip him of his undershirt. His chest was shaped, but not so much that it was out of proportion. He wet his index finger with spit and, giving a cheeky, suggestive look to Percy, he circled one of his nipples, ending by giving it a slow pinch.

Ahmed said something else to René and René nodded enthusiastically. Ahmed sat up on the bed and took René in his arms from behind, hugging him.

'We say that you are in charge. We do this for you, not for us. You must not be upset. You must say what we do.'

So, he was to have his own show. Percy's head was suddenly completely blank. He snatched around in his imagination for all the fantasies he had had when alone and found none came readily to mind. He suddenly wanted to be dirty – really dirty. He wanted to fumble with himself under the cover of his trousers and masturbate while these two wonderful men did unspeakable things to each other for his delight. He knew this, but he didn't know where to begin. He suddenly felt coy.

Strangely, this slight sense of shame was precisely what gave him his sexual charge. He was tongue-tied but, at the same time, his deepest desires were bubbling up inside him, now covered by the thinnest veneer of propriety and Englishness. He was willing and almost ready to cast his respectability aside and be as filthy as he had always wanted to be.

'Make him pull his shorts down. Just a little. Don't let him take them off yet. I want to see his stomach, but not his cock – not yet.'

This was relayed to René, who stood and eased the shorts off his hips. He wet his finger again and trailed it down from his navel, following the line of hair which started there and spread across his flat belly. At exactly the right point, just before his pubic hair was properly revealed, Ahmed stayed his hand and he stopped. René stroked his abdomen with his hand, circling round, and watched the movement himself with a kind of curiosity, as though that part of him belonged to another person and he was seeing it for the first time.

'I want to see his armpits again. Make him hold his arms up.'

It was lovely to see the huge tufts of black against the smoothness of René's skin. It was, Percy realised, youth: the first signs of manhood on one who had reached that stage only

31

a few years before. It was like seeing freshness and springtime: the first, full bloom of maturity.

Percy knew he was getting sentimental. Soon he would become sad because he had never possessed such beauty himself. His own twenties had been marked by every physical imperfection nature could have thrown at a young man: being slightly stout, having acne, losing his hair, suffering from pale skin which burnt at the slightest sign of the sun. This young man was what he himself had wanted to be. Ahmed was attractive in quite a different way. Percy felt safe with Ahmed because his beauty came from his quirky, broken looks. This René was utterly gorgeous.

René stood patiently with his hands on his head. He made sure that his armpits were exposed to Percy's gaze and he kept his eyes lowered to the floor. He didn't seem to mind at all, and Percy left him like that for a couple of minutes or more.

'Ask your friend what he likes to do,' Percy finally said.

Ahmed shrugged without consulting René. 'He like what you like. He likes to be told. He don't want to have to say himself.'

'Pull his shorts down at the back and put your tongue into his bottom.'

Ahmed did this with serious concentration, pulling the garments down slowly and carefully. His own cock was twitching, showing he was enjoying this game as much as the other two. Percy unbuttoned his fly and loosened his belt. His hand sought out his cock and he began to rub the end of it with his finger and thumb. He didn't want to go too far because he knew that, as soon as he had come, this whole scene would change from being exciting to being sordid. He didn't want it to appear so until all of them had had what they wanted from being together.

Ahmed gently positioned René, bending his back so his arse was sticking out near Ahmed's face. The shorts were now barely covering René's nudity. His erect penis was pushing them out at the front, seeming to be the only thing holding them up. His arse was exposed and near to Ahmed's lips. Ahmed buried his face in between the buttocks. Percy couldn't see from where he was sitting but he was content to let this go on for some time. He could supply the missing bits of the picture from his imagination.

All the while, René kept his hands on his head and even attempted to keep his armpits available to Percy's view. He was amazingly compliant and appeared to have no qualms about what was being asked of him.

Ahmed's hand went to his own cock and he began to slowly wank himself. Percy stopped him.

'No! I don't want you to do that. Not yet.'

Ahmed raised his head and winked. 'You come once. I come many times. Is OK. You allow me?'

Percy gave in to him. He knew it was true. Ahmed could come two or three times in a short period without any problems at all.

'Both of you must come a little closer,' Percy said. 'Place yourselves so I can see you better.'

Ahmed nodded quickly. He whispered to René as though what Percy had instructed was a secret which must be kept between them. René, not taking his hands from where they were placed, moved across the room and stood only a few feet away from Percy's chair. He bent down again and waited for Ahmed to spring across to him: Ahmed did so like a panther pouncing on its prey. He never moved slowly; it was always as though he were under orders to perform every task as a matter of extreme urgency.

He placed René's body so his arse was fully on view to Percy. Then he knelt on the floor and spread the buttocks with his hands and invited Percy to have a good look at the dark crack and the button of skin in the centre of it. It was wet with Ahmed's spit: glistening, moist and pink against the dark honey of the rest of René's skin. Percy eased himself to a better position in the chair, pulling his trousers down a little more so he might have a better hold on his cock. When he was comfortable, he indicated that Ahmed must carry on.

Ahmed pushed his lips towards the warm comfort of René's bottom and let his tongue flick lovingly around the hair. Up and down, licking it, lapping up the vestiges of sweat and plastering the black hair down against the skin. Every so often he drew back and pulled René's buttocks wide again so Percy could see the effect of his labours. Then he pressed his mouth against the hole once more and Percy knew his tongue was inside the other lad's anus. He could imagine the bitter taste, the heat, the smell. He slowed down the movement on his cock. He had nearly reached orgasm but stopped himself just in time.

Ahmed was pumping away at his own erection as he licked. In only a few minutes his body was tensing. His stomach flattened and his upper chest filled out as he held his breath. Then he released it in a long gasp before drawing it in again. His hand movement became disjointed: stopping every so often and then furiously rubbing at his penis again in short bursts. He raised his hips, as if he were about to get up – but he stayed there, frozen, for a second or so. Then he leant back from René's body and sighed as the creamy fluid filled his cock and then spilt over his fist. He panted slightly before kissing each of René's buttocks and wiping the semen on to them. He worked the lotion into the skin, slapping each buttock in between the caressing motions.

He looked at Percy for instructions. Amazingly, though his penis had gone soft immediately after he had come, it was already rising again.

Percy reached out for Ahmed's hand and pressed it to his lips, licking up the salty fluid that remained there. 'Now it is time for your friend to have some fun. Tell him to come near to me and pull his shorts down.'

René did as he was told. The shorts came off and his circumcised organ sprang forward. Just as Percy had hoped, the smooth, thin penis and tight sack beneath it were surmounted by a forest of downy hair.

Youth: in twenty years or so this young man would have hair all over his body and the smoothness of his skin would be long gone. He would, perhaps, have married and become paunchy. The summer of his life would give way to autumn and he would be like a lovely green leaf that weathers and wrinkles.

'What you thinking?' Ahmed asked. 'You look very sad.'

'I'm being very foolish,' Percy replied. 'I'm thinking about leaves and summer.'

Ahmed looked puzzled. 'Why?'

Percy shook his head. 'It doesn't matter. They are silly thoughts and quite embarrassing.'

'You are embarrassed? René isn't. He likes you to watch him. You enjoy seeing him?'

'Very much,' Percy replied. He let his hand wander fleetingly around René's pubic hair, over his shaft and under his balls. Percy could feel the wetness where Ahmed's tongue had been. René pushed his hips towards Percy, inviting him to go further. Percy declined and beckoned for Ahmed to come and attend to his friend's penis.

'Suck him, and drink his come. You understand?'

Ahmed certainly did understand. He knelt in front of René and closed his lips round the lad's dick. René breathed in deeply and, not sure of where he was supposed to place his hands, eventually brought them back to his head. He bucked his hips in and out, allowing Ahmed to caress his cock and making sure that Percy could get as good a view as possible.

Ahmed's hands wandered around René's body. First they had guided the boy's penis into his own mouth, then they stroked up and down his inner thighs, feeling around his genitals. Once or twice they rubbed the cock to give it extra sensation. Then they went up to René's chest, finally resting when they found his dark little nipples. Ahmed worked at these – clearly a source of delight for René, who closed his eyes and began to hiss through his teeth as he took in air. Unable to stop himself, René brought his own hands down to Ahmed's head and pushed it in and out, faster and faster. His eyes opened wide and he shouted something in Arabic. He gave two more definite thrusts and Ahmed gagged as his mouth was filled with come.

Without swallowing, Ahmed moved over to Percy and kissed him. The salty fluid filled both their mouths. In Percy's mind, all three were now united in this act of lust. He swallowed, as did Ahmed, and they smiled at each other; their mutual affection plain to all of them.

Ahmed told René to stand in front of them. He pulled Percy's trousers down and wanked himself and Percy in perfect time. Percy let the glorious feeling build in his cock while he gazed and gazed at the lovely young man before him.

When he knew he was about to come, he gripped Ahmed's upper arm urgently and tried to warn him. Ahmed gave him a brief kiss to let him know he understood and speeded up his own masturbation. The two of them came together and, as they did, they locked their mouths in a wonderful, passionate kiss. René grinned and knelt down with them, joining his mouth with theirs. Three tongues lapped around one another before a long, still embrace that seemed to Percy to last for ever.

'I must go,' Percy said. 'I have people to see at the Winter Palace. Is your friend . . .?'

'He go,' Ahmed said. 'But he see us again. He has enjoyed.'

He translated this to René, who nodded eagerly.

'Does he need some money?' Percy asked, his hand already inside his jacket pocket.

Ahmed seemed cross. 'No money. He is my friend. Now he is your friend. We buy him present sometime.'

Percy smiled. 'I liked your surprise,' he said.

Three

_____

'I really like Percy,' Graham said. He picked the sliver of lemon out of his glass and winced at the bitter taste as he swallowed it, peel and all. 'He's very good company and he sort of . . . Well, he just loves it here, doesn't he? He keeps smiling all the time and saying how wonderful everything is. Even when it isn't.'

He followed the lemon with a cube of ice which he crushed in his mouth and swallowed. Jeremy would have normally found this sort of behaviour to be quite unappealing, but there was nothing Graham could do that would possibly come under such a heading.

Two days had passed since their first meeting on the boat and at last Maria had taken herself off – and, amazingly, taken Mrs Dryden with her. They had gone to Aswan for a short stay. Maria had declared that the 'chaps' could come with them if they wanted, but they weren't really welcome as this was going to be an excellent opportunity for the 'chapesses' to rubbish them.

'She's out for an adventure,' Graham had concluded. 'I wonder what bright young thing has taken her eye.'

He had caught Jeremy's inquisitive expression and had deliberately misinterpreted it. 'Don't worry. Mrs Dryden won't be allowed to get in the way. She'll be packed off with the rest of the group to rummage through the joys of antiquity.'

So, Jeremy had Graham almost all to himself. Percy was in evidence, but was not a problem to get rid of.

Graham smelling of expensive cologne, sleek and utterly dashing in his white tuxedo and bow tie, his hair brilliantined back severely. Graham who had no idea of the effect he was having on his companion. Graham who had spent the last half-hour talking about his girl. Having concluded this, he was now starting on a paean of praise for Percy.

'Percy's all right,' said Jeremy. 'He can be very generous.'

'Forgive my saying this – I presume you and he are . . . Well, more than friends.'

Jeremy coloured bright red and took a gulp of his drink. Prior to this, no mention had been made of his attraction to other men. He had supposed Graham didn't know anything about it. Now it transpired that, not only was this supposition not true, but Graham had perceived beyond it. Jeremy wondered how much he knew. Did he assume he and Percy were lovers? Or did he know Jeremy was living off rich, middle-aged people: not only Percy, but Mrs Dryden as well?

Graham seemed totally at ease with having revealed this knowledge, even though it was obvious Jeremy wanted the subject to be changed and changed quickly.

'He's somebody I met on my travels,' Jeremy replied in answer to his question. 'Are we going to dine here or go native? I believe –'

'It's all right. Percy hasn't said anything. Maria told me. She's awfully intuitive. She gets it wrong sometimes, though. She said –'

Here Graham spluttered into his glass and waved his hand, dismissing the idea (whatever it was) as ridiculous.

'What did she say?'

'She said I had to watch you.'

Graham spoke the words with a crooked smile on his face and a twinkle in his eye. He pointed his finger at Jeremy with mock accusation and emphasised the warning as though it amused him beyond measure. 'I have to watch my step,' he laughed.

'She seems to trust us alone together,' Jeremy said. 'Look, I'm really sorry, but I don't think we should be talking like this in here. Somebody might be listening.'

'I have to go to my room and collect some cash,' Graham said, pulling back his chair and standing. 'I promise I won't tell,' he added. The singsong voice he used indicated that he found the secret to be very unimportant indeed.

Jeremy covered his confusion by blowing his nose. They walked down the corridor together. At one point, Graham dawdling some feet behind him, Jeremy turned. He would always remember the picture he saw at that moment.

Graham with one hand in his trouser pocket, standing easy and relaxed with his debonair, still-amused look. A cigarette in his other hand, with its smoke curling up into the air around him. This enchanting figure was framed by the French-colonial opulence of the corridor, with its high ceiling and grandiose decor. A potted palm tree stood just behind him. An artist would have spent hours drawing the image. Perhaps Graham would always look perfect, whatever his surroundings and no matter how he was dressed.

'You coming?' he asked as he moved forward, overtaking Jeremy.

His shoes clacked smartly on the marble floor of the foyer. His neat bottom and long, strong legs moved gracefully and quickly. His beautifully tailored tuxedo tapered into his waist and filled out around shoulders that years of rugby had produced. Jeremy followed him, still contemplating how damned appropriate Graham looked in these surroundings. They went upstairs.

The corridors of the Winter Palace never appeared to be

busy, no matter how many guests were about. The hotel was large enough to put all its occupants into their proper perspective. The ornate plaster on the walls and the whirring fans above; the gilt-framed oils of inappropriately dressed Victorians standing incongruously in front of Karnak Temple or the Colossi of Memnon; the tasteful Edwardian furniture in small alcoves here and there. This was a place of privilege and money. Jeremy knew he was a fraud in the midst of it all. Graham wasn't.

They passed a couple of Arab porters by the top of the great staircase. To these, as he had to the man at the reception desk, Graham delivered some pleasantry in their own language. His cigarette finished and no ashtray in sight, Graham had to suffer none of the clumsy, self-conscious palaver Jeremy would have had to go through – wondering if he would be discovered as he disposed of the butt in a flowerpot. He simply called some word in Arabic and, as if by magic, a boy appeared, bowing and smiling, ashtray in hand.

Jeremy considered his own (very slightly) ill-fitting evening wear. Previously he had thought it didn't look too bad. It would pass muster in most places. Now he decided he resembled Charlie Chaplin's 'Little Tramp'. He determined to complain to Mrs Dryden or Percy and get one or the other of them to furnish him with something a bit more modern and certainly something made to measure.

'What say you we go and ask your Percy to dine with us?' Graham said.

Jeremy could think of no good reason why not, other than the truth, which he could hardly put forward after what had been said in the bar. He tried to make his acceptance of the proposal as gracious as possible, enthusiastic even. In the event it came out as somewhere in between a grimace and a wince and prompted Graham to ask him if he was all right because he sounded strange.

Graham had reached the door of his suite now and was standing on the threshold with the same amused look on his face as he'd had in the bar. Jeremy realised he had been dithering for some seconds and this look was for him – yet again.

'Sorry,' he said. 'I was daydreaming.'

Jeremy had been in Graham's suite before, several times. Even so, it still made him wish again that he could afford such expensive comfort. The place would certainly not have disgraced a member of some foreign royal family.

It was dark: the blinds had been pulled down against the evening sun. Graham went over to the windows and immediately threw open the blinds and then the windows too. The room was transformed. All the colour came gleaming to life: the gold on the ornamental plasterwork, the deep red of the curtains and the furniture, the luscious green of the rugs. The noises of the street outside came to them clearly: shouts and cries, the clip-clop of horses' hooves. Soon the Call to Prayer would come wailing out from the mosque and evening would be upon them.

Graham tapped on the phone's receiver-rest and, again using more Arabic than English, he asked for Percy's room. Their date was soon confirmed: Percy would be delighted to join them. His driver would pick up all three of them in an hour and a half. Should he dress? Or perhaps they might prefer to go to some charming native place where, he guaranteed, the food would be quite safe to eat and simply delicious.

Jeremy would have told him to dress: he didn't fancy eating native food. Graham, on the other hand, was delighted at the idea. He sat down on a chaise longue and removed his bow tie.

'We'd better look the part,' he observed. 'Come on. You can't go like that. You can either dash over to your room or I'll lend you some of my things. We're just about the same size.'

Jeremy's room was easily accessible but it didn't occur to him that Graham's offer of clothes was unusual in any way. He was actually thinking of whether it would look out of place if he were to hang around long enough to see Graham remove his shirt. Now he might even get a look at his legs as well.

He reminded himself that Graham was interested in women

and he must not make him feel awkward by ogling his body too obviously. The only way this friendship had a chance was if Graham thought of Jeremy as a pal – a friend and no more.

Graham was now in his dressing room, taking the studs out of his collar and removing it. He had a prominent Adam's apple. Jeremy wanted to kiss his neck. He felt his cock stirring. Luckily his trousers were thick and loose enough to hide it, but this was going to be both a pleasurable and a difficult few moments.

Jeremy loosened his own tie and collar. He followed Graham's example and tossed his jacket on to a chair. Then, copying his friend, he removed his shoes.

Graham padded over to the wardrobe and selected what they would wear. His shirt was open, the tails of it flapping around his loosened pants. His braces were dangling. His chest hair was nicely framed in the curve of his singlet.

Jeremy thought to himself, not for the first time, how unselfconscious heterosexual men were about undressing in front of other males. He always felt eyes were upon him: criticising, comparing. This was contradictory: he was no weakling of course; in fact he thought he had a damn good figure and his face was respectably handsome.

He forced himself to look with fresh eyes upon Graham, who, by now, had opted for flannels and blazers for the two of them and was laying them out, ready to put on. He was handsome – yes, it had to be admitted – but could it be said he was honestly more handsome than Jeremy, or any of the other young men around for that matter?

Sadly, the answer was a resounding yes. Yet it wasn't his looks: it was his aura. He just had that certain touch of virile charm which Jeremy himself simply ached for. He was the sort of chap Jeremy would have adored to have as an elder brother. Then Jeremy could have enjoyed his company and his affection and there would be none of this inconvenient lust around their relationship.

Graham had divested himself of his shirt, undone his trousers and stepped out of them. He was wearing the sort of underwear that was popular in America. Jeremy had never seen the style before except in pictures. They looked like shorts but they were tighter and came to only halfway down his thighs: almost like swimwear, but white. His legs were rippling with muscle and were browned. His chest appeared to burst out of his singlet as if the tight material was only just able to contain it. He stood, holding up the two pairs of trousers for inspection.

'Which would you like? They'll both fit. I'm certain of it.'

Jeremy declared he didn't mind and Graham must choose. Graham threw one pair over to him and tossed the other pair on the chair by which he himself stood. Then he stopped and stood looking at Jeremy, who was only now taking off his shirt.

'So you like older men?'

Jeremy was startled. He wasn't sure he wanted to discuss his predilections with Graham. The conversation might easily have been suggested by Maria as a trap. He could imagine the scene:

'I'm quite safe with him,' (Graham would have said.) 'He only likes older people, like Percy.'

'All right then,' (Maria would have replied.) 'If you're so sure. Ask him and see what he says. I'll bet he gives the game away.'

'Very well. I will ask him. If it's as I think it is, then you can't object to my seeing him. And, yes, if it's as you say, then I don't need to see him ever again.'

Jeremy removed his shirt but did not take off his trousers just yet. He went over to the window and looked out at the river for a second or two. Then he turned to Graham and nodded firmly.

'Yes, I only like older men. You have no need to worry about being alone with me. I won't even notice your body.'

He'd gone too far. What he had just said made it very clear that he *did* notice Graham's body. Notice it! He could hardly take his eyes off it. Graham in his underwear seemed to be bigger than anything else in the entire room.

'Pity,' Graham said. 'I was hoping for a bit of fun while that little minx of mine is away.'

Jeremy started. He might have imagined what he had just heard. But no: Graham was running his hand suggestively up and down the front of his shorts. There was no mistaking the calm, steady look in his green eyes.

'Maria doesn't mind,' Graham said. 'She and I have a very modern sort of relationship. We're both interested in men *and* women. We decided to give each other some space to explore the other sides of our natures. But, of course, I'm barking up the wrong tree with you. I'm sorry. Let's finish getting changed and go.'

Jeremy couldn't think of anything to say so he simply threw himself at Graham and flung his arms round him. He slid down Graham's body, holding him tightly as though he might fly away at any second. Eventually he was kneeling upright with his cheek against Graham's stomach. He gripped him even tighter.

'Whoa! Whoa!' Graham said, holding his hands in the air in surrender. 'I seem to have taken hold of the wrong end of the stick. I thought, when you told me you weren't interested in me, that you weren't interested in me.'

Jeremy began kissing him: dozens of little, light pecks. He pulled Graham's singlet up and planted just as many kisses again on his stomach, around his belly button. He forbore to go further down just yet, but he was well aware of the swelling bulge in those tight shorts.

Graham took hold of Jeremy's hands and lifted him up so they were standing facing one another. He pulled Jeremy to him in an embrace that would have done credit to Rudolph Valentino. Jeremy melted into his arms and allowed himself to go limp as Graham brought their lips together. Jeremy's eyes closed as he enjoyed the feeling of having his mouth explored. Graham's tongue went around the back of his teeth, around his gums, flicking along his lips. Jeremy tried to compete but then gave up and surrendered to passivity.

Graham lifted him bodily, taking no more trouble about it than if Jeremy had been made of straw. He carried him through into the bedroom and deposited him on the cool sheets. Jeremy opened his eyes and found Graham's face still close to his, looking intently at him – almost studying him.

'You're quite a looker,' Graham said.

Jeremy usually protested at remarks like this, but for once he remained silent. He was content to let Graham do or say whatever he wanted.

'Let's get these damned trousers off you,' Graham said.

They were duly discarded. Graham lay on the bed beside Jeremy, letting his arm come round Jeremy's shoulders so they were holding each other close. Both men in their underwear; both with cocks that would not allow them to prevaricate much longer. Neither wanting to hurry, but both aware of the ticking clock.

'Suppose we go one stage further,' Graham ventured. 'I want to see what that chest of yours is like.'

Jeremy stripped off his vest and watched eagerly while Graham did the same. Graham's chest was not a forest of hair as Jeremy had thought it would be. He was smooth skinned apart from directly down the centre of his body. The hair was a thin trail, leading the eye downward, towards his crotch. His upper body had more hair, including a little tuft at the top, near to his throat. It was this that poked above his open shirt. His nipples were large and pink. They looked as though they needed to be kissed.

Jeremy followed his instincts and sucked on each in turn. He could tell by the resulting ecstatic moan that he was doing the right thing. He spent some minutes attending to that area of Graham's body and then began to slide downward, intending to take Graham's cock. Graham stopped him.

'If you're about to suck me, don't.'

Jeremy came away from his body and leant up on one elbow. 'I'm sorry. I didn't mean . . .'

Graham laughed. 'Hey! Hey! I don't mean to hurt your feelings. It's just that, let's face it, the women are good at that sort of thing. I would prefer it, now I have the opportunity, if we did something I can get only from a man. You follow my meaning?'

He didn't wait for an answer. He rolled over on to his front and pulled down his pants. Then he took a position on all fours, providing Jeremy with a first glimpse of his enormous prick, dangling between his legs like the phallus of an animal.

Jeremy's underwear was soon on the floor and he was kneeling behind Graham. He might have preferred to be fucked, to remain passive, but he was not about to argue. If this was what was on offer, he was more than pleased to take it.

He spat on his hand and wiped it into the hot valley between Graham's buttocks. Graham was bucking as if Jeremy's cock was already up him. Then Jeremy eased one of his fingers into the tight, burning hole. Graham's sphincter gripped round him as though it were the mouth of some tiny creature. Jeremy could feel Graham's insides pulsing against the invading digit. He looked down and saw his own hungry cock. Pre-come was oozing from the end of it and he used this to lubricate the hole as much as he could. Then he poised himself and pushed into Graham's backside in one slow, smooth movement.

Graham had been holding his breath for a few moments, waiting for the initial pain to come and go. He let the air out in a steady stream, exactly in time with Jeremy's push. His head went limp, as though his neck had been broken, and he collapsed the upper part of his body on to the mattress. His bottom and thighs remained rigid, easily able to take the pressing weight against them.

Jeremy sank his shaft into the encompassing grip of Graham's passage. He was still for a moment or two. He wouldn't begin to fuck him until he was quite ready.

Graham bucked gently, encouraging him. Jeremy leant over his back and pressed his palm hard against Graham's open mouth. Graham immediately got the idea and licked Jeremy's hand eagerly.

'Good boy,' Jeremy said. 'You be my little dog and lick your master's hand. Good boy.'

Graham whimpered, but he carried on licking until the hand was withdrawn. Then he stayed still, waiting for Jeremy to dictate what should happen next.

Jeremy had been confused by this seeming reversal of roles at first. He had always assumed that men who were able to be attracted to women just had to be dominant. He had never conceived of the thrill it would give him to actually see a real he-man whimpering like a puppy and, even more, being fucked up the arse by him, Jeremy.

He savoured the moment, running his hands over Graham's powerful back and allowing him to bite very gently on his finger. Then, without any warning, he fucked that wonderful, masculine hero of his – hard and without any concessions to his yelps and cries. It was like riding a stallion, but this was a stallion that made his cock surge with pleasure. Jeremy loved every moment, every slap of his stomach as it hit Graham's buttocks, the swing of his own balls as they rocked back and forth with the motion, the sweat building where their bodies connected.

He was near to coming. He took this last bit slowly, tantalising himself by prolonging the feeling that he so wanted to release into Graham's backside. He thought about his semen boiling away inside his balls, eventually surging up his dick and out through his piss-hole, filling the dark inside of the beauty beneath him.

Jeremy lay gasping for a few moments with his prick still inside Graham. It was going soft, but he didn't want to pull out. Graham didn't want him to either. He brought his arm around the small of Jeremy's back, pressing him closer to his own body. Then, sure Jeremy was not about to withdraw his penis, he took hold of his own huge member and wanked himself, staying as he was, on all fours.

His pants and gasps built into involuntary shouts as he too approached those few seconds of bliss. Jeremy kneaded his fingers into the flesh of Graham's back, making the action harder and firmer in tandem with Graham's evident build to climax. Then he felt Graham's body stiffen. He stayed still himself, letting Graham's come splash on to the bedspread.

The two of them rolled into each other's arms and lay there kissing and just looking at each other: each enjoying the sight of the naked body he held.

'You're quite something,' Graham whispered.

Jeremy felt he was in heaven. He squeezed Graham's hand and then pressed it to his lips.

'Better than Maria?'

Graham gave him a look that said, 'None of your business.'

'Come on,' Graham said aloud. 'The lovely Percy will be waiting for us. I don't think we have the ghost of an excuse for keeping him waiting. Do you?'

Four

—————

René El Sab was bored. He had been in his father's alabaster 'factory' all day and had done his best to make enough bowls and other ornaments to keep the old man happy and thus prevent another family row. Yesterday there hadn't been enough.

He'd sat cross-legged in the heat, grinding away with a hand-held drill at the soft, semitranslucent stone. Despite his efforts, he had not even managed to produce as many as he'd done the previous day. His mind wandered and time passed easily and quickly, without anything being done. Because of this, he'd found it necessary to escape from home before his father returned from the shop which he owned with René's uncles.

René's aunt, who ran their domestic affairs, had been in the women's part of the house with his two sisters and her own child. They were busy preparing the evening meal; even the little one would have been helping as much as she was able. René had shouted to her that he was going to eat at a friend's house.

This was not acceptable behaviour: the family meal was the bedrock of their lives together. It followed strict tradition. After

René's father and uncle had served themselves, René would be next in line, then the trays would go to the back room for the womenfolk. This patriarchal system, which westerners might see as strange and unfair, was one of the many reasons René's mother had left them and gone back to her native France.

René was out of the door in a trice. His aunt had not had time to rise from where she was squatting over a mortar and pestle and apprehend him. He had pretended he hadn't heard her yelling. He just wanted to get away.

So, not having eaten since daybreak, and unable to find the usual crowd of youths at the coffee shop, he had suffered the (no doubt) wise advice of an ancient gentleman whom he'd met only once before. The old man had claimed he knew René's trouble. He was not above presuming to repair the damage René was doing to himself. The man claimed he knew how difficult youth was: he had made the same mistakes himself when he was René's age. How old was René by the way? Twenty-one – or -two? Yes, he had guessed so. René must listen to the old for they have trod the path of life before . . . And so on.

Unable to take much more wisdom, René had sauntered down to the Nile bank to see if he could find any tourists who would give him some baksheesh. This was a word most foreign-ers understood well enough – a tip or even a free hand-out. Maybe some rich woman would want a guide and he could make some real money.

Sometimes René found a man from abroad who would pay him for his cock. René enjoyed this sort of job most of all. He found it curious that the most pleasurable activity was the one he could charge the most money for. Surely sitting on the ground all day, making stupid pots and bowls for foreigners to buy – things they didn't want – surely that should warrant more than the pittance he received for doing it?

René thought about his fruitless day and realised he was sulking. This was not going to be the sort of attitude that would get him trade of any kind. Luxor was full of Europeans; last week it had been Americans. White men expected the Egyptians to be all smiles, 24 hours a day: it was expected of them.

He kicked his heels for an hour or two, approaching everybody who crossed his path. At the end of this time he had three piastres, a broken fountain pen and a couple of French cigarettes. Time to head for home and face the music.

The road to the bazaar, beyond which he lived, was alive and bright. The gaslight from the small shops on each side of the dust-filled path lit the scene: Luxor at night. The sun had set as though it had been popped quickly into an envelope. Sunset was always perfunctory here, no matter what time of year it was. René had never been anywhere else and did not know why the foreign people commented so much upon it.

There were plenty of tourists about in this part of town, strolling about as if they belonged. Normally René got on all right with everybody, but he had had enough of holidaymakers for one day. The poorest of them possessed wealth René could only dream about and not one of them was willing to part with a decent amount of it.

If only he could find some American who wanted his cock. (Americans were René's favourite, but he would settle for any white male.) Last year he had managed to meet three men during the high season. With the proceeds, he had bought a scarf for his little sister and some jewellery for his aunt. For himself, he had the memory of white skin and trembling hands, of his own dark, engorged penis sinking in between those pale lips and gleaming teeth.

Behind the row of shops was the looming silhouette of the ancient temple. This was something the visitors loved. To René, it was so much old stone. Even the magnificent statues – the gods, the Pharaohs – even they were so familiar to him as not to be in the slightest bit remarkable. He was willing to indulge their European guests, but he failed to understand their fascination with everything that was old. One might as well be fascinated by the sand of the desert: that was even older than the tombs themselves.

Despite this, the temple had one big advantage. It was an excellent place to go at night. Men wandered around, sometimes white men who had money. Sometimes René would find somebody local whom he knew.

His Arab friends would rather go with a foreigner (for the money of course) but, if an Arab youth had no girl waiting at home for him and there were no punters to pay for the honour of relieving him, he would think very little of offering his cock to a good friend. It was a thing men had to do; it meant nothing and it gave him pleasure. He would not discuss it of course: René knew himself to be one of a very small minority who preferred messing around with other men to the prospect of finding himself a wife.

He knew several others: there was Ahmed for instance. They had fallen out recently because Ahmed had a rich Englishman in tow and had kept him all to himself. Then he had relented and let René join them for sex. The two Arabs had done things while Ahmed's friend from abroad simply watched. It had been wonderful, but the Englishman had not payed René anything for what he had done. René suspected that Ahmed had told him not to, for he had seen the man reach for his wallet. This had caused another rift between them and they hadn't spoken since. Ahmed's parting shot had been to suggest René should go and live in one of the whorehouses. Male prostitutes occasionally banded together under the patronage of some rich older man. René knew of an Englishman named Welch who ran several such houses. He was frightened of him and would never have even considered such a thing. He'd been insulted by Ahmed's taunt.

But he was willing to make it up now. He remembered Ahmed's lovely body and how good he had felt. Europeans were strange. They were not content to enjoy each other for the sake of it: they had to pretend other things to stimulate them. Ahmed's friend had apparently wanted René to act as though he was being forced to display himself. It had only meant Ahmed bossing him around a bit. René had found it sexy; he didn't quite know why. He had spent most of the time in an attitude of surrender, like he'd seen prisoners adopt before they were handcuffed. The English visitor had liked that.

Ahmed was besotted with this man but René liked the younger sort. Tonight he didn't care.

René liked to dress as the westerners did. He was wearing a pair of beautifully pressed cream trousers and a dark-green silk shirt. It was attire that would maybe look a little outlandish on a real Frenchman, but René's skin had more of his father's colour than his mother's. He was happy to stand halfway between the two cultures that had given him life.

He was idly wondering if he might have more luck by the hotel when Ahmed's voice stopped him in his tracks.

'Hello! You must come for a drive with us! There are two more Englishmen for you to meet.'

The fat man was staring at him like an old hen with René his newly born chick. Ahmed was driving the calash and turned round only in order to point things out to the visitors. The fat man liked René's looks far more than Ahmed would be comfortable with if he realised it. Luckily, the fat man was sitting with his back to the horse, opposite René and the Englishman René fancied most: the blond one. The dark one was nice as well – René would be happy with either of them – but the fair-haired one was best.

He was not quite sure where they were going. The atmosphere in that gilded, gaudy coach was simply charged with sex. An Egyptian would acknowledge this and go somewhere to do whatever they had to do. Not so these people. They were making some pretence of having to go down to Karnak to see the other temple there. Then they might come slowly back along the river. Ahmed translated this to René, chuckling all the while.

'Are they going to suck us?' René shouted to him. 'It's not a free gift for your friends this time. I want paying properly.'

'It's fine. You can have as much money as they want to give you. I will even add some from my own poor pocket if you like.'

This wasn't true and René knew it. Ahmed was always promising things. Still, at least they were clear about tonight. The fact that the young men were so handsome did not mean their charms would not be increased by having them empty their fat wallets a little. They both seemed very happy and appeared to be lovers together. Ahmed had denied this was the case.

'My friend, Percy says the dark-haired one is only interested in women,' he told René. 'We will get rid of him and then we'll have one man each.'

'It's not true.' René was confident in this. The dark-haired youth was quite clearly aroused by his blond friend. 'Your friend Percy is wrong.'

This annoyed Ahmed and he turned round to give René an earful. In doing so, he was able to get an overview of the relationships between his passengers. He saw, not only that René was quite right, but that Percy was displaying too much interest in René. He said something in English to Percy, who immediately became conciliatory. The blond Englishman looked slightly puzzled and awkward; the dark one was grinning at the two Arabs as though he understood every word they said.

'I have to be careful what I say in English,' Ahmed explained to René. 'Percy thinks we must not talk of sex or love in front of one another. We might find out where our interests lie and this would be a dreadful thing. Of course we can *have* each other's body as long as we do not speak of it.'

This was a fine joke between the two of them and they laughed conspiratorially, dismissing the temporary cloud. Percy averted his eyes and pretended a great interest in the sights. He was now playing guide to the other two white men. They were evidently not interested in what he had to say, but Percy had nothing else to occupy him now René had been declared out of bounds.

By this time, René had a hard cock. He was an impatient youth and, usually, if he had an erection, he would either find a man to pleasure him or he would simply take himself off somewhere and masturbate. It was like scratching an itch, but much more fun of course. Being with these people was frustrating. You had to waste so much time pretending sex was the last thing on your mind. It was almost getting to the stage where René was going to give up. Was there any chance of anything happening?

He drew closer to the blond boy. He pushed his leg a little further in, so their thighs touched. The Englishman flashed him a look, very briefly, but it was appreciative. René read the thoughts going so quickly over his open face. The blond had been hoping to take his dark-haired friend into his bed, but the older man must have intervened. Now it was either going to be an adventure for all of them or no adventure at all. René knew the older man just liked to watch. Perhaps he, Ahmed and the fair one could provide him with a fine show.

'We're going back to Mohammed's restaurant,' Ahmed announced. 'These people want food in their stomachs. You and I will wait outside.'

'I'm very hungry,' René complained. 'Mohammed could feed us all and your friend could pay. He owes me money.'

'We will share the horse's hay,' Ahmed said. He might almost have been serious. 'Mohammed would not like us to sit at a table with white men. We would be seen by all as whores.'

They were pulling up outside Mohammed's restaurant as they spoke. It was a splendid establishment in their eyes (and in Mohammed's), but the visitors seemed doubtful. After some persuasion, mainly from Ahmed, they resolved to go in. René got out of the calash with them, still hoping to be invited along.

They disregarded his presence and were just about to go in. Ahmed indicated that he would wait. All was just about settled. The fat one and the dark one entered the place, but the fair one turned back.

He asked Ahmed something. He was whispering in English, though this was not necessary as it was clear that René did not speak the language. René saw the man point at him and he saw a wide grin spread over Ahmed's face. Ahmed began nodding furiously. Still smiling, he climbed down from his driver's seat and hurried over to René.

'After they have eaten, his friend with the dark hair is going back to the hotel. The fair one is lonely and does not wish to be with my Percy and me because we are not so attractive to him. I said he could have you for a price and he has agreed. I get one third for making this arrangement. Is it agreed?'

It was agreed.

They nearly took Ahmed's suggestion of going to a hotel. If only they had, things would have been very different. In the event, it was a mixture of Ahmed's enthusiasm (which the fair one evidently saw as avarice but was in fact genuine), and a lack of communication caused by the fair one's bad French and René's terrible English. The temple was near at hand; René was used to taking people there. He linked his arm into the Englishman's, was told off for it by Ahmed, and finally, somehow, steered his conquest in the direction of those looming dark shadows.

As soon as they were off the road, the atmosphere changed. The fair one put his arm round René's waist and his whole demeanour was more forceful than it had been. This was the real man: gut feeling, not polite pretence. They had gone only a few steps when he stopped and pulled René towards him, safe in the darkness of centuries. He plunged his mouth on to René's and they held together tightly.

But this wasn't the best place. Somebody might come. René

said so in French and the fair one seemed to understand it. Accepting René's hand, he allowed himself to be pulled further and further in.

Here there was almost complete silence. The distant noises of humanity could just be heard, but seemed very far away. The moon was the only illumination. It bathed their surroundings in silver, black and grey-blue. Small animals scurried nearby and bats swooped about overhead. The majestic columns which had once been the dominating splendour of this courtyard stood some yards away. They looked as though they had been arranged by an artist. René had seen people painting that very view during the daylight hours.

Outside the area where they stood, and away from the ominous statues of Osiris and Ramses II, there was a more open, less delineated space. René could not remember what it had been and he didn't care to. Archaeologists had found some important things there: huge lumps of old stone covered in worn hieroglyphics.

They were soon near to these: arrayed neatly before them, labelled and waiting to be shipped to New York, Berlin, Paris – wherever. The site was deserted now.

Of course, they were not the only men who had come to the temple to worship the male body. There were many others, but they generally confined their activities to further in, where it was darker. René had reasoned that nobody would be likely to come anywhere near the excavation until the morning. There would be no reason to. They were safe.

The fair one was trembling visibly. René stroked him and showed him his concern in his face. The man smiled nervously and looked around. René sought to reassure him they were not overlooked by pulling off his shirt and guiding the man's hands to his breast. Once the hand was there, albeit tentatively, René opened his arms wide and turned his body to the right and left, demonstrating the vacant space around them: 'See,' he was saying. 'Nobody has come to hurt us.'

The man dared to bring his hand lower down René's body. The cock was rigid underneath the flimsy cotton. The man pinched gently along its length and then gripped it through the material. René kissed him to encourage him further.

He pulled René further into the shadow of one of the great stones and placed him against its cold surface. René enjoyed the coolness on his naked back. He assisted the fumblings of his companion by undoing the buttons at the top of his own flannel trousers and letting them fall to the ground. He was wearing underwear, but it was soon off him. He was naked.

The evening air caressed his skin and he longed to have this man naked with him. He wanted to hold him and eventually be taken by him, but he knew this probably wouldn't happen. Most white men knew nothing better than to grope inexpertly for a few moments and then suck cock, masturbating themselves as they did so. When their own needs had been met, they rarely stayed around to give pleasure back. Money would change hands and that would be the end of it.

'I am Jeremy,' the white man said. René nodded to show he understood.

'René,' he replied.

René didn't expect this man to be any different from others he had had. He was surprised then when Jeremy began by stroking his face. He was studying it in the moonlight, careful seriousness in his own expression. He traced René's eyebrows with his finger, then the bridge of his nose and along his lips. René took the finger in his mouth and sucked on it. Jeremy pushed it gently in and out. Was he asking permission to put his cock in there, René wondered?

He undid the buttons on Jeremy's shirt, going inside with his hands as soon as there was room for him to do it. He stroked the skin, enjoying the firmness he found there. He let his hands go everywhere, even around Jeremy's back. At this point, he tried to pull Jeremy towards him so they could kiss. Jeremy resisted, looking around fearfully as though this confirming gesture was more detectable to prying eyes than what they were doing already. René laughed at the irrational fear and pulled him forcefully into his own body. They kissed.

Locked as he was in this embrace, René eased Jeremy's shirt from his shoulders and let it fall into the dust at their feet. Jeremy was the more manly of the two and René felt pleasantly vulnerable because of it. He would be safe with this man; here was somebody who would protect him.

If he had been honest with himself, René would also have admitted he looked upon his new friend as an acquisition that he could show off in the town: one that would be bound to make all his friends jealous. Europeans meant money, sometimes even a passport and an invitation to travel across the world and see lands that, otherwise, the Arab people could not even hope to glimpse.

René's hand slid down inside the back of Jeremy's trousers. It was difficult to determine exactly what he was feeling there because the cloth was tight against Jeremy's body. Eventually he found a place that was damp with sweat and rough with body hair. It was hot too. He squeezed the end of his fingers in between the gripping buttocks and eased around until he found the hole which he knew was there.

Jeremy tried to pull away slightly and grunted his protest. In response, René kissed him even harder and used his free arm to pull Jeremy closer to himself. Jeremy's body lost its tension and he allowed his buttocks and arse to be probed. He even assisted by hurriedly scrabbling around with the front fastenings of his trousers, loosening them, so René could have freer access to his backside.

Soon Jeremy's trousers were in a bunch round his ankles. René took full advantage of the freedom he now had to explore around inside Jeremy's underpants. All the while, they continued kissing, not sure now which of them was leading this dance. Jeremy was by turns hungry, dominant, melting, nervous. René didn't care. He knew where he wanted all this to lead. He knew too that he must get what he wanted soon, before his beautiful man either came or allowed his nervousness to take over and spoil things.

He took Jeremy's hand from where it was curled around his waist and guided it downwards, using his own hand, still safe in the valley of Jeremy's arse, to indicate what he wanted Jeremy to do.

Jeremy copied René's actions. His fingers probed into the warm cleft of flesh, finding the entrance to René's body and pushing into it, forcing the muscle to part and allow the invasion. Then, with only the briefest of hints from René, he slid his finger in and out. René pulled away from Jeremy's lips for the first time and let his head fall back, rocking his hips against the motion of Jeremy's hand.

Then he eased away from Jeremy completely. He was going to ready himself for what he really wanted. Jeremy looked slightly confused, but, when René lay on his back on the ground, he was soon kneeling in between his open legs. He wanted it just as much as René did.

Leaning up just long enough to pull Jeremy's underwear down and free his enormous pale cock, René lay back and raised his hips, parting his legs as wide as he could in the process. He liked to think of himself as being a woman and his arse being that part of the female that he had never seen. He wanted to see this man as a woman would see him if she were being fucked by him: on top, sweating and pounding downward on to his conquest.

Jeremy seemed to know what René wanted. He lay on top of him first of all. He kissed him again, briefly, and then let his body rub against René's, pushing his cock against René's skin meaningfully.

René's back was being scratched by the rough sand underneath him. The mild pain this caused him was adding to his pleasure. It was a sharp contrast to the caressing he was getting on top. Pain and pleasure: to be loved physically was such an achingly slow experience that it needed hard grit to put an edge on it – to give the emotion somewhere to go.

It didn't hurt him to be entered. He had thought it would because of the size of Jeremy's cock, but the Englishman was mindful of René's reactions as he went in. He allowed him time to adjust to every push. When they were complete together, René sighed blissfully and dug his nails into Jeremy's shoulder: sharp claws, scratching the skin because of the sheer joy of human touch.

Jeremy was poised above him, waiting for his consent. René shifted himself, testing. The living thing inside his arse almost slid out; he immediately wanted it back. He moved again and was filled by it as before. Jeremy said words to him in English. Though he understood none of them literally, he knew they were words of passion and he responded in his own language.

Jeremy fucked him slowly and deliberately. He went in with sharp, sudden jabs and withdrew as though he was being sucked back against his will. At the point where his cock was about to become free, he plunged down again as though resisting the force that had caused him to withdraw. René felt the enigmatic glow, deep within him. It was building, spreading to his stomach and into his chest. Where actual visceral feeling stopped and glowing fervour began, he neither knew nor cared. He surrendered himself to those minutes of his life and tried to record them in his mind so they would always be there for him.

Jeremy took hold of his legs, and raised them into a V shape. He held them there, high up, so René's buttocks were completely available to him. He quickened his pace. In this position, René was able to touch his own erection and he did so immediately. The glow inside him was soon completed by the thrill in his cock. It surged and surged until he knew he could not hold off any longer. Jeremy pulled himself out of René's arse and brought his hand on to his own dick. First Jeremy and, a few seconds later, René: the come splashing on to René's stomach and forming pools across his skin. They rolled over together and kissed again.

Holding each other tight they eventually fell asleep in each other's arms.

Bleary with sleep, and not entirely sure where he was and how long he had been there, René was woken by a foot, poking him in the back.

It was still dark. Jeremy was awake too. He was sitting up, frozen with fear. They were no longer alone.

Two uniformed men stood over them and both were clearly delighted with their discovery.

Five

————

Graham had long since retired for the night. He had lain in his bed for hours, turning his body this way and that, trying to get comfortable. He was used to Maria being in the next room. Though no doubt many of their friends would have been entirely shocked if they knew, he would often creep through when they were both undressed and squeeze into bed beside his fiancée.

He didn't do this every night. There had been times when he had, to use his own phrase, 'indulged himself by having a little adventure'. There had been times aplenty when she had done the same. They secretly prided themselves on the adult way they conducted their lives. They found the prudishness of the society they were part of to be nothing more than a huge joke.

Graham's little adventures seldom meant anything very much to him beyond physical gratification. They were a way of expressing the side of him that he'd always known to be part of his emotional make-up. Even his brief time with Jeremy, still fresh in his mind, was not what was keeping him awake. The truth was, he wanted more and he wanted it now.

He tossed back the covers and lay there feeling the breeze

which came through the open window. It was a warm breeze and, this night in particular, he could have done with cool air. He removed his pyjama jacket and threw it on the floor. His night clothes were silk and this felt nicely sensual against his erect cock. He didn't want to masturbate. He didn't want to waste this feeling: he wanted company.

He fleetingly considered going into the bar (it was still open for he had retired early) and getting outrageously drunk. No, he thought, that would never do. He rose and crossed to the liquor cabinet. There was nothing in there that he fancied drinking. For some reason, he had a craving for a Martini. He asked the operator for room service. Once through, he ordered one to be sent up.

The young waiter who eventually appeared was a little over-sure of himself for Graham's tastes. Graham harboured an opinion, which he knew to be snobbish, that waiters and servants and all their kind should be deferential. He was, after all, an Englishman with status and money. This young man was a waiter who was paid to bring him a drink. He was acting like a flirtatious whore who expected to be serviced. He was all smiles and suggestive looks. He might even have winked at Graham, but maybe that had been imagined.

Certainly, the sight of a half-naked guest with, it had to be admitted, a visibly hard cock was not something that bothered this youth in the slightest. Was this how such transactions always happened in this country? It seemed to be so taken for granted. It was so coarse.

Graham retired to the other room, ordering the waiter to follow. He flopped back on to his bed and immediately wished he hadn't because this encouraged the waiter to come far too close to him. The young man posed with the tray as though he were offering goods for sale.

'You like it here?' the waiter asked. He flashed what was admittedly a most charming smile. All these people smiled all the time. It was really quite irritating. Graham knew he was being most unreasonable but found himself utterly unable to help it.

He took the drink off the tray and placed it on his bedside cabinet. Then he rolled over and searched in the drawer for some change to give as a tip.

'No need for baksheesh,' the waiter said. 'I am happy to be of service. I asked, do you like our country?'

'Very much indeed,' Graham said grudgingly. 'But I am too hot.' He fanned himself to convey his meaning more clearly. 'Too hot!' he said loudly, as though this might help the man's comprehension of his English.

'I know the English language,' the man said. 'I studied in New York. I will soon be taking up a responsible position of employment in Cairo. Until then, I bring your drinks and anything else you might want from me.'

This was a blatant invitation. Graham couldn't help putting aside some of his bad temper and contemplating the possibility of accepting what was so clearly being offered.

'How much?' he asked at last.

The waiter frowned, affecting not to have understood this. He must have been pretending, for none of the Egyptians Graham had met had any difficulty at all with those particular words.

'I'm asking you how much you want,' he said.

'For what, please?'

'Oh come on!' Graham howled. 'We both know what we're talking about! I don't believe you don't understand me. Do I have to say it in words of one syllable?'

'You are a bad man,' the waiter said sternly. 'You think we're all just to be bought and sold like cattle. I have come to you with a drink. Perhaps that is where we should leave our communication.'

His English was excellent, even though his accent was heavy. Graham could have kicked himself for being so damned British. He had made the fatal mistake of assuming all these people were in some way different from, less intelligent than, the English. What a dreadful opinion they must have of their visitors. Not just him: there were worse people. There were real twits about the place who would, no doubt, make the lives of their hosts hell and would not be worth shit if compared to the Arabs.

'I'm so sorry,' he said humbly. 'I have had a very bad day. No, that's a lie. I'm just in a stupid mood and I've insulted you when I didn't mean to. Please accept my apologies.'

'I accept,' the waiter said. 'My name is Ali. I will do anything I can for you. But do not treat me as though I were your property. I speak my mind now.'

This was not only well put but brave too, and maybe perceptive. If Graham had wanted to, if he had been one of those inflated English twits, he could have this man sacked for his 'impudence'. But Ali had seen through the bad temper and the bluff and appreciated Graham for who he really was.

'I would still like your company,' Graham said. 'I like you.'

Ali climbed on to the bed beside him and laid a hand on Graham's chest. 'I like you too,' he said. 'You are very athletic, I think.'

'I have been known to be.'

'May I see your legs? I would like to.'

Graham eased his pyjama bottoms down and lay there naked. Ali spent some time just looking at him. His eyes went up and down Graham's body, not taking in his face, but committing to his memory every inch of that muscular form.

Graham's shaft was sticking upward as though it didn't belong to him. It suddenly looked entirely ridiculous. He laughed and waggled it about. Ali looked reproving.

'Why are you laughing? Are you ashamed of what you have between your legs?'

'No,' Graham said. 'I just thought it looked funny, that's all.'

'Not funny,' Ali said. 'It is the part of a man that is the most beautiful. It should be respected. See, here is mine.'

He opened his trousers and felt inside them. His cock

appeared, long and thick. He pulled on it slowly and then reached across and took hold of Graham's. Graham lay back and let him feel as much as he wanted. Then he had a pang of conscience. He was doing it again. He was treating this man as though he were a whore, not a lover. He raised himself and placed both of his hands on Ali's shoulders.

'Let me give you pleasure,' he said quietly. 'Lie back and think of Egypt.'

His mouth brushed over Ali's cheek and down his neck. He flicked his tongue against the hot skin before unbuttoning the tunic and the shirt beneath it. Ali was wearing a vest underneath. Graham lifted it up and was pleased to find a slim, smooth chest with not a blemish on it.

He kissed Ali's nipples, each in turn, and then again. Then he concentrated on one of them, licking, sucking, nibbling. Ali reached over and tried to feel Graham's own nipple, but their positions were awkward now and he couldn't do it. He tried to adjust himself so they could, but Graham was intent on showing his contrition and all but pushed him out of the way.

'You must be taught how to make love,' Ali said. 'For you it is not a sharing thing, but one man doing to the other only. Here we give the honour of our attentions back and forth so both are united in their passion.'

Graham stopped what he was doing. 'I'm sorry,' he said.

'It is not to be sorry. It is to learn,' Ali replied. 'Are you willing to learn?'

'I'm just dying to learn,' Graham said. 'Absolutely.'

It was at that moment the phone rang. It was Percy Gilbert.

Graham met Percy in the bar some half an hour later.

'I didn't imagine you might be in bed,' Percy said.

He was flustered: half of his attention given apologetically to Graham; the other attempting to attract one of the waiters in the lounge. He had in fact ordered a drink, but quite a long time ago and nothing whatsoever had arrived.

'I'm so sorry to disturb . . . Really! These people are so very admirable in many ways, but they have no idea whatsoever of how to give proper service to their guests.'

Graham couldn't help but grin at this after what Ali had said – and indeed *done* to demonstrate his brand of 'proper service'. They had broken off Graham's lesson in love but Ali had promised to continue it at some other time. The fact that Graham had a female sexual partner neither surprised nor worried Ali. He took the information as being a quite normal state of things which was only to be expected. He would, he said, be 'most discreet'.

Graham caught the eye of the man behind the bar and mimed to him to send somebody over. His bad temper having evaporated completely and his friendly demeanour now attractive to all and sundry, he succeeded immediately. Percy was impressed.

'I thought I was the one who had the knack. You, no doubt, have charisma. I think that's the correct word. Yes, you certainly have that. I know it . . .' His conversation trailed off and he looked lost all of a sudden. He saw Graham looking at him and blushed. 'I do apologise. It's just I'm so worried, you see. Jeremy has been out with our friend, René, an awfully long time and Ahmed doesn't have the faintest idea where they might have ended up.'

He accepted the drink and swallowed a mouthful of it too quickly, making himself cough. Graham saw a good-hearted man on the later side of middle age who was driving himself frantic because his friend was late for their nightcap together. Jeremy Oakland was behaving like a cad, but it was nothing. It was trivial.

'He'll be back,' he said. 'He's probably riding a camel off into the desert.'

Percy patted Graham's hand. It was intended to be a surreptitious gesture but it caused several raised eyebrows around the room. Percy coloured and mopped his forehead with his handkerchief.

'He must surely have done this sort of thing before,' Graham went on. 'It's hardly uncommon and – don't worry – the Egyptians are very fond of the English. He'll come to no harm. I'm certain of it.'

'I'm keeping you up,' Percy said. 'I do thank you for your kind words. I suppose I must seem very foolish to you.'

Graham squeezed Percy's hand, much to Percy's astonishment and the disapproval of those raised eyebrows around them.

'Nothing has happened to Jeremy,' Graham said.

It was Wednesday at dawn. Jeremy's mind was crowded with practical strategies, none of which seemed remotely helpful. Flashing into his brain like a beacon was the one message that he wanted to hold on to: 'I am a British citizen. They can't do anything to me.'

It wasn't enough to take away his terror. He had been caught doing what was surely highly illegal, no matter which country one was in. He had no idea what the penalty would be. Ridiculous images insisted on visiting him: of being publicly flogged, or held in some ghastly prison until he was old, or even being shot by firing squad. No amount of reasoning with himself could dispel his fear. He hugged his knees into his chest and hid his face, trying to find comfort, if only for a second or two.

He was alone. They had taken René somewhere else. He might be in the next cell, or he might be in some tiny interrogation room with a light shining in his eyes: 'How do you know this man? What did you do together? Was it at his suggestion?'

At the time of their arrest, he'd protested: he'd said they were just sleeping. He wasn't sure whether René had understood, though he'd tried to say it in such a way that would be clear to him as well as to the policemen. They hadn't appeared to be interested, either in his excuses or his later demands to be allowed access to a telephone.

The two prisoners had had their trousers thrown at them, but the rest of their clothes had been kept. In this humiliating state of undress, they had been handcuffed and pushed into the back of an ancient car. Jeremy had tried to hide himself from the inquisitive looks of passers-by, much to the amusement of the two officers. They didn't appear to be unfriendly, but their matter-of-fact attitude had a hint of menace about it which was unnerving.

No comment had been made apart from an offhand 'OK, OK' every time Jeremy had demanded his shirt, or a telephone, or tried once again to explain how they had come to be lying naked at the back of the temple. Perhaps the guards did not speak English. René had kept up a stream of angry protest which was similarly ignored. Jeremy had wanted him to be quiet. Antagonising these people seemed like the height of folly. Then again, Arabs always shouted at each other, and nobody seemed to mind it.

The police station was as basic as might have been expected. The gas mantles threw shadows against the undecorated, rough walls and the concrete floor. Unsurpisingly, there was no glass in the windows, just plain bars. It was, in short, the archetypal prison, its plainness underlining its function. There was a desk at which sat a middle-aged man who chain-smoked and continually shifted forms, stamping them officiously for what seemed like no good reason other than it making him look important.

Without taking any more notice of the two prisoners' complaints than his colleagues had, he'd taken Jeremy by the arm and manhandled him into the cell where he was to spend the rest of the night. Once inside, Jeremy had been freed from the handcuffs. The rest of his clothes – Graham's clothes, in fact – had still not been returned to him.

There was a mattress on the floor with a crude, grey blanket to cover it. In the corner was a bucket which presumably was to serve as a lavatory. There was a window which looked out on to a yard and, beyond it, a brick wall. Jeremy had nothing else to distract him from his anxiety. He felt as though he had been plunged into hell.

And yet he was indignant. What harm had they done anyone? Two men who found each other attractive had rubbed their bodies together and fallen asleep. It was, he found himself saying out loud, 'hardly in Al Capone's league'.

He was rocking now. Back and forth, like a lunatic in an asylum. He had to get a grip on himself. He had to think of a plan.

If he had any guilt it was not for himself, but for René. René would suffer because of this far more than he would. René had to live in this place long after Jeremy had returned to England. René would have a distraught mother and a family who would see his arrest as the ultimate shame. No amount of reasoning seemed to help. Yes, René must have known the risks; yes, René had been just as willing as Jeremy; yes, he was a grown man who must take responsibility for his actions. It was no good. Jeremy felt wretched.

Footsteps. Jeremy sat up too quickly. It made him dizzy and his head was still swimming as the key turned in the lock.

It was one of the officers who had arrested them. As his face came into focus, Jeremy was disgusted to find his instant reaction to the lean, handsome features which gloated down upon him was one of attraction.

The man was about his own age and, though a little too slender for Jeremy's taste, was also lithe and fit. He was crisply dressed in the same khaki uniform he had worn the previous evening. He was bare-headed, his hair shaved close at the sides of his head and round the back of his neck. This severity was softened by the soft black hair on top. He was short, and cocky. His whole attitude was bullish. Even the fuzz on his upper lip (an attempt at a moustache that hadn't come off) was indicative of his personality. This was a man who enjoyed the power his job afforded him. He was not one to be appealed to.

'Stand,' he ordered.

Jeremy did so.

The officer came close, so close as to be uncomfortable. Jeremy tried to keep his eyes fixed on a point behind the man's head. It would not do to meet his eye for that might be seen as confrontational. He was aware the man was smiling, but it was not a pleasant smile.

'You are a pervert,' the officer said, making it a statement of fact which was not to be contradicted.

'You are English?' he added after a long pause.

Jeremy swallowed hard and nodded. He was sweating now. He could feel the beads of perspiration falling from his brow and running down his arms.

'Your new prime minister, Mr Stanley Baldwin, sends us his perverts. Is that so?'

Jeremy nodded again. He was too frightened to do anything else. The officer pushed his clenched fist into Jeremy's bare stomach. It wasn't intended to hurt. He was testing: seeing how far he could intimidate his prisoner. He ground his fist into the soft flesh and, seemingly satisfied with the resulting panic on Jeremy's face, took it back again.

'Winter Palace Hotel, yes?'

Jeremy was eager to affirm this. It might mean they were going to contact his friends. Maybe this whole thing could be dealt with by offering a huge bribe to these people. Percy would know what to do – or Graham.

'I have companions there. They will be worried about me. Please –'

The officer tapped him on the cheek with the flat of his hand. He was enjoying himself. This was no more than a game to him.

'Yes. You have companions. I know. Is OK.'

'But will you –'

Again the light slap on his cheek.

'Kneel.'

Jeremy wasn't sure. He hesitated and soon wished he hadn't. The man slapped him hard across the face and, for a second or two, genuine anger surfaced.

'I say, "Kneel." You kneel!' shouted the guard.

Jeremy did so, terrified. The officer stood directly over him with his legs slightly apart. For all the shortness of his stature, he seemed to tower above Jeremy. His hands went to the front of his trousers and paused there, making the significance of the action plain.

The bastard wants to have me! Jeremy thought. He's going to make me suck his cock. Part of his fear disappeared instantly. A 'pervert' who disgusted these people by what he had done would have had no chance. A man who had been caught doing something his captors did themselves could at least level with them.

His own penis was responding. He was more aware of it because of not wearing his underclothes. The looseness of his trousers felt pleasant as his shaft brushed against them. He had at least been lucky enough to be arrested by a handsome officer. Had it been the man on the desk he would have found forced sex to be a far greater ordeal.

The officer reached inside and brought out his cock. It was neither hard, which Jeremy was relieved to see, nor was it exactly huge. If he was going to be made to suck it, he would do his very best to please this man. If he performed well, maybe they would let him go.

But the officer didn't put his cock anywhere near Jeremy's lips. He took hold of his prisoner's hair and yanked his head back so his face looked up to the ceiling. Then he bestrode Jeremy with his penis hovering over Jeremy's face. He held it at the base, gently shaking it up and down.

Drops of urine splashed over Jeremy. A spurt came next. The guard tensed, holding back the full flow. Jeremy collapsed inside, horrified. The guard seemed pleased. Keeping hold of Jeremy's hair, he pointed himself so he could better hit his target before letting go of the full stream of piss.

It splashed over Jeremy, a concentrated jet of warm, salty fluid. He had plenty of it inside him and the force with which it came out indicated he had been saving it.

Jeremy's horror was mingled with a growing feeling of abandonment. He was a prisoner, kneeling to take a man's piss. He couldn't escape it and maybe he didn't want to. If he was going to please this bastard, he would have to accept his position and demonstrate that acceptance. He dared to open his mouth.

The stream of piss filled him and he drank from it. Yes, his mind was racing with doubts, but he quashed them. He had heard, and believed it to be true, that urine was not a dangerous thing to drink. He felt amazingly charged with lust. Sex, power, submission: it was all one. He closed his eyes and surrendered. The piss didn't taste of anything – it was just hot liquid – but it meant so much. It meant he was nothing to this man; nothing but an object. This was the man in his dreams. The man he had been sold to so often. He was a slave at last.

The man finished pissing, but he didn't move and Jeremy dared not either. He could smell the urine on his own skin; splashes of it stained his trousers. He hung his head to demonstrate his subservience and waited for what might come next. He was still not entirely sure this man was after sex. It might be that he wanted to piss on him simply to demonstrate his opinion of homosexuals. Whatever the case, it seemed politic to be as obedient as was possible. The officer grunted loudly and gave a curt, 'Hey! Pervert!'

Jeremy looked up and was rewarded by a gob of spit in the face. The officer was really enjoying himself and, to Jeremy's relief, his cock was lengthening. This didn't mean he wouldn't add to his pleasure by causing Jeremy pain. Jeremy had heard of unspeakable tortures being visited upon prisoners in these sorts of places. He wondered how King Fuad felt about perverted love – probably more open-minded than the British representatives in Egypt.

He allowed the spit to run down his face without attempting to wipe it away. This amused the guard and prompted him to spit again. This time he bent over and himself wiped it across Jeremy's face. Then he took Jeremy's chin firmly in the cup of his hand and deliberately twisted his head to the right and left, examining Jeremy's features. He seemed pleased because he grunted and patted Jeremy's shoulder. Then he poised his cock by Jeremy's lips.

'You good dick-sucker?' he asked.

Jeremy responded by taking the guard's, now hard, cock into his mouth and devouring it hungrily. He licked carefully, but kept up a hard suction which he knew from experience was satisfying. He could tell he was giving pleasure because the officer had closed his eyes and relaxed considerably. Jeremy dared to bring his hands round the back of the man's legs and he felt up and down, trying to bring a little love into this brutal scene. The man took this for some short time but then became impatient. It was evidently too gentle for him.

He pushed Jeremy away roughly and undid his own trousers, letting them fall to the ground. Jeremy had a fleeting image of himself the night before and wryly recollected this was exactly how he had begun the terrible crime for which he'd been arrested. Next, the officer went for Jeremy, pulling away his meagre covering as though it were the last wrapper in a 'pass the parcel' game. Jeremy was soon naked.

The man pushed him over on to all fours and pressed his upper body down to the concrete floor. He was grunting over and over again, like a satisfied pig. He knelt behind, keeping his hand on Jeremy's shoulder so was continually reminded that he wasn't to attempt to move. Jeremy prepared himself. He had no doubt this man would have no finesse in fucking him. This was going to be hard and short and would probably hurt like hell.

It did at first. Jeremy yelled and received a cuff across the back of the head for it. He remembered to take deep breaths and try to relax his anus so the pain might ease. It lasted only a few seconds before he found he was loving the feeling inside him and was even making responding noises to those intermittent satisfied grunts.

'You like?' the guard said. 'You like me inside your bottom?'

It might have been his use of this word that amused him, or it might have been the appropriateness of his fucking a man whom he had arrested for fucking somebody else. Whatever the case, the officer laughed to himself as if the whole thing was highly comical. All the while he never let off fucking his prisoner. It was a rhythmic stabbing which, though it was not intended to, was stimulating Jeremy's gut and bringing his penis to full hardness. He wondered if he would be allowed to come; he somehow doubted it.

As it happened, the officer had no apparent desire to reach orgasm himself. He pulled out of Jeremy's arse and stood apart from him, milking his cock, but not in such a way as to finish his pleasure.

'Stand up.'

Jeremy stood. He lowered his head respectfully.

'Look at me!' This was said angrily, as though Jeremy's attempt at subservience was directly disobeying some order he had been given.

Jeremy raised his eyes and met those of his tormentor. He wished he could level with this person: tell him he was perfectly willing to give whatever sexual service the guard wanted as long as he was allowed to go free at the end of it. He wondered if René was undergoing similar humiliations with the other officer.

'You are in trouble, Englishman,' the man reminded him.

Obviously, 'hypocrisy' was not a word in this monster's vocabulary. Jeremy had a rush of blood to the head and, without actually knowing what he was doing, or why, he flung himself on the floor at the feet of the officer and began kissing his boots fervently. He kissed them with all his passion. When the guard shifted away, Jeremy pulled the foot back to his mouth and carried on insistently.

'Why you kiss my feet?' The voice sounded puzzled and had at last lost some of that sneering edge which had marked it hitherto. 'You crazy man. What you doing?'

'Let me serve you,' Jeremy said hoarsely. 'You understand? I want to serve you.'

The guard pushed him away with his boot as though he were an irritating cur trying to rub himself against his leg. He still looked wary, but his lips had curled into a mocking smile once again. He pulled up his trousers and buckled his belt.

'You crazy,' he repeated. 'I no want crazy person.'

'You like my body?' Jeremy asked. 'It's yours. You can do what you want with me. I can make you feel good.'

For answer, the guard, who was now fully dressed again, shouted something and blew a whistle. Footsteps came running and Jeremy tried in vain to cover his nakedness. He wasn't quick enough. The door of the cell opened and there stood the other young policeman from the night before.

There was a brief, animated conversation between the two of them and much pointing and amusement. The second officer was nodding eagerly, his eyes never leaving off looking at Jeremy. Jeremy for his part decided it would be best to keep absolutely still and try not to meet those eyes. He knelt on the floor and waited.

The newcomer came into the room at last and circled him as though Jeremy were an exhibit in the museum. With any luck, he had simply joined them in order to have his own piece of the cake.

Jeremy could not make out anything of what they said one to another. They were enjoying themselves; that was all he could tell. He wondered how many other officers there were in this place and whether they all knew exactly what went on, or whether fucking a prisoner was something the first guard would try to hide from his colleagues.

The second guard squatted down beside him and reached into the top pocket of his shirt. He brought out a folded piece of paper: something torn from a magazine. He licked his finger and found the edge of it, unfolding it slowly. All this time he continued to fix his attention on Jeremy, studying his every reaction and finding all his nervousness interestingly comic. He thrust the paper under Jeremy's nose and said something in Arabic which his friend translated.

'Look at picture. He wants to know if you like.'

Jeremy looked. It was a picture of Rudolph Valentino with Agnes Ayres in the famous clinch from *The Sheik*.

The guard was grinning inanely as though what he was showing Jeremy were something precious of which he was very proud. Jeremy muttered that it was very nice. He wasn't entirely sure this was the desired reaction.

'Which one?'

This was, again, a translation of what his mate had said. Jeremy didn't comprehend for a second or two and then it dawned on him. He was being asked if he found women or men attractive. They were trying to find out if he, presumably like them, would be willing and able to have either gender in his bed.

'They're very nice,' he said again. 'Both of them.'

He hoped this was noncommittal enough and polite enough for the subject to be dropped and the guard to be satisfied. The second officer was looking from Jeremy to his friend. Though his only means of communication was through his companion, he appeared to want to be physically close to Jeremy: intimate. It made him all the more threatening.

He put his mouth close to Jeremy's ear and whispered conspiratorially. Jeremy looked towards the other man, who may or may not have heard what had been said. He joined them. Jeremy was still kneeling and both guards were now squatting each side of his naked body. He was thoroughly intimidated.

The second police officer was only a little taller than the first, but he was thicker set. He was almost burly. He had the tracings of a beard under his chin, but no moustache. He had very bright eyes, his brows close down over them. The effect was to make that part of his face serious, no matter what his mouth did to contradict the expression. He wore a peaked cap, far back on his head, like a schoolboy who had been required to wear a uniform but who refuses to conform. He had uneven, broken teeth, but he was not unattractive.

He took hold of Jeremy's penis and felt its weight in his hand. He stroked it absent-mindedly; it might have been some bauble he was considering purchasing. He suddenly squeezed it hard and was clearly appreciative of the sharp intake of breath this caused. Then he took some of Jeremy's pubic hair between his finger and thumb and pulled sharply. The tug was fast enough not to hurt very much, but, nevertheless, it caused Jeremy's eyes to water. The man wiped the tear away with his own hand, took Jeremy's cock again and turned to consult the first officer.

They had quite a long conversation. All through it, the second guard never let go of Jeremy's penis. He squeezed it and rolled it about in his hand, using it like he would a lump of clay which he intended to soften for sculpting. Jeremy eventually closed his eyes, listening to the fast, energised jabber of words which meant nothing to him and feeling the constant manipulation of his cock. He was a prisoner (in his mind, a slave) in between two handsome men, one of whom had already used his arse. Soon the other one would want to have his fun. He wanted to be pleasing to them. He wanted to give himself.

His face was slapped to make him open his eyes. The first guard was holding out the picture again.

'He want you to have this.'

Jeremy was completely nonplussed. The guard was thrusting the paper towards him and the one who had first produced it was nodding encouragingly.

'You say you like. It is Valentino. He very famous. Take.'

Hesitating, for he had no idea where this was leading, Jeremy took the paper and bowed his thanks to both men. He had nowhere to put it of course, so he laid it reverently on the floor beside him and placed his hand on top of it to show how very much he valued it.

The second guard took hold of Jeremy's hand and brought it to his lips. He kissed it romantically and then threw back his head and laughed at this ridiculous travesty of courtship. He spoke again; again his words were translated to Jeremy.

'He says you woman and he Valentino. He take you in sands of desert.'

'He can take me here,' Jeremy said. 'You both can. Then I must return to the hotel or they will come looking for me. I don't want to get you into trouble.'

The first officer's face clouded over and he dealt Jeremy a hefty blow across the face. He explained to his companion what Jeremy had said and the other man tut-tutted sadly. Jeremy held his smarting cheek and waited for the guard's anger to calm.

'You threat?' the man shouted. 'You threat me? I arrest you! You are pervert! I not pervert! They look for you and I tell them you arrested for being pervert. Then *you* in trouble. Not me.'

This altercation had meant the second man letting go his hold on Jeremy. He continued to look sadly at his recalcitrant charge, but he took hold of Jeremy's cock again and rubbed it back to its full stiffness. This time he accompanied the attention by rubbing the front of his own trousers, bringing a noticeable lump to the fore.

Jeremy assumed they were playing a psychological game with him: the nice one and the nasty one. They were trying to completely unnerve him, maybe for their own amusement, maybe for some other reason. He resolved to simply go along with whatever they wanted and try to please. He would not attempt to leave until they were ready to let him. After all, they couldn't keep him here for ever. It had to end somewhere.

'My friend think it would be good to have present from you. He given you something. Now you give him something.'

Jeremy wondered what on earth the man could want. He had no money. Presumably any he'd had in his jacket had already been taken by these two. All he had to give was his body. Maybe this was what they meant.

Very slowly, making it clear that he wasn't trying to do anything to trick them, he moved away. He fixed his eyes on the second officer, mentally urging him to pay attention. The man did pay attention. He was transfixed.

Jeremy turned his back, still with very slow movements so as not to alarm either man. Then he bent over and raised his bottom up off the floor, inviting the man to have it.

This seemed to meet with both men's approval. Jeremy had his eyes closed and wasn't about to risk offending either man by trying to find out what they were doing. He could hear them moving behind him. He assumed from the sound of undressing that one or the other of them was going to fuck him again.

When he sensed one of them close to him, he took deep breaths and pushed his arse further towards them so their access to his insides might be even easier. He was determined to be a good boy, a model prisoner.

It wasn't the warmth of flesh which came into contact with him. It was cold, hard and smooth. Jeremy only had to think for a second or two before he knew he was being poked by the baton he had seen dangling from the second officer's belt. He wasn't forcing it in, but the push against him was firm and demanding. The implication being that Jeremy should impale himself upon it.

He reached behind himself to guide the thing inside him. It was made of polished wood, thicker at the top end than it was further down. It had a ridged handle with a disc-shaped fist guard round it. He placed the bulbous end of the truncheon against his sphincter. His arse was still relaxed from having been entered only a few minutes before.

The baton went in without trouble and was swallowed by Jeremy's gut as it tapered down towards the handle. The fist guard met with his buttocks and he knew the truncheon was fully inside him. He moved about carefully, feeling the obstruction and loving it. The guard twisted it. This was slightly uncomfortable. Jeremy let out a short gasp. It betrayed to his captors that their prisoner wasn't completely immune to their sadism and this seemed to go down very well indeed. It was twisted again, this time more viciously. Jeremy had adjusted to the movement after the first time and the second twist felt good.

He wisely decided to pretend hurt and therefore let out a cry of pain which prompted even more twisting. Then the guard started to fuck him with the thing. Jeremy realised that any movement on his part would show he was enjoying it and so he tried to stay absolutely still. He gave out small yelps and whimpers every so often to let them think he was in pain.

His inner fluids had lubricated the phallic implement fully. The polish and the smoothness of the wood presented no obstruction. Jeremy even wondered if he could find one of these things to take home and use on himself. It was certainly reaching his prostate and making it increasingly difficult to keep his joy of it to himself.

It stopped abruptly. There was more scuffling before Jeremy felt the hard wood being removed swiftly, to be replaced by the warmth of human flesh. He could tell it was the second guard who was inside him by the smell of his body. He was more careful than his friend, slower and more leisurely.

After the truncheon, Jeremy didn't get as much pleasure from his cock, but it still felt good. He risked a very small movement against it to give more thrust. The guard slapped his buttocks playfully, then harder, then harder still. Soon the slapping was stinging him, but not so he couldn't take more. He grunted and sighed, letting the attention his backside was receiving take over his mind.

The guard was now hitting him in the same rhythm as he

fucked. The slaps came each time he went in and indicated how close he was to spilling his come. The other man came to Jeremy's side and reached under for his cock. He wanked him while his friend brought himself to the point of no return. The man's hot wetness spurted into Jeremy's gut and he felt the cock soften there. It was over.

The first guard still hadn't come, and neither had Jeremy. There was a silence. The second man was mopping himself on Jeremy's trousers. He was proud of his performance and was giving all his attention to his cock, which was glistening with semen.

The other was looking at Jeremy. After some time he spoke.

'Is not enough. You are our pervert. You must give us money. Much money. We want present from England.'

'I don't have any money,' Jeremy said. 'I don't have anything.'

'No,' the guard conceded. 'Not here. But your friends: your important friends at hotel. They have money. Will they pay to have their pervert back with them?'

Jeremy wasn't given chance to reply. The second man, now having cleaned himself to his satisfaction, spoke in broken English for the first time.

'The men at hotel. Yes. They have baksheesh for us.'

Jeremy was finally going to be allowed his telephone call.

Six

––––––––––

Graham had breakfasted that morning on the veranda over-looking the gardens. It was still early enough to be cool – as it might be on a fine summer afternoon in England. At one point, he caught sight of Ali. He was no longer in his tunic and was, no doubt, on his way home after the night shift. He was in deep discussion with another Arab man who was wearing a smart suit and dark glasses. He looked like a decidedly shifty individual, but seemed to be taking everything Ali said deferentially.

Afterwards, Ali looked up and waved at him. Graham felt the warmth of affection and it occurred to him he wasn't such a fuddy-duddy old European after all. To prove this to himself, when the waiter brought his coffee, he tipped him far too much and absolutely refused to listen to his profuse thanks.

The women were due back today. That would please old Oakland, thought Graham sarcastically. Jeremy was a very nice bloke, but it was obvious he was playing a dangerous game with the affections of two wealthy people. Graham supposed it highly unlikely Jeremy would have had the courage or the opportunity to have an arrangement with Percy and Mrs Dryden such as he and Maria had.

He was looking forward to Maria's homecoming. No, he couldn't say he'd missed her. The beauty of their relationship was that each separation gave them opportunity for diversity and no toes were trodden on in the process. Their only rule was Graham must not sleep with women other than Maria and Maria must not sleep with men other than Graham. It was perfect.

The world seemed a very nice place to be that morning. Until Percy turned up.

'There you are,' he panted as he approached. 'I looked in the dining room and in your room and . . . Oh dear, you see . . . I've nobody else I can turn to. I do hope you don't mind my worrying over your breakfast.'

He sat down and presented a face of such consternation that Graham put aside his excuse (which he'd formed as soon as he had seen Percy approaching) and, instead, invited him to take coffee.

Percy was absent-minded and the invitation took some seconds to sink in. He came to, briefly, in order to say, 'What? Coffee? Oh, yes, yes. Thank you, my dear chap.' Then he sank back into his fretful gloom.

'His bed hasn't been slept in,' he said at last. 'I know I'm being a mother hen and I really do not wish to be. But I can't help but worry. I really am very concerned.'

'He doesn't deserve you,' Graham said. 'He's very naughty.'

Percy tried to deny both sentiments. He was only a silly old man and Jeremy was very caring and thoughtful. That, indeed, was why he was so worried at Jeremy's nonappearance. It simply wasn't like him.

'What say you we take a calash ride? Your friend, Ahmed, seems to know what's what and who goes where.'

Percy had spoken to Ahmed already and Ahmed knew nothing of what had happened to Jeremy. He had been round to René's house and found no one at home, but that was not unusual. The working people in Luxor were up and about long before the holidaymakers. Ahmed was going to make enquiries, but had seemed to think the pair had absconded for 'some reason'.

'Some reason' was Percy's euphemism. He was still being circumspect about all things sexual. Graham had thought he had made his own position clear, but maybe not. This gentle soul was evidently still not entirely sure of whether openness would offend.

'You mean they're having fun?' he ventured.

Percy avoided Graham's eyes and nodded, guilty and anxious to change the subject. 'Yes, yes, that's right.'

'Look,' Graham said. 'Forgive me, but you don't perchance labour under the misapprehension that Jeremy stays faithful to you?'

Percy blinked at him in genuine surprise. 'Faithful? To me?'

'I don't know anything about your relationship, but Jeremy is something of the bumblebee going from flower to flower – if you'll forgive my stupid attempt at metaphor.'

Percy relaxed somewhat. Though nothing had been said directly, Graham was gratified to see he had said the right thing and put Percy at his ease.

'These things are so difficult,' Percy said. 'One never really knows who knows, if you know what I mean.'

'For my part,' Graham said, 'you can be quite candid with me. I am not the sort to go screaming to the police as soon as I see two men kissing each other.'

'The police!' Percy said, seizing on the idea. 'Do you suppose we ought to contact them and report Jeremy missing?'

'Not at all,' Graham said as soothingly as he could. 'I tell you, he's fine. He'll deserve slapped wrists and bed with no supper for the trouble he's caused, but he's not on the critical list. Not just yet.'

One of the staff approached. He was a rotund chap with a waxed moustache. He was anxious not to let the message he had to give interfere with his guests' enjoyment of breakfast. This difficult balance, it seemed, was best achieved by bowing an awful lot and taking an awfully long time to get to the point.

'I sorry, Mr Percy Gilbert. Forgive this intrusion on what is your time, please. I hope you enjoy your food. But I see you have not yet had food – or maybe you have finished?'

Percy was far too mild-mannered to let his anxiety change to irritation, but Graham could see he was verging on exasperation and the situation needed rescuing.

'Have you a message for Mr Gilbert?' he asked. 'We are having a rather important conversation and we really haven't time for chat. I do so hope you understand.'

'I understand, I understand . . .'

The man 'understood' many times over, the words gradually losing their meaning with the repetition. Now Graham was getting exasperated too, and he was not so mild as Percy.

'The message?'

'Is delicate, perhaps. Not here. Perhaps we must go to the inside of the hotel, where I might have a private word with Mr Gilbert.'

Percy was already halfway out of his chair, but Graham stopped him. After asking for and receiving Percy's permission, he told the man he was to speak in front of both of them. He had a growing sense of unease. This had to be about Jeremy. What had the little fool gone and done?

The man coughed politely before asking, 'Mr Jeremy Oakland is your *habibi* – friend?'

Percy affirmed this to be true.

The man went on: 'I fear there has been some trouble and Mr Oakland has requested the pleasure of your company at the police.'

The messenger didn't know what the nature of this trouble was. He was so very sorry to be the bearer of bad news. Perhaps the gentlemen would care to come into his office? There, he could offer them a strong drink in a place where they wouldn't be seen indulging at this early hour.

This was refused, but the man still hovered. He was perhaps keen to discover what the drama was all about. Graham had no doubt all persons in his profession were lovers of gossip.

Neither he nor Percy bothered to stay and listen to his carefully prepared assurances that everything was surely perfectly all right. They were already on their way.

The attitude of the officer they faced across the desk was quite intolerable. He was supercilious and really quite impertinent. Had it not been for Graham's presence, Percy would certainly have lost his temper. This was not the treatment Englishmen should expect from these people.

He and Graham had arrived as quickly as they could. Percy had fretted all the way and had insisted their driver was taking them by the longest route. This had provoked a row which Graham had only just managed to calm. Percy had taken his fractious mood into the station with him – he admitted it – even if such an attitude did go against Graham's good advice.

They had waited for an eternity; they had begged, threatened and pleaded. Percy had explained to the man on the desk – and he thought he'd done so clearly, concisely and reasonably – what their demands were: they insisted upon knowing exactly what had gone on; they needed to see their friend and this must be arranged straight away.

The brutish fellow (not the night officer whom Jeremy had seen, but very much of the same type) had smiled, showing all his yellow teeth, and then simply returned to reading his newspaper. It had taken a hefty wad of notes before he would even condescend to raise himself from his chair and ring the bell to summon his colleagues.

Once these two horrors had arrived, they too had to be paid similarly large amounts of money. Their shift had ended at dawn, they said. They had stayed only in order to look after the prisoner. This they expected payment for.

The money changing hands had not – as Percy had expected it would – solved the entire problem. Evidently it was just a stage in the game. They were out to make as much as possible from the situation. Graham had whispered a cautionary word or two: if Percy demonstrated he was willing to keep on dipping into his wallet, they would surely exploit him for all he was worth. He would be better off pretending Jeremy was not worth all that much to him. In this way they had a chance of securing his release for the lowest amount possible.

'I do appreciate your advice,' Percy had said somewhat irritably, 'but I must be allowed to do all I can to get Jeremy out of this situation. If that means throwing money at these devils, then so be it. At least it's something I'm relatively good at.'

After His Majesty, the Union Jack and England had been invoked several times, the guards had decided they would allow their prisoner to talk for himself.

'He is an Englishman who the English would rather not have on their island. He is not your good John Bull,' the guard had said. When he spoke, he had a vile habit of chewing on a toothpick which he used for its proper purpose every time he paused. Percy found him to be utterly revolting. Graham seemed to quite get on with him, but Graham was evidently not as close to the situation as Percy was and could therefore afford to be objective.

'I have no idea what you're implying –' Percy had begun.

Graham had laid a restraining hand on his arm and taken over. 'Are you saying our friend has done more than inadvertently broken some local law? Is – How can I put this? Is someone else involved in this problem?'

This had amused the guard enormously. He had translated it, first to his colleague and then to the man on the desk, who had enjoyed the joke every bit as much as the two officers. Percy had felt he was going to explode. To his annoyance, Graham had actually joined in the laughter as though he understood what it was all about.

'Really! I know we have to be diplomatic, but there is no need whatsoever to be quite so accommodating of their rudeness,' Percy said angrily.

Percy was stopped by a flash of seriousness across Graham's face which was immediately supplanted by the genial laughter it had interrupted. Percy kept his petulant comments to himself thereafter. Graham was obviously aware of exactly what he was doing.

Graham had approached one of the guards. He had grabbed hold of his hand very tightly, still smiling away. He had whispered something that Percy could not hear. The guard suddenly looked shocked and both Egyptian men stopped laughing as though their merriment had been switched off like a light. The change in them was violent and immediate, but it apparently had not affected Graham's attitude towards them. He had whispered again and both the guards had left the room immediately.

'What . . .?' Percy began. Graham shook his head quickly to indicate he should hold his tongue until later.

The man on the desk had gone very quiet. He was pretending to read his newspaper but he kept looking up towards Graham somewhat warily.

Then one of the guards, the senior one they supposed, returned. He was pushing Jeremy in front of him and occasionally prodding him with a truncheon. Jeremy was looking more wretched than Percy had ever seen him in his life. Whatever had happened to him in that squalid little prison had changed him absolutely. He looked like he had suffered the torments of hell. He was barefoot, in loose trousers and open shirt. His hands were cuffed behind him and his face was ravaged. He was a man who had been deprived of sleep by fear and torture. He had been pushed into the room as though he had no more rights than an animal.

Percy felt a lump coming up into his throat and it was all he could do to prevent himself burying his face in his hands or availing himself of Graham's manly shoulders.

Jeremy immediately sank to his knees and began to sob uncontrollably. Percy went over to him and patted his head as fondly as he could without it looking effeminate in front of these hateful people. Graham knelt down beside Jeremy and actually took his face in both hands and kissed him fully on the lips. Neither of the two Arabs now present seemed to react to this. One read his newspaper and the other stood and looked on impassively.

Percy, quite beside himself with rage at the unnecessarily harsh treatment his friend had received, angrily threw down a couple of banknotes and all but stamped his foot as he said, 'I expect you'll require payment of some kind before you'll have the decency to remove his handcuffs. There! I trust that should be enough!'

He hoped the contempt in which he held them was clear enough. Whatever the case, the guard first picked up the money and then took a key from his pocket and freed Jeremy's hands.

Jeremy was helped to his feet and guided slowly out of the room into a calash outside.

'René!' he said as they set off. 'I've left René in there. I must get him out.'

They were safe in Graham's suite in the splendid comfort of the Winter Palace Hotel. Jeremy was already subtly transforming his version of the night's events into a good yarn. Graham, who was alone with him now, was an excellent listener; Jeremy was actually beginning to thoroughly enjoy himself.

'He did what?' Graham said. He had a look of fascinated horror on his face and edged further towards Jeremy in the manner of a small boy thrillingly horrified by a ghost story.

Jeremy smiled at him. He really did feel much better now – in clean clothes, having bathed and shaved. Even apart from its value as a conversation piece, he was beginning to view his unfortunate adventure as something really quite exciting. He was aware of a raging erection whenever he thought or spoke of the sexual treatment he had been forced to accept.

'He urinated all over me and in my mouth. I had to drink it.'

Graham made a face and swigged a mouthful of whisky as though this might eradicate the taste he was imagining.

'Actually I enjoyed it. I felt very . . . complete.'

Graham looked puzzled for a moment and then shrugged. 'Ah well,' he said. 'Each to his own. Just don't expect everybody to want to take part in such activities. Most of the people I know would run a mile. And for God's sake don't tell Percy. He's had about as much as he can take.'

Prior to this conversation, Percy had been given the bare bones of the story. Then he'd been sent to his room with an aspirin and a cup of tea laced with something strong. Jeremy was in no fit state to talk to him properly; this he had accepted. Percy had promised to make a phone call to the police station to see what had happened to René. He'd wanted to do something and this was the most practical way in which he could help.

After he had gone, in Graham's company, Jeremy had managed to regain his dignity. Especially when Graham had told him how he'd looked both handsome and heroic in the police station with his chest bared, his hair mussed, his chin covered in stubble and his hands cuffed behind his back.

'You looked like a man in an adventure story I read when I was a small child,' Graham said. 'In the illustration he's tied to a tree and about to be eaten by cannibals or some such thing. He had this impossibly powerful chest and they'd ripped his shirt open, so they could get a better cut of meat I suppose. I always thought I wanted to be that man. Needless to say, he was bounding away through the jungle by the time you got to the next chapter. He was amazing.'

'Talking of lucky escapes,' Jeremy said, 'I don't suppose mine was totally to do with luck and Percy's money. Apparently, according to Percy, you were wonderful with those policemen. What did you do?'

Graham looked bashful. He smiled a little and then walked over to the window to look out at the river.

'Come on,' Jeremy said. 'I have to know. It will spoil the story of my adventure if I don't know – and I intend to tell everybody.' He realised what he was saying and qualified it immediately. 'I shan't tell everything over dinner, of course. Well, not unless I'm having dinner in a male brothel.'

Graham laughed and turned back to him. 'I took a bit of a risk,' he said at last. 'It might not have worked, but we were lucky. I told the officer you had a sexually transmitted disease and it would be best for them if they let you out as it was very easy to catch. He's probably being examined by his doctors even as we speak. With any luck that will also be a good reason why they shouldn't want to hang on to René. They'll think he's contaminated as well.'

'I must find out where he is,' Jeremy said. The thought of René still locked up had been nagging him. Now, bringing him into the conversation had made Jeremy serious. He had a responsibility to make sure René was all right.

'Later,' said Graham. 'Percy said he'd do what he can. I've no doubt it will just take a phone call and a load of his cash. After all, if they've let you go, they can't really hold on to him. René's probably perfectly fine. Percy wants to play the hero and bribery *is* probably the best way to get results in this country.'

This all sounded totally reasonable but Jeremy was suddenly overcome by melancholia. Graham caught the change in his expression and moved closer to him. He put his arm round Jeremy's shoulder and hugged him. It felt safe and comforting.

'Come on, old chap,' Graham said. 'It may never happen.'

Of course he knew the remark was a facile cliché but it was intended to cheer Jeremy, who tried his best to respond to it. Then, with a sudden pang of guilt, Jeremy realised he could no longer sit with Graham and ignore what René might well be experiencing.

'It's no good,' he said. 'I know Percy will have done his best, but he did say he'd let us know if there was any news and he hasn't. I think René is still in that horrible place and I have to do something to get him out. It seems to make it worse that I'm in this lovely hotel and . . .'

He stopped himself just in time. Graham knew what he had been about to say: that he was with such a lovely person too – and that he was finding himself increasingly attracted to that person, even though that person was not available and was intent upon marrying a woman.

Graham answered him by giving him a long and careful kiss. He held Jeremy very tightly as his lips caressed him. Jeremy went limp with the emotion it caused inside him. He suddenly wanted to cry. This was how silly females reacted to love. He was a man and should be able to shoulder his feelings without giving in to them. Graham was a good-looking chap who, luckily, didn't mind a bit of sexual fun with other men. That was all. Any other attitude towards the situation would certainly lead to disaster.

Graham seemed to have read his thoughts again. 'You're just wound up because of what's happened,' he said. 'In the morning you'll be thinking I could do with using a skin cream and my neck's too long and –'

Jeremy stopped him going further by planting another kiss on his lips.

'Let's go and see if Percy has heard anything first,' Graham said eventually. 'We might as well have all the information before we go in like the cavalry.'

Percy had all his curtains drawn and was lying in the dark with a wet flannel over his forehead. His cup of tea had long been drained. Now he was clutching a bottle of spirits, most of which had also been consumed. There was a full bottle waiting for him on the table by the bed. His words were slurred and didn't make a great deal of sense.

'These Arabs are fine people, but they aren't English, you know. One has to be very careful not to upset them. Like the French: never trust a Frenchman unless you're related to him. Course, the French are not a bit like the Arabs.'

'Come on,' Jeremy said. 'He's pie-eyed. Percy, we'll see you later on. We have to go out now.'

'Never did go there,' Percy said, then he appeared to be asleep. As they reached the door he began talking again, but not about anything sensible.

As usual there was a ready line of calash drivers waiting outside the hotel. The one they chose seemed surprised when asked to go to the police station and tried to persuade his guests to take a drive to Karnak instead.

'Police station not nice place to see,' he said. 'We go temple. Very nice temple. Alexander the Great was there.'

Once persuaded they were determined to be taken where they wanted to go and not where he thought they might prefer, they were soon on their way.

The evening was beautiful. That carriage ride, with his handsome friend beside him and all his recent problems, bar this one, behind him, would have been wonderful for Jeremy. But his conscience would not let him enjoy the glittering sparkle of the moon on the river, nor the smiles and shouts of a gang of interesting young men who were sitting at the side of the road. He smelt delicious local cooking and the curious aroma of incense and spice, but he hardly noticed them. He didn't respond when their driver asked them where they had been and whether they enjoyed Egypt. Graham was able to keep up the pleasantries in such a way that conversation was kept at a minimum.

Jeremy didn't feel fearful. He knew these people were susceptible to bribes and what he and René had been arrested for was generally accepted, if not acknowledged. Their only crime had been to be found out.

He didn't even worry that the guards might want to have sex with him again. In fact, the more he considered this, the more attractive the idea became. He could really let go and be the weak and helpless prisoner now without feeling there was any real danger. He kept thinking of what Graham had said about the book illustration. Yes, he could be the intrepid adventurer taken prisoner by sadistic foreigners. He could withstand any torture, any torment. He had to go and rescue his friend from their clutches; he was being the true hero.

Needless to say, part of his mind realised that these notions were ridiculous. When it came to it, he would be able to do little more than try to reason with the policemen. He could hardly burst into René's cell brandishing a revolver and carry him out over his shoulder.

They pulled up outside the police station and dismissed their driver, who was terribly reluctant to go. He made no bones about letting them know how curious he was to know their business.

'You tell me what happened and I not charge for waiting.'

He eventually drove off, shaking his head sadly and muttering to himself that they were 'crazy people'. 'Crazy' was an adjective all Egyptians seemed to use when a westerner refused anything which was offered.

Inside the police station, all was exactly as before. It was as if no time had passed since the earlier events of that day. The single light bulb still lit the desk where sat the same man they had left. He was reading the same newspaper. It might even have been the same page.

Jeremy strode up to the desk confidently. He banged the flat of his hand against the wood to bring the officer to attention. In fact, the noise had no immediate effect at all. Taking his time, and making it clear he intended to finish the paragraph he was reading before condescending to look at his visitors, the man placed the paper on the desk in front of him before raising his head enquiringly. Jeremy was leaning in to him, trying to look forceful but feeling rather silly.

'Englishman,' the officer said, 'you wish a room with us for another night perhaps?'

'We wish to see my friend. The one you brought in with me. Is he still here?' Jeremy tried to say this clearly and loudly, following the commonly held theory that volume makes up for lack of vocabulary. The officer responded by raising his own voice as though Jeremy might be similarly helped.

'Yes, he is still here. He like it here. Maybe you wish to join him again?'

Graham came forward and quietly discussed the matter, using a mixture of Arabic and English. Jeremy was very impressed by this, but he was also slightly resentful of his leading role having been snatched from him. Graham had a way of assuming command of any situation without actually making any great effort at all. Though this was admirable and extremely sexy, it was also galling. Graham was so sure of himself. He even handed the man a business card, saying his name loudly and clearly in a voice that suggested it should open any doors.

The officer apparently accepted whatever proposal had been put to him. He nodded several times and then rose and rang a bell. There was a long pause during which Graham kept squeezing Jeremy's arm. For some reason Graham was nervous. He was drawing his breath in uneven gasps and Jeremy could feel his friend's heart beating rather too quickly.

'What's going on?' Jeremy said. 'Are they bringing René out?'

Graham shook his head briefly and told him to wait. The man on the desk was regarding the two of them with a cool, amused look which sent shivers down Jeremy's spine.

After five minutes, a policeman entered, presumably in response to the bell. It was the officer who had urinated over Jeremy. He greeted him as though they were long-lost friends.

The sarcasm behind his attitude was quite evident and Jeremy tried to retain his dignity.

'You have come back for your *habibi* – your friend? That is good. He has been asking about you.'

'My name is Graham Etherington.' Another business card was produced, looked at and pocketed. 'We can pay money,' Graham went on. 'We want you to drop the charges against him.'

The guard discussed this in Arabic with the man at the desk, who looked very doubtful that anything could be done so easily. He tutted and shook his head.

'Will you perhaps like to see your friend? For some money, of course. Then we will talk further.'

Graham handed him some cash. The officer took it but kept his hand outstretched for more. Graham shook his head.

'That's all you're getting. We wish to see our friend and then we will talk more.'

The man walked towards the door. When Graham followed he held up his hand to prevent his going any further.

'Not enough,' said the officer, displaying the note. Graham tried to snatch it back but the man was too quick for him. 'I need more. Then you see your friend and then we talk.'

He disappeared through the door, slamming it behind him. Graham looked at Jeremy.

'Looks like I've blown round one,' Graham said. 'But there is always round two.'

He walked over to the desk and started to speak with the man. What was being said was making the desk sergeant angry. Then he shrugged and changed his attitude. He would, he said, see what he could do, but his colleagues were 'bad men' and he didn't advise it. More money exchanged hands before Graham rejoined Jeremy.

'I think we'll get René out of here,' he said in a whisper. 'But you're going to have to trust me and you're going to have to leave.'

Seven

Graham looked back on that moment many times throughout his life. It was the first time he could actually remember feeling he was crossing back and forth over the line between fear and desire. Within minutes of having spoken to the man on the desk, his brain was a heady mixture of the two emotions.

He heard his own voice tell Jeremy to wait outside, but it didn't sound like himself any more. The tone was deeper than normal, more throaty, and he thought the words he used were ridiculously melodramatic.

Jeremy gave him a curious look and Graham read in his face that, though Jeremy might trust him, he did not trust the guards. He was very worried by the situation. Here Graham exuded such an air of heroic command – and he did so quite purposely – that Jeremy acquiesced and left. He turned at the door and told Graham he would wait for only one hour. When that time was up he would come back to see he was all right.

Then he was gone. Moments later, Graham found himself alone with the desk sergeant and one of the officers who had arrested Jeremy. The one on the desk appeared to be mostly unconcerned and Graham guessed the younger one, the handsome one he now faced, was the more senior of the two. He still chewed on the toothpick and still managed a sarcastic grin, which was surely his practised way of striking terror into those he confronted.

'I am not prepared to meet any demands you might have here,' Graham said. 'We will have to go somewhere else. Somewhere neutral.'

'OK, OK.' This phrase was a favourite among the Arabs. It could mean all sorts of things, only one of which was that they agreed to a proposition that had been put to them. In this case it meant: 'Shut up and listen to me.'

'I do not want no tricks,' the guard said. 'You want someone get out of here. I have them. You do as I say. It is not for you to say.'

'Before anything happens, my friend must go free. Then I will do what you ask.'

'With this there is problem. How do I know you are a man of your word? Englishmen are not always such people.'

Graham went to the desk and clicked his fingers before pointing briefly at a pad and a pen. The desk officer may very well have resented being treated in such a perfunctory way, but he grudgingly handed them over. Graham wrote on the pad and gave the paper to the guard.

'I have there made a confession to the same offence as my friend is charged with. When I have fulfilled my part of this bargain, I expect the paper to be returned. I trust you to do that. But my friend must go free before we proceed.'

The man read the confession carefully, following the few lines with his finger. When he had apparently finished reading, he nodded sagely as though he thought this a wise compromise. Graham attempted to take the paper back and the officer slammed his hand down on it. Graham smiled.

'I have not yet signed it,' Graham said. 'Would you like me to read it out to you before I do?'

'OK, OK.'

Graham cleared his throat. He could feel his temple throbbing and knew that he had gone bright red. He told himself neither thing would be detected in this dull light. The pressure faded and he was able to think again. He began, 'I, Graham Etherington, hereby confess that I committed a sexual act of gross indecency with another man whom I refuse to name. This was done publicly in the town of Luxor on the evening of Tuesday tenth of February 1925. I deserve and accept the full penalties for this act and set any other rights I may have absolutely aside.'

He looked at the guard for approval and was given a nod of assent. Then he signed the paper and passed it back. The man folded it and locked it in a drawer of the desk. Still the desk officer sat there, apparently engrossed in his newspaper. He was listening – Graham knew it – but he no doubt understood only snatches of what was being said. He knew his place: so be it. Graham was managing things so far and his plan was working.

René was eventually brought from his cell. He looked drawn and haggard. He protested he was fine and just needed to know he was free and his family would know nothing of what had happened.

He practically ran over to where Jeremy waited for him outside and both evidently thought their brush with the corrupt law enforcers was at an end.

For them it was, but Graham had more business to attend to.

'I told you to trust me. I have to stay here. I have to keep my bargain. I'll see you back at the hotel.'

Of course Jeremy tried to reason with him and then tried to plead with him. No, Graham was resolute. He would see this thing through. He did not add he was actually looking forward to the last part of the adventure.

They went to a backstreet rooming house. Graham had agreed to pay both the bill and, though the man had made a fortune out of them already, for the guard's time and trouble. The officer warned Graham he must include two of his colleagues in the bargain, for they would be difficult to placate if they were left out of it. Graham insisted on seeing them first but, once he had, he was ready and willing to allow them to go with them.

The proprietor of the hotel was cringingly accommodating. It was likely this favour was letting him off the hook for some other small transgression. The four men were shown up two flights of stairs into a plain room in which there was a washstand, a bed, a table, two hard chairs and nothing else.

'From this time, you must be prisoner. You are in place of your friend and must no longer be fine English gentleman. You understand?'

Graham did understand. He wondered briefly if *they* understood. They probably thought this 'sacrifice' of his was utterly foolish and completely altruistic. Could they possibly comprehend how much he wanted it? The irony was, if they did comprehend, would it still be possible to have it? Would they be able to be as brutal with him as he desired if they had an inkling of his willingness to take it?

'You will strip and fold your clothes. Everything must be taken off and placed on the bed. Here.'

The guard pointed to the desired place, making it clear in the definite way he did so that no other part of the mattress was going to be acceptable. Graham loosened his tie and began to fiddle with his collar studs. The guard slammed his truncheon into Graham's stomach – it hurt, but was not sufficient to wind him completely.

'You will do as I say quickly! You will not be slow.'

Graham breathed deeply and looked the man fully in the eye. This resulted in a slap across the face which stung badly.

'You are not permitted to look at me in such a way. You will face the floor and strip yourself naked.'

Graham lowered his eyes and tore at his shirt, not caring if the material ripped. He kept his vest on while he removed his shoes and socks. Then he pulled that off as well. Now, bare-chested, he knew he was a good enough specimen for them.

They would perhaps want to linger over the next stage. He pulled in his stomach and pushed out his chest before reaching for the buttons of his trousers. They were all three watching him: he knew this even though he kept his gaze respectfully averted. The two junior officers were sitting on the chairs behind their leader, who was standing, legs apart, with ramrod back, directly in front of Graham.

He could feel their eyes burning into his body as he let his trousers fall to the floor. His trunklike legs were slightly parted. He widened the distance between them, mirroring the guard's stance. It was not a provocative action; it was one of subservience. It said, 'Here is my body. It is yours to do as you wish with. I will not try to protect myself.'

Even so, he was still wearing his underwear. He knew from experience this last piece of covering was best removed slowly, and he meant to teach these men something at least. The guard yelled at him in Arabic: he must strip naked. Naked did not mean wearing underwear.

He inched the fabric down so his pubic hair showed above the waistband. Then he slowly turned his back on his aggressors. He pulled his underpants down at the back, giving them sight of his buttocks. Then, keeping his legs spread, he raised his arms and placed them against the wall. They were the ones who must strip him completely. He belonged to them now.

The guard cursed and drew close to him. His arms came round Graham's body and pinched his flesh. Then, with another curse, he tore the underpants down. Graham had to adjust his stance to allow them to come off, but he put himself back in the same position immediately. His cock was bobbing in front of him, drooling pre-come. He gently let it press against the cool wall.

He wanted to voice his subservience but thought better of it. In another minute it was too late anyway: the guard gagged him with his torn underpants, tying them into place with his own belt. It wasn't tight enough to hold, but Graham bit into the gag and held it in place himself. He wanted to be denied speech. He wanted to be abused completely.

The guard passed his hand over Graham's cock and tested its firmness. He laughed as he rolled his finger over the head of it. He explained to the other two that the Englishman was another pervert: did all these foreigners enjoy such treatment? The guard spat on Graham's back. Graham felt the saliva running down in between his shoulderblades.

Another gob of spit and then another.

The first cock that entered his arse belonged to the youngest officer. He was maybe just past the age of twenty and was slender. His cock prised into Graham's muscle without problem: it actually felt comfortable. The guard did not strip – he just unbuttoned himself – and humped his prize as though Graham were some whore taken up against an alley wall. He had little skill, but it didn't matter to Graham. This experience was not about physical satisfaction for either of them. It was a demonstration of power and subordination. Its pleasure was entirely rooted in the mind, and Graham was completely given over to it.

He knew he could have taken the man on in a fight. He was stronger, older, more intelligent. This man was learning what it was like to be in complete control of another human being. Graham wanted him to understand that he was a willing victim, but he also wanted the guard to have utter dominance: the power that does not care whether the other man is compliant or not.

He stayed silent, but tightened his arse to give the young man the most pleasure he could. The officer came in a minute or two, shouting out as the semen spilt. The two others had been encouraging him, egging him on with joking taunts. Now they all but applauded. It was the turn of the second man, the next in rank.

'Our young friend has only just joined our little family,' he said. 'He is to be married next week. His wife will be the next to have him inside her. You must be grateful to him that he can spare so much of his juice for such a worthless pig.'

This was said quickly in Arabic and Graham understood only some of it. There was more, but he guessed it amounted to the same sort of sentiment. Graham bit on his gag and readied himself for the next penetration. He did not have to wait for long.

First and foremost, this man appeared to be fascinated with Graham's skin. He ran his hands over Graham's body all the time, letting his thick member rest inside his prisoner without movement. Then, still stroking and prodding, he began to rock gently in and out, moaning as he did so. He called Graham names in his own language. Some of them Graham understood: the tone he used belied the words. He was calling Graham a pig and a pervert. He said Graham was less than a female, less than a convict. He was going to teach him how filthy he really was. All this was said in a voice of quiet urgency as though he were declaring his love for his victim.

The swelling feeling of completeness in Graham's mind and his stomach was filling him just as the man's cock filled him physically. It was like a warm flame building to a fire within him. The words, whispered directly into his ear, were just as much part of it as the hot groin which pummelled his buttocks.

He let the guard's pace build before responding himself with hard, quick movements to meet the man's penis. This was not to be allowed and he received a sharp reprimand. The guard pulled out suddenly and whacked him across the arse with the flat of his hand. He followed this with another slap and, after a pause, several more. The senior officer approached them again and, after a few words with his friend, took over the verbal communication.

'You have gone too far. We think you are not to enjoy this as much as perhaps you do. You must bend over and hold your legs – so!'

He took hold of Graham's body and forced him to hold his ankles, keeping his buttocks up. Then, satisfied, the senior guard told his colleague to 'make the pervert understand'.

The man used a belt across Graham's arse. It was not hard to take at first, but it stung. When he had been dealt several blows, Graham began to give some muffled voice to his pain. This provoked the man to lay on the strap even more ruthlessly, until Graham's backside felt raw. He didn't have to hold back his shouts of anguish: the gag stopped him and he was grateful for it. He started to shift his position to get away from the beating, but the other two were quick to attend. They held him firmly, one at each shoulder, until the guard was satisfied. Then, without the other two letting go of him, and without giving him time to let the air cool his inflamed skin, the guard resumed his assault on Graham's insides.

This time it hurt, but the pain of it and the whipping he had endured was adding to Graham's sense of fulfilment. He was mentally telling himself he was indeed a pig, a pervert and an utterly lowly thing. If he could not sink so low, how could he know he had any other side to him? This was as much a part of himself as that suave, sophisticated sportsman who had ordered these people around. He thought of Ali back in the hotel and wondered if this would help when next that gentle human being took him lovingly. Would it also help him when he next lay down with Maria? Would he ever be able to tell her he had enjoyed this?

When this man had spilt into him it was the turn of the last one. Graham knew he would be the most brutal. He felt his knees grow weak and was almost glad when he was told to lie on the bed. He was to be taken on his back with his legs raised. This, said the guard, was how he fucked all his whores.

The officer's cock looked hungry. He never left off chewing his little splint of wood. By now, Graham's arse was loose enough to take the monster. Had they fucked him in this sequence out of deference to his comfort? He doubted it

106

somehow, but he was grateful fate had put them in that order of seniority.

It burnt as it went in and Graham could feel his guts instinctively attempting to expel it. He resisted the feeling; tried to allow the meat inside him so it wouldn't hurt so badly.

It worked and he was given new tolerance as his muscles stretched. The guard gave one last push and his cock completely engaged; he immediately began to fuck.

Graham had placed his hands wide above his head so he was still demonstrating his inferior status. Now, as the guard pushed in and out of his body, he couldn't help himself. His arms rose as though of their own accord and reached for the man's shoulders. Amazingly, the officer did not resist it. He allowed himself to be pulled down upon Graham's body and, though he never left off his thrusts, he let Graham hold him. Had he not been gagged, Graham would have kissed him. This, he knew, would not have been acceptable, but he thought about doing it and that was enough for him.

Their closeness made the man's body movements awkward and jerky. Though this was clumsy, it did not seem to prevent the officer building to orgasm. Graham could sense the man was about to come even though he gave no outward signs of it. The cock inside him stopped moving abruptly and the man lay quiet for a second or two.

Without any more indication than this, and Graham's sense of yet more fluid mixing with that already inside his arse, the guard pulled out. He wiped his cock on Graham's shirt and buttoned himself up. The other two did the same. The ordeal, if that's what it had been, was over.

'You have done,' the guard said. 'We have finished.'

Graham looked at his own naked body and his still-hard shaft. He had hoped they would allow him to come before they released him. He didn't want to have to wank himself. He wanted them to do it as part of this ritual. He stroked himself briefly, inviting them.

'We are not perverts,' the guard said in reply to this. 'You must attend to yourself.'

Graham pulled himself off the bed and grabbed the officer's arm. The other two men stiffened, ready for a fight. Firmly and, he hoped, unthreateningly, Graham forced the officer down beside him. He was still gagged and he wanted it that way. He pushed the man's hand between his legs and pressed the strong fingers round his cock. The guard looked uncertain but the steady look in Graham's eyes persuaded him. He gave a few slow strokes. He turned to the other two for confirmation. They shrugged and turned away.

The guard gave Graham what he wanted. He lay down next to him and, holding him round the shoulders with one arm, he wanked him with the other. Graham closed his eyes and let his own pleasure surge upward and out of his throbbing cock.

Eight

When Graham arrived back at the Winter Palace, Jeremy was relieved to see that he had a smile on his face. The nightmare scenario of having Graham play Sidney Carton and do his 'far, far, better thing' vanished from his mind with a welcoming hug from the man Jeremy now considered to be his very best friend.

'How did you do it? What happened?'

His questions were dismissed with a nonchalant wave of Graham's hand. It wasn't important. The main thing was that all of them were safe.

René had gone back to his family. He was shamefaced at having, in his words, 'Brought nice people to such trouble.' Jeremy had appeased his own conscience by accepting this version of events. If René had not suggested they go to the temple, all would have been well. It was not Jeremy's fault, and Jeremy was happy to rid himself of blame.

It was much later that Graham gave him an edited version of his diplomatic skills.

'They wanted a confession from me, saying in writing I'd

done what you had been accused of. Once they'd got it in their grubby hands, they released René. It was that easy.'

Jeremy nearly exploded, 'You did *what*?' This was not at all what he wanted to hear. Was Graham out of his mind? He could be frogmarched back to jail at any moment! Had he really been so stupid? 'I can't live with myself, knowing I've got you into trouble and worrying every time I see a damned police officer . . .'

Graham drew in a breath to speak. Jeremy stopped him.

'I know, you're about to say you'll be leaving this filthy country before it comes to anything. But, Graham, they could come for you tonight. What the hell did you think you were playing at? This isn't going to help at all. What the devil shall I tell Maria?'

Graham looked smug. He waited for the tirade to die down. 'I said they *wanted* a confession. I didn't say I gave them one.'

Jeremy stayed silent, waiting for him to go on, but with his heart still drumming away inside him.

'Think about it. When we arrived I gave everyone a business card. I also said my name out loud. Why do you think I did that?'

Jeremy didn't have the faintest idea.

'The business cards I gave them were some of these.' He handed Jeremy a small square of paper which declared that Percy Gilbert Esq. lived at Beach Mews, Brighton, England.

Jeremy began to see the light.

'I was merely ascertaining whether our little friends could read English as well as speak it. I hope Percy doesn't mind my having pinched these. I shall of course return the remainder to him.'

'So, because they didn't ask you why you carried another man's card, you knew they weren't able to tell what you wrote.'

Graham smiled.

Jeremy felt momentary relief. Then he panicked again. 'What *did* you write?'

'Old chap, it was so much nonsense. Well, not nonsense exactly. I wrote, "I confess . . ." and then I gave them a rather exciting bit of Shakespeare. I would imagine the authorities would be very interested to know that they have found a man who is so remorseful at having been involved in the assassination of Cæsar.'

The two women arrived back during the afternoon of the next day. Jeremy and Graham did not need to say anything to each other: a look between them was enough. Nothing was to be said about what had happened between them, or what had happened at the police station.

Percy was another matter.

'You have gone through such a lot, my dear,' he said to Graham. 'Surely your lady ought to know what you've done to help us. There is absolutely no reason why you should play the diffident hero. You *are* a hero. I think the least Jeremy and I can do is acknowledge the fact. You do deserve it.'

Graham smiled sweetly and told Percy that, if he whispered to Maria one word of what he knew, he would never speak to him again. Percy was reluctantly silent.

Mrs Dryden was full of their trip. She twittered about everything that was irrelevant and had apparently not noticed the fact that she was in Egypt and not Kensington.

'There were absolutely no shops as such. Just little stalls with those funny little creatures attempting to force all sorts of knick-knacks upon anybody who was foolish enough to stop and listen to them. They were like flies. And the weather! So hot! I really think they ought to warn you . . .'

Indeed, everything would have returned to normal. Egypt would have been nothing more to any of them than a story to be told at dinner wherever open-minded people gathered and required scandal.

But then Khalid came back into Jeremy's life.

★

Jeremy was sitting on the veranda, gazing across the gardens and wishing that Graham was not the marrying kind. He had, he decided, fallen in love. Mrs Dryden, who claimed she had completely fallen for the darling little Percy, left that man and came over to Jeremy's table.

'I really think you ought to take yourself off for a walk, Jeremy. It really is quite pleasant by the river. There's a most refreshing breeze.'

Jeremy wanted neither a walk nor a breeze, but, since he did not want to listen to Mrs Dryden's good advice either, he rose and, pleading a headache, took himself off. He strolled down to a coffee shop and went inside.

He was the only white man in there. It was cool and dark. The brilliant, sunlit street was framed by the open front of the building. He was brought a coffee and was then given a hookah, which he had not asked for, but he found the gentle smoke pleasant enough once he had become used to it. The Arabs sat around him, paying him no heed other than the odd sly glance and, he suspected, comment. He might have left but something made him order another cup of coffee.

'*Habibi*!'

It was a cry of delight and was accompanied by a thump on the back which nearly knocked him across the table.

Khalid was wearing western clothes and too much gold. He was older, stouter, but just as gorgeous to Jeremy's eyes as when they had first met all those years ago. He sat down and launched into a hundred questions without pausing to allow an answer to any of them.

Jeremy just grinned happily. Already he was planning where they might go and what they might do together. He wanted to dispense with catching up and get on with it. He needed to be physical.

'We can talk later,' he said, once he was able to get a word in.

Khalid roared and banged the table in approval. 'You want to go and annoy the birds on the river?'

Jeremy shook his head. 'I want to take you somewhere very private and see how your body looks after all this time.'

'We go,' Khalid agreed. He was already standing, his hand extended. Jeremy grasped it and the two set off.

Khalid had a share in a house, he explained. A young man whom he coyly called 'a friend of gentlemen travellers' used it as well. Mustapha was at home when they got there, but he was happy to vacate the place for an hour or so.

It looked humble enough, but Khalid was inordinately proud of it. There were only two rooms and almost no furniture. Matting covered the earthen floor and a few huge cushions on softer mats served as a bed. Khalid lay down and looked at Jeremy, who was hovering over him.

'You are like angel from heaven,' Khalid said. 'You are gold and light. But there is something wrong.'

Jeremy waited: he knew this was not a comment to be taken literally.

'Angels do not wear clothes!' Khalid declared at last.

Jeremy unbuttoned his shirt and quickly rid himself of his shoes and socks. His jacket was already on the floor.

Khalid watched him closely. 'I think you must go much further for me.'

The shirt followed the jacket on to the floor. Jeremy was now standing barefoot in only his trousers and vest. He was aware of feelings that were almost narcissistic. He knew how his muscles bulged through the singlet and how good and strong his arms were. He knew his eyes were sparkling and his blond hair flopped over his forehead. He looked good and he was going to take his time.

'Everything must go. I want to see *you*.'

Jeremy raised one eyebrow quizzically. He was fully aware this looked cute because he'd often practised it in front of a mirror. 'You want me naked?'

Khalid nodded.

'I won't do it.'

Jeremy lay next to Khalid and reached across to him. Khalid was already sulking. He turned his back to Jeremy and hugged his knees to himself, silent.

'I just wanted to see if you still did that when you don't get your own way,' Jeremy said, laughing. 'I only said that *I* won't do it. You can do it for me.'

'I make you nude?' Khalid turned towards Jeremy. There was a glimmer of a boyish grin on his face.

Jeremy nodded eagerly. 'You must be the man,' he said. 'I will do what you wish me to do.'

Khalid didn't need this to be explained. Jeremy sat back against the wall and raised his arms so his vest could be pulled off him. Khalid sat astride Jeremy's legs and felt along the sides of his torso through the vest. Then he leant forward and licked the hair on Jeremy's armpits. It felt like a small animal tickling and caressing. When he had thoroughly attended to one, Khalid went to the other. His hands were now taking the material of the vest up with them, pulling it out of Jeremy's trousers. Once he felt flesh, Khalid abandoned his licking momentarily in order to strip Jeremy of his top covering.

Then Khalid traced a path with his tongue, licking Jeremy's firm chest, taking care to visit each of his nipples on the way. Jeremy sighed and closed his eyes. He could hear Khalid ripping off his own shirt and soon felt the silky skin of his friend's chest close to him. Their lips came into contact and then their tongues. Arms entwined: hot, passionate bodies finding each other.

Khalid went down to Jeremy's crotch and pressed against his dick with the heel of his palm. Jeremy responded by lifting up off the matting to maximise the pressure. His trousers could not be left on his body: Khalid unbuttoned him and pulled them down. Jeremy attended to his underwear. Khalid had soon achieved his purpose: Jeremy was lying with him – naked.

'I make love to you,' Khalid announced simply.

He sucked on Jeremy's cock for a long, long time. His soft lips manipulated the blood-engorged shaft, driving Jeremy to distraction. He wanted to use his own hand: the need to come was so urgent. Khalid wouldn't let him: when he reached down, Khalid's strong hands grabbed his wrist and forced it up over his head. Jeremy liked that; it made him feel helpless and secure at the same time. He wished he was still handcuffed. That would be the best way to exorcise any mental demons that might still lurk in his mind. He could lie there with metal round his wrists, knowing that this handsome youth would not hurt him, but also knowing he was completely powerless.

'My tie is in my pocket,' he whispered. 'Will you get it for me?'

Khalid raised his head. He was puzzled.

'Just get it,' Jeremy said hoarsely. 'Please.'

Khalid did so.

Jeremy put his arms together and held them out. 'Please, tie my hands.'

Khalid evidently thought this was marvellous fun. He tied Jeremy so tightly that he had no chance of escape. 'You wish to be my angel prisoner?' he said.

'I'd like you to fuck me. You put yourself in my behind – yes?'

Khalid didn't need to be asked twice. He grabbed Jeremy's body and lifted him as though he weighed no more than a small child. Then he laid him on his front. Some moments later, Jeremy knew Khalid had his own penis out. He heard him spit and rub himself to lubricate it. Then the wonderful feeling of Khalid's body lying full length across him. Then a stabbing pain in his arse as the cock went smoothly inside him.

Jeremy tested his bonds again. He was still unable to free himself. He let his mind drift as Khalid fucked him.

The drab little room they were in became the palace of some beautiful Pharaoh. Men stood all around, some of them slaves, some of them masters. They were almost naked: just simple cloths round their waists. This was important to Jeremy because he knew he was one of only two people who were actually naked. He had been brought in and stripped in front of all these men. This was done in order to humiliate him absolutely and he accepted it. Then he had been bound and laid down for his master's pleasure.

Khalid was then brought in. He too was a slave. He arrived without clothing for he was nothing more to the watching men than a stud who was to give them the show they desired to see.

The Pharaoh was sitting on a great throne somewhere above Jeremy's head. He read out their sentence; Jeremy could hear every word in his mind.

'You are slaves and it is decreed you be made to mate in front of the assembled household. You shall be like animals and afforded no dignity. Since you are both men, you, white man, will be taken up your anus. You will have no dignity and, when it is all done, you will be taken to the market and there sold.'

He wanted to share this fantasy with Khalid but knew he was better advised to keep it to himself. He kept his eyes tightly shut and concentrated on the feeling of being nude in front of so huge an audience. He was being fucked. He could feel Khalid's huge shaft going in and out of him. He could feel Khalid's breath and sweat.

Khalid pulled out and grabbed Jeremy's chest from underneath. He lifted him so the pair were kneeling, close together. Khalid's hands found Jeremy's cock and he pumped it in time with his own. Jeremy saw the men in his mind moving closer to them. They wanted to see his come spurting out of him. They wanted to see if he was worth buying when the time came for him to be put up for sale. He raised his bound hands upward, to the back of his head, an attitude of complete surrender.

Then he came and relief swelled through him like an ocean of water cascading through his body.

★

They spent the rest of the afternoon together, lying in each other's arms. When early evening came, Khalid wanted to go out on the river. They took a felucca and held hands as the sun set over the Western Desert. The man who owned the boat took no notice of their intimacy. He didn't even look up when they kissed, lying down together in the belly of the vessel, feeling the water rocking them gently. The sky blazed above them as though it had been drenched in gold, then red, then the black of night and a million stars.

The boat was now still. They had reached the reeds on the western side of the Nile. Somewhere in the dense, mysterious void which lay beyond, the Pharaohs slept in their tombs. Maybe among them was the very man who had visited Jeremy's mind. Maybe he was not of the imagination but a ghostly visitor come back from the underworld.

'You are my golden angel,' Khalid said.

Despite Khalid's misguided attempts at fine western-style clothing, Jeremy knew he would be discouraged from bringing him into the auspicious confines of the Winter Palace. He thought he'd got away with it by agreeing to the pleasant alternative of the felucca trip, but Khalid had other ideas.

He grabbed Jeremy's hand and set off in the direction of the hotel as though this had all been agreed beforehand. Men holding hands occasioned no comment in Luxor, but a white man and an Arab was strange to see. A group of lads shouted words of mocking derision; a woman who had been sauntering with her child picked it up and hurried past as though some disease was in the air. Jeremy let go of Khalid's hand and stayed where he was. It was some moments before Khalid realised he was walking on alone. He ran back to Jeremy.

'We go to Winter Palace. You buy me alcoholic drink.'

'I can't,' Jeremy said.

'Why not?'

This question was asked petulantly: Khalid could see no

reason why not and Jeremy could have no possible excuse for refusing him. Jeremy tried to tell him there were certain places where it was best for two men not to be seen together. This was not an acceptable explanation.

'You have been there with men. You told me you and another man stay there. You drink with him. Why not me?'

Jeremy tried the 'you have no tie' excuse. He knew as soon as he'd uttered the words that this too was transparent.

'You wear no tie now. You get one for yourself from your room, get one for me also. Or is it you have only one tie in Egypt? I think not.'

Jeremy put his arm round Khalid's shoulders and, ignoring the group of lads, who had been thoroughly entertained by the exchange they had witnessed, he led Khalid a little way up the road.

'All right,' he said. 'I'll come clean.'

Khalid did not understand the phrase, or at least he pretended he didn't. When it had been explained, he spent some time repeating it to himself, committing it to memory. Then he gave Jeremy his attention once again.

'Yes, now you come clean.'

'The people who own the hotel would not let you in. They would think you were like your friend at the house.'

Khalid waited patiently for this to be explained further.

'Your friend – the one who looks after the gentlemen tourists. They would think you're one of those and I've . . . well, they'd think I've . . . picked you up.'

Realisation lit Khalid's face; he did not appear to have been overly offended by the truth. Thank goodness, Jeremy thought. He really didn't want another long sulk to cope with.

'This is fine! There is no problem,' Khalid said.

'You're sure you understand?'

'Of course. I understand.'

'In that case I must be getting back.'

Khalid linked his arm and they walked back towards the

hotel. Jeremy expected Khalid to leave him on the road, but he proceeded with him to the foot of the winding staircase which led to the main doors. He didn't part from Jeremy even as he began to mount that staircase. Jeremy's heart sank. Khalid was going to try to embarrass him by taking his leave at the very door of the hotel. Jeremy disengaged himself and attempted to summon up a reasonable tone of voice.

'Khalid, this is where you must go home.'

He was put in mind of some pet animal who follows you on to a main road and, for its own good, has to be sent off home. Khalid's face clouded over.

'You buy me alcohol in bar!'

'No,' Jeremy retorted. 'I can't. I told you why and you said you understood.'

'I understood,' Khalid said. 'You say they think I am like my friend and you pick me up. This is truth. I *am* like my friend. You *do* pick me up. If they think what is true, why should I not come in bar?'

Jeremy was somewhat exasperated, but he tried to keep calm. 'They'd hurt your feelings,' he said. 'Not everybody is as nice as Egyptian people are.'

'You are ashamed of your race? OK. I don't mind.'

This wasn't a surrender: he meant he wouldn't mind Jeremy's shame or their rudeness and therefore another block had been removed.

'I can't take you in,' Jeremy said. He was now openly frustrated. He knew Khalid was aware of the real reason and he was attempting to force it out of him. All right, Jeremy thought. He knows anyway, I might as well tell him.

'You are not wealthy enough,' he began. 'You don't have the right clothes. You look like a prostitute. All right, you *are* a prostitute and I picked you up, but, when I'm with English people, I pretend to be what I'm not. They don't like men who go with men. Even the ones who do it themselves don't like it to be seen. You'd show me up.'

Khalid had hung his head like a small boy being told off by his schoolmaster. When he raised it again, his face showed genuine sympathy. He brushed his hand across Jeremy's cheek.

'Poor Jeremy. It is difficult to be English. It is difficult to be what you are not. I could not do it, not even to be in bar and drink alcohol.'

He turned and sadly moved off down the steps. Jeremy heaved a sigh of relief and went into the hotel.

Mrs Dryden was there. She was sitting in an armchair in the vast foyer. She appeared to be waiting for someone and that someone turned out to be Jeremy himself.

'You are a wicked boy,' she said as soon as he was through the revolving door. 'Why didn't you tell me?'

'Tell you what?' Jeremy tried to sound innocent but her words had sent him into panic. Who could have told her about his arrest? Percy probably. The man could never keep his mouth shut.

'You must come with me to my suite,' she said. She was more commanding than he had ever seen her. She rose and swept off down the corridor. He followed at a distance, his head swimming with possible ways of dealing with this latest disaster.

'Heaven knows how long I've been sitting in that chair waiting for you,' she said as soon as they were in her room together. 'Where on earth have you been?'

'Just for a walk,' Jeremy replied. He had opted for a 'none of your business' approach to the whole matter. This, he knew, would not solve any problems, but it would make him feel better and he already felt like a little shit for having had to dismiss Khalid. There was only so much guilt a chap could deal with at any one time.

'I've been talking to Mr Gilbert,' she said through pursed lips. 'He has explained one or two things to me.'

Jeremy hoped the shame he felt was not perceptible to her.

120

He sat down and tried to look relaxed but was aware that his leg was shaking and his hands were unsteady.

'And what did Percy have to explain?' he asked.

'I will come to that presently,' she said. 'First, I think you ought to pour me a stiffener. I think I'm in need of one, though, heaven knows, I'm not a great one for drink.'

His hand trembled as he poured the drink and handed it to her. He knew she'd noticed this but no comment was made. She sipped the drink quietly while he poured another for himself.

'I might remind you,' she said tartly, 'that what you drink here is on my bill. I have no doubt that the drinks in your room will not be, but this has not yet been made clear to me.'

He stopped, amazed. 'What did you say?'

'There is nothing the matter with your hearing.'

Jeremy put the drink down untouched. She had not finished, for her lips moved briefly. Then she thought better of what she was about to say and took time to reframe the thought.

'I – I have been hurt greatly by your actions. I regret having to tell you this, but I think enough of you to know I must reproach you if we are to continue to be friends.'

'What have I done?'

'Mr Gilbert is a nice man. I see that. I see also that he thinks a great deal of you. However, I have been made aware that he is – how shall I put this? – that he is not the marrying kind.'

Light began to dawn. This might have nothing to do with recent events. This might be a case of old chickens coming home to roost. Jeremy had feared it when they first came to Egypt, but other things had made that fear seem irrelevant. Now it came back to him it had lost a lot of its impact.

'I see in Mr Gilbert's attitude towards you a man who is being deceived. Yes, deceived. I'm sorry to have to use such a word.' She bristled with indignation for a second or so before going on. 'You must know he has formed some sort of emotional attachment to you. You are aware of that, I trust?'

Jeremy nodded.

'I do not criticise others for the way they wish to lead their lives. I used to, but I have seen things in my travels which have taught me I was wrong to do this. He has been kind to you – I mean financially – has he not?'

'Yes,' said Jeremy. 'Percy has given me cash when I was stuck. But I intended –'

She stopped him. 'What you intended is beside the point. I happen to know that, because of unfortunate circumstances which were beyond your control, you have no actual money of your own. Therefore I cannot think good of your intentions for I know I would be the one who has to pay for them in the end.'

This hurt. It hurt because Jeremy knew it to be true. He went back to the drinks table and took the whisky he had poured out.

'I'm sorry,' he said. 'May I?'

She gave her curt permission and he drank it quickly.

'Why did you not tell your friend that you have been recently bereaved?' she continued. 'Why did you not tell him that he must not hope for a closer friendship with you? All he could talk of this afternoon was how worried he was about you and how he hoped you would find a – I hesitate to say it – a gentleman who would be good to you. He thinks you're a queer! He thinks it because you have allowed him to think it. I suspect you have done so in order to take money from him. If I am right, and I hope to God I am not, then these are the actions of a cad and a rogue. There! I've said it.'

How could he explain? Jeremy almost blurted it out, almost said she was seeing the situation completely upside down and she, not Percy, was the one he had deceived. He was abject, but to mend the situation he would have to hurt her even more than he had done already.

'I appreciate what you say, and you are right,' he said. 'I have been dishonest. Please believe me when I say I was forced to be like that because I had no money. Percy is no fool. He knows what I am. You must believe that.'

'He thinks you're a queer!'

'I'm bisexual.'

It was the best compromise he could come up with. After all, he had never pretended that he was going to jump into bed with Mrs Dryden and she had never suggested that she wanted him to. She had said she was uncritical of the way others chose to lead their lives. Maybe this would pacify her.

It didn't.

'Leave my room, please. I cannot take any more of your duplicity.'

He attempted to explain himself further but the words wouldn't come. She turned her head away.

Percy did not seem to have the least idea of what he had done. He claimed he had simply expressed his deep concern for Jeremy and had certainly said nothing to imply anything about his own, or Jeremy's, sexuality.

'But, my dear. This is surely a good thing, isn't it? It's out now. You have no need of pretence,' he reasoned.

'She thinks I'm some sort of leech,' Jeremy wailed. 'She even made me ask before I had a drink – reminded me of who was paying for it.'

'Such is the way women behave,' Percy said sagely. 'They get over these things. Tomorrow, all will be forgotten.'

'I told her my girlfriend had died,' Jeremy confessed. 'She still thinks that's true.'

Percy took the information calmly. 'If the mythical young lady is dead then she cannot be much of a problem. Oscar Wilde had one of his characters do much the same thing with a Mr Bunbury.'

'I'm sure Mrs Dryden would understand that perfectly,' Jeremy scoffed. 'Oscar Wilde! Look where he ended up.'

'Paris, I believe! Yes, most unfortunate for him,' agreed Percy.

'We are all forced to live our lives secretly,' he went on. 'It is the nature of our society.'

Percy looked around the room and managed to catch the eye of a lovely bartender, who flashed him a wicked and knowing smile. Jeremy scowled.

'Sometimes,' said Percy, 'I think the Egyptians have the right idea. They are the sexual equivalent of the lilies of the field.'

Jeremy had no idea what he meant by this and said so.

'They do toil and spin, of course, but the rest of the quote holds true: "That even Solomon in all his glory was not arrayed like one of these."'

'You're barmy,' Jeremy said.

Jeremy was soon able to put aside his problems with Mrs Dryden. Two people were now dancing around his mind, vying for the prime place in his affections. Graham represented so much that Jeremy desired and he was at least English; but he was engaged to be married, albeit to a bisexual who was willing to allow him his freedom. Khalid held the mystery of his exotic surroundings. He was a different fantasy, but no less powerful. He was available, but only for the time Jeremy remained in Egypt. Each man could have satisfied something within him that he needed desperately, but he had no real hope of either becoming permanent in his life.

Since his arrest, Percy and Mrs Dryden had both become irritating to him. He meant them no harm and tried to disguise his annoyance, but he resented having to go to Percy for money, and he still felt awful about having deceived Mrs Dryden and being found out.

She was deliberately polite to him. She was conventional enough to regard extended unpleasantness as socially distasteful. Even so, he knew she was still critical of his relationship with Percy. There was definitely unfinished business there.

Percy had evidently elected to keep Jeremy within his sights as much as possible. It became something of a game between them. Jeremy would sneak away like an alcoholic in search of a forbidden drink. Percy would find him in the act of leaving the hotel and declare, unconvincingly, that he too wanted some air and would accompany him.

It was on such an occasion that Jeremy met Khalid again. Percy stayed close, determined to act for Jeremy's better interests despite any hints that were given.

'Percy just came out for a walk,' Jeremy explained to Khalid. 'He must leave soon. They'll be expecting him for dinner. Is that not right, Percy?'

'I have no appetite tonight. Khalid is very kind to allow me to accompany you,' he said to Khalid. 'You don't mind, do you?'

Khalid looked at Jeremy to see whether he should mind. Jeremy didn't have time to give him any indication of what he should answer. Percy went on.

'Good, that's settled then. It really is most accommodating of you both. I suppose you'd like a walk along the river and then, maybe, coffee? I should think some coffee would be a most excellent idea.'

They walked for a while in silence. Then Khalid sneaked his hand into Jeremy's and was checked with a loud 'Hem!' from Percy. Khalid fell into a sulk and continued a few steps in front of them.

'Percy,' Jeremy said quietly, 'I know you're trying to protect me from hordes of dangerous Egyptians, but I do know this man. He's all right. He's not about to get me arrested again. I absolutely promise.'

'I really do need the air,' Percy insisted. 'I know you are quite able to look after yourself. I should hate you to think I was patronising you.'

'They have the Whirling Dervishes and the snake charmer performing at the hotel,' Jeremy reminded him. 'You said you particularly wanted to see them.'

'They'll be there again next week. I checked.'

Jeremy stopped walking, calling to Khalid to wait for them a moment or two. He turned to Percy, anger building inside him. He tried to check it.

'Am I to have no further sex life? This is the man I told you about, whom I met last time I was here. It will be very insulting to him if . . .'

Words failed him here. He knew what he wanted to say, but it would hurt Percy and confirm some dreadful unspoken opinion he had of Jeremy's character.

'I am playing gooseberry,' Percy said sadly. 'I am doing so deliberately. I must admit to it.'

'Why, for God's sake? I don't nanny you everywhere you go.'

Percy had caught Jeremy's angry mood and was reflecting it back at him. He was quivering slightly and he spoke with genuine emotion. 'I do not end up in the local police station. I do not have my friends sitting up all night worrying about what's happened to me.' He paused before stammering, 'Do you know, young man, how much I went through during your little adventure? I know we are not – how should I put it? – We are not close in certain ways –'

They were interrupted by a group of children who flocked around them like flies, holding out their dirty hands and chattering in high, whining voices. Khalid came to their rescue and shooed them off.

'This is neither the time nor the place,' Percy said. 'I just want you to know that I will not be prepared to come to your aid a second time. If you end up in a prison cell, it will be entirely your own affair.'

Jeremy sighed and attempted to reach out to Percy to calm him. Percy pulled away and glared at him.

'And do not think that a few smooth words will change my mind. I warn you. If things go awry, you will have to look to yourself or some other person to sort it out. I have had enough. Enough! Do you hear?'

He walked away as smartly as he could. Jeremy watched him:

a little man bursting with righteous indignation. Jeremy felt terrible. Must he always do this? Surrender his true instincts in order to appease these people who had money enough to support him? Was there such a thing as an equal relationship between a wealthy man and an impecunious one? Was he being entirely fair to expect Percy to foot his bills and yet remain apart from his private life?

He didn't know. He felt tears coursing down his cheeks.

Khalid was watching him with a kind of curiosity which was not devoid of sympathy. 'There is bad feeling?' he said.

Jeremy wiped his face with his sleeve. 'Oh, Percy will come round,' he said. 'He's very upset about something.'

He looked at Khalid, who was obviously thinking himself to be the cause of this altercation.

'Not you,' Jeremy said. 'It's not about you. I'll try and tell you about it as we walk.'

He forced a smile. Khalid responded readily and they set off down the road.

How much Khalid understood of what he said, Jeremy had no idea. He looked across at him every so often, but, though he nodded each time to show he was still listening, he didn't interject in any way.

Jeremy told him how he had very little actual money. He told him about his parents back in Camden Town. He described the house in which they lived before realising that, poor though it might be, it was far more than Khalid could ever hope to achieve. He then tried to explain the difference between being poor in Egypt, where everything was so cheap, and being poor in England, where images had to be kept up if one was to succeed in life. He confessed to having sponged off Percy for a long time and even mentioned the time on the steamer when Mrs Dryden had opened her purse for him so often. He told Khalid how often he had thought of him and how much he had been looking forward to seeing him. He also explained that, though he might have money enough as far as Khalid could see, he was not the wealthy Englishman he had pretended to be. At present he had twenty Egyptian pounds in his pocket. That was a fortune over here; in England, it was nothing.

He stopped. They were far down the road, near to Karnak. Beyond this the street divided: two dirt tracks led out of the town. The temple was some few hundred yards over to their right. Its huge pylons, looking like the sloping walls of a gigantic dam, could be seen. Palm trees dotted the route that led to the twin avenues of sphinxes which guarded the sacred building. The sun was beginning its descent over the Valley of the Kings: soon it would be dark.

'It was at this time of the day that we first met,' Khalid said. 'We went for a sail to watch the sun go home to bed.'

'And I was frightened we would be seen by the birds,' Jeremy answered, smiling. 'I was very new in Egypt then.'

'You are not so very old now. You still do not know how we think here.' Khalid tapped his head meaningfully. 'You have to think as we do. Then you not feel so bad about your friend and no money. Such things not important.'

'Maybe not,' Jeremy agreed. 'But it seems so at the moment.'

'You have twenty pounds.' Khalid grinned and delved into his pocket. 'I have fifty.' He brought out the notes proudly and waved them at Jeremy. 'Me and you – we are not so different as you think. You have rich Englishman to pay for your wishes. I too.'

Jeremy wasn't sure he wanted to hear this. Khalid had picked up some rich old effeminate and was being paid money to fuck him. Jeremy had realised something of the sort, but he wasn't sure he wanted to know the details. After all, if Khalid was just a prostitute, it didn't say much for their special friendship.

'You do not think it right that I should have friend pay for me. Is OK for you, not for me?'

Jeremy claimed Khalid didn't understand. It was clear to both of them he understood all too well.

'This man pays for the house which I share with my friend.

We pay him and he pays us. We are safe and he makes much money. Homosex is very profitable.'

'He's what we call a pimp,' Jeremy told him.

Khalid liked this word greatly. Jeremy groaned. It was now going to be quite difficult to stop him saying it every two minutes.

'Will you meet with the pimp?' Khalid asked pleasantly.

'Not if I can help it,' Jeremy replied.

Nine

Anthony Welch was about to be forty and he hated the fact. He looked at himself every day and was so far relieved to find assurance in what he saw. He was slim: he'd taken after his father in that respect. Judging by the shape the old man was in now, obesity was one worry he could strike off life's little list of torments. He had grey hair, but it had gone that colour in his early twenties, so he didn't associate it with age. He checked often for signs of thinning. All so far was well, but Welch Senior was totally bald, so his son had that to look forward to. Welch was tall and had a craggy face which some people found attractive and others said made him look like a refugee from a Wild West Show. He wasn't sure whether this was a compliment or not.

Anthony Welch lived for his own comfort and wasn't all that bothered how he achieved it. He had decided, early on in life, he would eventually live outside England – a country in which he had little hope of achieving his aims. To this end he had, during his teenage years, run away to Rhodesia: the newly named land of the white man's dreams.

He had been relatively prosperous there. Then the Boer War

had broken out and he had left, worried the trouble could spread and he might lose everything. He had lived comfortably in Ireland until the next great conflict interrupted his calm at the age of 29. He wanted adventure. So, like so many others, he enlisted and, like so many others, found 'adventure' in the trenches was not to his taste.

He had been lucky. A bullet lodged in his shoulder. It was a bad enough wound to send him back to England, but not bad enough to incapacitate him entirely. He sat out the rest of his war in a beautiful convalescent home in Kent, claiming shell-shock and getting away with it. His shoulder continued to trouble him, but he was grateful he had not ended up buried beneath the fields of Flanders.

The war had changed him. He had not been a violent man before. Now he thought very little of international conflict and had no particular loyalty to any cause or country. He was sufficiently fatalistic about life not to worry if the means by which he maintained his fortune was illegal or dangerous. He led a charmed life and he would not be discovered.

He found Egypt in 1922 and he liked it.

He had prospered. So what if the guns he ordered and dispatched were being put into the hands of Nationalist revolutionaries? Did it matter if their cause was just? Did he care if Egypt remained in the hands of the English, the Arabs, the French or whoever chose to rule it? What if the young men he employed were living in squalor? He creamed off enough from their earnings to make the arrangements he made with them viable. And, of course, these arrangements included a proviso that meant Welch never had to go looking for sex.

He would go his own sweet way and, as long as there were people who had money and a need of something he could obtain, he didn't trouble his conscience about it.

He eased his aching body off the bed. Mustapha, the young whore he had just ejaculated into, was still lying there. He was waiting to be dismissed. Welch knew Mustapha wanted to go home now. He was not attracted to Welch and the feeling was reciprocated. Mustapha was too slender and smooth to be of very much interest to his employer. Welch would have preferred Khalid, but Khalid was out with 'a friend'.

Welch tended to feel disgust for men who were willing to give their bodies. Sex for him had become too easy. He liked to think there was something of the conquest in procuring his men. This one, who was older than Khalid but looked younger, had not even questioned his demands. After Welch had rid himself of his spunk, he usually wanted to be rid of the man as well. Tonight was different. Tonight he'd left Mustapha waiting.

He'd half decided to go back with him to the vile hovel Mustapha called home. Welch wanted to find out what Khalid was doing later. He was still annoyed at having earlier been denied his first choice of whore. He wanted Khalid and Khalid he should have.

Khalid was, in fact, Welch's great success, and not just as a prostitute. He knew people who knew people and had been more than useful for business purposes. Mustapha had made pathetic attempts to 'protect' his friend from Welch's influence, but Khalid was too fond of cash to take any notice.

'I go now,' Mustapha said. 'You promised give me baksheesh.'

'You do as you are told,' Welch replied. He reflected that he must be going soft. Why on earth had he offered money? He wasn't about to give Mustapha very much, of course, but it was still inadvisable. He might get above himself, think he was worth something. Give them an inch . . .

He lit a cigarette. Mustapha reached out, asking for one. Welch tossed it over and it fell on the floor. The lad crawled off the bed and scrabbled for it. It had rolled underneath. The sight of his smooth buttocks sticking out made Welch's cock twitch again. He went over and pushed his finger up Mustapha's arsehole. The other stiffened his body and waited. He looked both ridiculous and damned inviting at the same time. Welch pulled him out from under the bed.

'You sit on bed,' Welch said. 'You open legs and I put my finger up your arse.'

Despite everything, the renter was pretty. Yes, a bit too pretty for Welch's tastes, but not too bad at all. He had a clear, unblemished face with large, dark eyes which looked frightened all the time. His hair was thick and curly. He had a slim body which was adorned with tufts of jet black under the arms and at his groin. His legs were smooth as silk and as slender as a girl's. His arms were too thin, but that could be overlooked.

'I said, legs – open.'

He pushed Mustapha's legs apart and pulled him to the edge of the mattress so that his arsehole was easily available. Welch stuck his finger into it without bothering to lubricate it first. Mustapha closed his eyes tightly and tried to remove the finger; tried to give himself a chance of accepting it without pain. Welch grunted and insisted it stay where it was. Gradually the young man's face relaxed and Welch smoked his cigarette while probing around inside his 'purchase'.

Welch's house was akin to a miniature mansion. It had belonged to some foreign diplomat and had been built with style. It was beautifully cool and spacious: white walls and large arches throughout. The building formed the four sides of a courtyard in which there was a small fountain and one forlorn palm tree. Welch had hired an American cissy to decorate the place. He readily admitted to having no taste himself, but he wanted his little palace to look good to whoever visited him. In truth, he thought the whole decor to be a bit prissy: white, muslin curtains which billowed out in the breeze; cushions scattered here and there; plaster reproductions of tastefully draped Greek athletes.

He looked around the room, fingering Mustapha's arse all the while. Life was not so bad. Had he stayed in England he would not have been able to achieve anything like this opulence.

Mustapha lay back. He had managed to light his cigarette and was blowing smoke rings. He appeared to have accepted the probing finger now. Welch wasn't sure this was what he wanted. He pushed another finger into him. The lad stiffened and then allowed his body to become loose once more.

'I please you?' Mustapha asked.

Mustapha had leant up. He was searching Welch's face for some sort of approval. Welch glanced at him and discarded his cigarette. He looked down at his own prick, not even sure whether it was hard or not. It was rising again.

'Not so much that you're getting any extra,' Welch growled. 'I might need to take you again. Don't think you're running away just yet.'

The young man didn't respond. His face suggested he didn't approve of Welch in the slightest. There was fear there too, but underneath it Welch detected censure.

He considered beating the whore's arse. He liked that idea. It would be satisfying to have that slight frame bent over his knee; to hear the cries and feel his body squirming about. It might even be a better idea than fucking him again. It would also mean he wouldn't have to worry about maintaining his erection.

'I may pay you more if you will do something for me,' he said. He had to make sure the little bastard wouldn't go screaming about assault. 'Something special.'

The lad nodded and drew on the cigarette sharply. 'What you want?'

Welch withdrew his finger and pushed Mustapha's legs up into the air so he was forced to roll back on to the mattress. He stroked the flesh of Mustapha's arse briefly and then brought his palm down on it with a very light slap. Mustapha remained where he was.

Welch gave him another slight smack and then allowed him to sit up.

'I do this properly and you get another two pounds. Do you understand?'

The young man did not appear to understand in the slightest. He seemed to be utterly confused by what Welch had done.

'Properly? You feel me underneath properly?' the boy asked.

'Like this,' Welch said in reply. He pushed the boy back again and dealt him a proper smack. It was hard enough to hurt, but this was the only way to demonstrate what he wanted and the whore would have to put up with it.

'You want hit me?'

'I want hit you,' Welch confirmed. 'Two pounds.'

The young man considered this. He soon came to a decision. 'Three,' he said.

'Two.'

Three would have been a fair price, but Welch had an in-built antipathy towards paying in full for anything. He knew now the lad didn't mind being spanked. Welch was not about to let him think he was in a position to make demands.

'OK,' Mustapha said. He turned over on the bed and pre-sented his arse to Welch. This would not do. Welch wanted him over his knee.

Welch sat as far away as possible: on a hard wooden chair in the corner of the room. He beckoned Mustapha over. When the lad stood up, he growled at him, 'On your bloody knees!'

Mustapha did not understand this. Welch was therefore required to go over and show him what he meant. He pushed the young man down, giving him the impression that he was required to lick Welch's boots. When he began doing this, Welch thought it a good enough sight to allow him to continue.

Satisfied with one foot, he presented the other. The lad kept looking up at him – not moving his head but rolling his eyes upward. It was most appealing: it showed real commitment to the task in hand. He was, in fact, checking that his master approved of what he was doing.

Bored with this, Welch showed the renter what the English word 'crawl' meant. Mustapha's dick was by now as hard as his master's. He did as he was told. Deliberately and slowly, he approached the chair where Welch had seated himself once more.

He tried to get his tongue on to Welch's shoes once again, but they were pulled back before he could. He ended up with his face against the cold marble floor. Welch placed his foot on top of his head: a gesture of his power and one which was evidently appreciated.

Mustapha was told to bend his naked body over Welch's knee. Welch almost resented the fact that they were both naked. There was something so satisfying about pulling the trousers and underpants down to reveal the vulnerable cheeks beneath. However, there were compensations here: the touch of naked flesh, the feel of the lad's hot genitals. His slender arms were stretched out, one hand gripping Welch's leg for support. Welch was going to enjoy this.

He ran his hand over the lad's nudity, enjoying the smoothness of his skin. Then he kneaded the flesh of Mustapha's buttocks. They were poised perfectly – slightly raised – round, firm and with a tantalising rift of hair to make the crack more inviting.

The time had come. Welch spat on to his palm and rubbed the saliva over his target. He brought his hand down hard, bringing a red glow rushing to the surface of the lad's skin. His victim squirmed and made some sort of noise, but not anything to indicate he had suffered real pain.

Another whack. This was carefully aimed to hit exactly the same spot as the first, so as to maximise its effect. The resulting moan was a more rewarding reaction than the first muffled cry. Welch brought a third slap down and the body he held tensed. The lad raised his head and yelled freely.

Welch clapped his free hand over Mustapha's mouth and held it tightly. The young man carried on yelling, using Welch's hand to push against. Welch felt the wetness from Mustapha's mouth against his skin and punished him for it with another three smacks.

His arse was now beautifully reddened. Welch felt lightly over it and was pleased to find it hot to the touch. The gentleness of this action made Mustapha fall back into his former position: loosely bending over with his head down and his neck relaxed. Welch wiped the spittle from his hand into Mustapha's hair. Vexed at having had to do this, he brought his hand down on to Mustapha's backside, again, and again, and again.

Welch knew from experience that there is a point when the slaps cease to hurt and become pleasurable. When this point is reached, it is possible to stretch the limits of a person's pain threshold. He felt underneath Mustapha to see how hard his penis was. It was half-erect; his touch made it stiffen a little more.

He pushed Mustapha off his knee as though he were a useless rag doll. The lad rolled on to the floor and Welch was gratified to see tears in his eyes.

'I want money now. I go now,' the boy said sulkily.

'You'll get what I promised you when I say so, not before,' Welch replied. He left the room: he needed to piss.

It was pitch black in the room. Jeremy clung on to Khalid's body and pressed his face against the peaceful rise and fall of his chest. Jeremy couldn't sleep. His mind was too full of things. He was beginning to think it was time to do something about his life. Maybe he would go back to England and start up in some respectable business. By the time he reached Percy's age, he might have money enough to help some good-looking young chap along life's path in the same way as he had been helped by Percy. It would be the right thing to do.

Then again, he might continue as he was and probably end up drunk in some alley in London. The prospect was not terrible to him. In fact, it had the air of romance about it: a wasted life. There had been other such tragedies – famous ones. People were always happy to read about them. Maybe he had been born to be one of the losers.

Maybe he would talk to Graham about it. Graham was assured and sensible. He would advise wisely.

The thought of confiding in that paragon of British manhood gave Jeremy a warm feeling. He squeezed Khalid and then wished he hadn't. Khalid opened his eyes and kissed Jeremy lightly on the forehead. Jeremy was being unfair again, thinking of one man while cuddling another. It would have to stop.

'I must go,' he said. 'They'll be waiting for me and I don't want Percy to be worried again.'

Khalid sat up. 'You come back to me?' he asked. 'You not angry about pimp?'

Jeremy declared he wasn't in the slightest bit angry. What right had he to say how others should act? He scrabbled around for his clothes. Khalid stopped him and lit the lamp.

'Now we are not blind with night,' Khalid said as the glow illuminated the room. 'Now I watch as you dress yourself.'

Jeremy had got as far as putting on his trousers. He was looking for his socks. Footsteps approached.

Khalid grinned. 'It is only Mustapha. He come back home.'

Jeremy nodded and continued his search. Mustapha called from the outer room. Khalid yelled back. Then there were some words in Arabic and Khalid's mood visibly changed.

'You must dress quickly,' he said. 'Pimp is here.'

It was too late. The door opened and a grey-haired, wiry man in his early middle age stood before them. Behind him, Mustapha was cowering. Jeremy had finally met the pimp.

'Good evening,' the man said. 'I don't believe I've had the pleasure.'

His voice was croaky; he probably smoked too much. There was the merest hint of a foreign accent in it, but Jeremy couldn't place where it was from. The man wore an expensive suit and had a sparklingly white felt hat in his hand. He looked like a gangster.

'I'm sorry,' Jeremy said. 'We were just having a lie-down. I have to be off soon. I'm due back at the Winter Palace.'

'I see,' the man said. He sauntered around the room as though he owned it. 'My name is Anthony Welch,' he volunteered after a long silence. 'Khalid, introduce your friend to me.'

Khalid did so. There didn't seem to be any reason why he was so frightened of this man. If what he had said earlier was true, then he and Jeremy had been doing what was to be expected of them in such a place.

'Perhaps you'll leave your money with me,' Welch said to Jeremy. 'We prefer cash to cheques. I'm sure you understand.'

Money? What was he talking about? Jeremy felt himself becoming angry. The man's whole attitude was threatening and insulting.

'I'm not quite clear why I owe you anything,' he answered.

Welch moved swiftly across and caught Khalid by the hair. Khalid squealed. Jeremy was about to go and rescue him and then thought better of it. Welch was probably a thug and was just the type to conceal a knife about his person.

'Please leave him —' Jeremy began.

'This man is my property,' Welch hissed. 'I have paid for him and you have helped yourself. You do not do that and leave without settling your bill. I have my standards.'

'I'm not a customer. I'm an old friend. Look, can't you leave him alone? He's done nothing to hurt you.'

Welch was silent but his face still spoke of menace. Jeremy despaired. It seemed likely Percy's warning had, after all, been pertinent. Did trouble have to be such a regular visitor? Was Egypt really populated by sadists, whores and corrupt officials?

'Thank you, God!' Jeremy muttered under his breath.

Welch yanked Khalid's head viciously. Khalid's face was creased in pain and he was trembling. Jeremy reached down to the floor for his jacket in order to find his wallet. He had only one note and that was worth twenty pounds. It couldn't be helped: he could scarcely ask for change.

He was stopped by Khalid's other friend.

Mustapha came into the room. Previously he had been quaking in the doorway. He walked determinedly over to

Welch and placed his hand on top of the one that still gripped Khalid's hair. 'I am the oldest. If you need hurt us, you hurt me.'

Welch's facial expression changed from malice to derisive amusement. Even so, Mustapha's words had their effect and he let go of Khalid, who retreated to a corner of the room and huddled there. He kept his legs up in front of his genitals and, for further protection, his hands over his head. Mustapha remained where he was. He was clearly frightened, but he was standing his ground.

'Look,' Jeremy protested. 'This is my fault. There's no need to hurt anybody. I'll pay you. Will that do? We'll say no more about it, eh?'

Welch wasn't listening to him. 'Quite the little Christian, aren't you?' he sneered. 'What makes you think you're suitable to be had twice in one night? I didn't even want to have you the first time.'

'To *have* is different. *Hurt* not what good men do. You do not hurt my *habibi*.'

'I'll pay,' Jeremy insisted.

Welch snorted and pushed Mustapha aside. His brave intervention had worked: Welch's previous anger had been dispelled somewhat. Mustapha went to Khalid and put his arms round him. They watched warily as Welch took further stock of Jeremy.

Jeremy was holding his jacket, but he had not yet brought out his wallet. He wondered if all this had just been a frightener. Would he manage to escape without hurt for a second time? Maybe fate wasn't as cruel as he first supposed. Maybe it put him in danger only to prove he was immune to it.

Welch stopped circling him, which was a relief. He'd stopped very close to Jeremy's face. His manner was hugely intimidating.

He placed a hand on Jeremy's crotch and squeezed his testicles until it brought water to Jeremy's eyes. He tried to remain as impassive as he could, but eventually he was forced on to his knees by the pain. Welch followed him down, still not letting go of him.

'I'll take your balls off if you try anything clever,' Welch said in a matter-of-fact way. 'What makes you think I want your bloody money?'

Jeremy gasped. He held his stomach tightly and gradually recovered his equilibrium.

'I have more money than you'll ever have,' Welch went on. He glanced over his shoulder. 'Haven't I, Khalid? I have much money.'

Khalid agreed hastily and then went back to hide behind his hands. Welch took Jeremy's chin in his cupped hand and examined the face before him.

'What *do* you want then?' Jeremy asked. He already knew the answer, but he thought it best not to offer himself in case it might be considered insulting in some way. Men like Welch didn't like it to be assumed they were queer.

'I don't know yet,' Welch replied. He appeared to be debating the question. Eventually, having thought better of availing himself of Jeremy's charms, he rose to his feet. 'You say Khalid is a friend of yours?'

Jeremy nodded. He mustn't give too much away. There was no telling what might offend this fellow.

'You're not a government man, by any chance?'

This was a surprising thing to ask. It obviously meant Welch had something to hide. Whatever it was, Jeremy had no intention of finding it out.

'Do I look like a government man? No, I'm not. Certainly not!' Jeremy replied.

Each denial was carefully monitored by Welch. Suspicion still hovered over his face, but he seemed to accept Jeremy's word – for the present at least. He bent down again and pushed his thumb into Jeremy's cheek as though he were a piece of malleable clay. Jeremy allowed this without protest.

'No. The government ones are far more uppity than you

could ever be,' Welch said finally. 'I believe you.' His whole
demeanour had changed: he'd actually become genial. The last
few minutes might not have taken place.

'Good,' he said, smiling now. 'Mustapha, I think you ought
to offer your guest a cup of tea.'

Mustapha was on his feet in a trice. Jeremy declined, he
hoped politely.

'I really have to be going. I'm sorry if I upset you. I didn't
mean it. It's not Khalid's fault either. You mustn't blame him.'

'Khalid can do what he wants,' Welch replied capriciously. 'I
don't mind in the slightest. Just as long as he remembers which
side his bread's buttered.'

Khalid was still not convinced of this freedom. He stayed well
back in the shadows, whimpering every time he heard Welch
mention his name.

Jeremy thought it best not to leave him alone with Welch.
The man was obviously unhinged. He claimed he didn't know
the way back to the hotel and would it be all right if Khalid
accompanied him? Welch saw through this immediately.

'You needn't worry. I'm not staying in this benighted place a
moment longer than I need to. Khalid!'

This last was an order. Quivering, but afraid of the conse-
quences of disobeying, Khalid stood.

His beautiful body was something to behold in the flickering
candlelight. Shadows caressed the hollows and hills of his
muscles; orange mixed with the brown of his skin and his eyes
shone white. His genitals were only just discernible in the
darkness which cloaked them. Jeremy could just see the tip of
his cock, lit where it rose out of his groin.

'You have something for me. You get it now,' Welch
demanded.

Khalid ran into the outer room and reappeared with a piece
of paper.

Welch cast his eye over it and seemed satisfied. 'These good
men?' he asked.

'Oh yes,' Khalid agreed. 'They very rich. They meet you where they say and do good business. Is OK.'

Welch accepted this assurance. He gave a brief nod to Jeremy before leaving.

The following evening, in a café where it was known foreigners were not welcome, a group of four men sat smoking and drinking. They wore loose robes and had the traditional head-coverings of the sheiks. They were bearded and their faces were wizened by the desert sun. Their teeth and their fingers were nicotine stained. They appeared to be engaged in intense discussion.

An observer might have noticed a change in their attitude as eight o'clock approached. They had finished their private discussion and were now in agreement. A minute or two later, an Englishman appeared and stood just inside the doorway, looking around the room.

The ringleader of the four pulled up a chair from a neigh-bouring table and invited the stranger to join them. The observer, had he known these people, would have been sur-prised by this, for they were not given to entertaining white men, Englishmen especially.

The group went into another huddle, the stranger with them. The visitor was respectful and never spoke until he was addressed, but he also had about him the air of one who holds the better hand of cards. The four men were by turns angry, agreeable and solicitous. A deal was being made.

Some ten minutes later, the group shook hands and, declining their offer of refreshment, the stranger left them. He walked out with far more confidence than he'd had upon entering. The deal had gone in his favour.

The four men huddled once again. One accused the other of having thrown their money away. Another reminded him they were in no position to bargain.

Their leader was sanguine. They might have lost this battle, but what was money? The Englishman was vital to them if they were to succeed – and succeed they certainly would.

'Then he, and his kind, will be no more here in Egypt,' he said. 'I smell the blood of many such as he and, my friends, I like the smell of it.'

He spared a thought for the various people who brought such Englishmen to them. They were not always honourable men: this latest was perverted with strange desires, but he had been useful and that should not be forgotten.

'We deal with the filth of our country and the rats of theirs,' the leader reflected. 'So be it. We must follow where our destiny takes us. The man Khalid has one of his feet in the sewers. It is there we will find others such as Mr Welch. We must take care he and those like him do not slip from our grasp.'

Ten

The next day began bright and early for the more adventurous of the tourists at the Winter Palace. They were to cross the river at the crack of dawn. There, those who were able had camels waiting to take them to the Valley of the Kings. They were preparing to taste the excitement of a discovery that had given rise to a craze.

Over 130 centuries ago, the boy-king Tutankhamun had lived his brief life and been laid to rest. His spirit might well be safe with his ancestors and his gods, but his treasures were, by all accounts, as beautiful as when they were buried. Howard Carter, the famous archaeologist, and his team were still coping with the celebrity which their discovery had brought them. The mysterious death of the Earl of Carnarvon had added uncanny drama to the find.

There was a deal of speculation about what might be seen: 'probably nothing' was one opinion; 'you can bribe these people to show you anything' was another. The consensus was it would be enough to say one had been there.

The more sedate of the company could ride in calashes, but

however they made the journey it was a trip they were urged not to miss.

Mrs Dryden didn't want to go: she knew Jeremy would be with them and she had no wish to speak to that particular young man until she could do so without emotion. She was eventually persuaded by Maria and Graham. Percy, they told her, ever independent, had elected to take a calash of his own. He hated being part of a group. Besides this, his fear of water meant he needed to steady himself before crossing the river. He could be prevailed upon to share the carriage with her as long as she pretended not to notice his embarrassing fear.

Graham, Maria and Jeremy were determined to try their hands at riding the 'ships of the desert'. The group was setting off at half past five, to get most of their sightseeing in before the sun became too hot for them to cope with.

The lobby of the hotel was crowded with bags, picnic hampers, servile staff and, like sheep in an unseen pen, the intrepid tourists.

Jeremy had no desire to converse with any of them. He was still worried about what had happened two nights ago, though he'd not spoken about it to anyone – not even to Graham.

He found his friend and Maria and was pleased to learn that Mrs Dryden and Percy were already en route. He wouldn't have to face either of them until lunchtime.

They boarded the *Nefertiti*, the paddle-steamer that had been commissioned to take them over the river. It was surrounded, even at that early hour, by chattering, pleading children and the insistent traders who followed the tourists everywhere.

Further down the river, the local ferry was about to set off. It was little more than a floating raft and was already full to overflowing with livestock and people. Percy's calash was visible in the centre of it. Judging by the interest it attracted from the Arabs around it, the two older people were hiding somewhere under the hood. Graham was highly amused by this. Apart from speculating on Percy's horror of the ferry sinking, he was certain

146

Mrs Dryden was regretting her decision. She would be wishing she was travelling on board the larger vessel with genteel twits to minister to her.

'Poor old trout,' he said. 'She thought she was going to get away without seeing a single black face all day. She probably thinks we knew all along she was going to end up being stuck with all that lot.'

Maria gave him a reproving look. Whether this was for his opinion of Mrs Dryden or his opinion of the native population, she did not say. He was sheepish and turned his attention to Jeremy to change the mood.

'What have you been doing with yourself recently, old chap? Anything interesting?'

They were leaning over the rail, watching the people below and enjoying the fresh breeze which the river was good enough to provide for them. They had all taken good advice and covered themselves well. Maria had on a full-length cotton dress and she was wearing a hat with a silk scarf round it. Jeremy and Graham had blazers and flannels and good, thick shoes to protect them from those nasty little blighters, the scorpions, which apparently lay in wait in the sand, ready to take nips out of the legs of innocent tourists.

'Tell you later,' Jeremy said nonchalantly.

Maria was instantly inquisitive. She assured Jeremy she wouldn't tell a soul. Had he had an adventure? Was it true what she had heard about Arabs selling their bodies for sex? Graham tried to stop her but she waved him away.

'I had to cope with your "old trout" for all that time in Aswan,' she declared. 'I've no doubt you had enormous fun while we were away. Come on, Jeremy, give me a bit of scandal. I'm practically gagging for something interesting to happen and I've been awfully good about keeping out of the way so far.'

Jeremy was saved by the bellow of the ship's horn. There was

147

a flurry of activity below and, with a cheer from the watching crowd, the *Nefertiti* heaved herself into action.

'Oh well,' Maria said when they were away from the east bank. 'At least I'll be able to avail myself of the ship's bar while you two go galloping off into the sands. Sometimes I wonder whether I might just as well declare undying affection for Mrs Dryden and show her what Sapphic love is all about. You chaps seem to be having all the fun.'

A camel is a difficult beast to mount. Jeremy was brave enough at first, but the gnashing teeth and the hiss which came from between them persuaded him the animal was not agreeable to being ridden. They each had a handler to help them, but these teenagers were enjoying the visitors' discomfort so much that they were not very useful at all.

The animal rises with its back legs first, plummeting its rider downward so it seems as though he is going to fall on to his head. Then it heaves the front part of its body upward, giving its human a dizzying vision of sand and sky. When it has corrected its stance, it seems (it did to Jeremy) the rider has said his last goodbye to terra firma. There appears to be no hope of ever getting down without the assistance of a ladder.

Maria thought it all utterly marvellous and kept saying so. Graham pretended he was used to this sort of thing and attempted to appear comfortable, which they all knew was an impossibility. Jeremy was not proud and openly admitted hating his camel, Egypt, and everything around him. Similar reactions were happening all around them. The Arabs allowed themselves the luxury of having these people in their power for once.

The ride was bumpy, but, once Jeremy was used to it, not unpleasant. The morning was still reasonably cool and, once away from the sugar plantations which bordered the river, the scenery was impressive in its awesome bleakness.

The mountains known as the 'Theban Crown' dominate the Valley of the Kings. The tourists were tolerated, but not welcomed by those others who had a more serious purpose in disturbing the Pharaohs' peace. The Arab guides kept them well away from where most of the archaeological activity was centred.

Once inside the narrow corridors of the tombs, the dazzling reflection of the sun on the sand seemed like another world. These were airless, dark places. The lamps illuminated wondrous paintings. Some were unfinished: life having departed the monarch before his everlasting house could be made ready for his corpse. The pictures, familiar from countless reproductions, were more vivid than could be thought possible. The three friends and their companions were walking back over centuries.

'It makes the Tower of London seem like a modern building,' Maria commented. 'I don't think I will ever think of ancient history in the same way again.'

Inevitably, they became immune to their wonder. After an hour or so, they were talking in terms of having 'seen one, seen the lot'. This was utter sacrilege and they knew it. It was time for a break. But there was nowhere to escape from the heat which had built up during their time underground. All three were ready for a drink, but they didn't trust the water that was offered to them at exorbitant prices.

Percy and Mrs Dryden were nowhere to be seen. Either they were here and 'doing' different tombs – just missing the three friends all the time – or they had decided to visit other sights of interest first in order to avoid the larger group.

They sat on a stone wall outside the entrance to the valley and debated what to do. They had the best part of a week in Luxor to go. There would be time to come back and view what they had missed or revisit what they had already seen.

'Let's not become jaded,' Graham advised. 'I want to have a peek at the Colossi of Memnon. Are you two game for that?'

They would have left then, but on the way to the queue of

carriages they were apprehended by a breathless figure running towards them: it was Khalid.

He had gone to the hotel in search of Jeremy; he hoped Jeremy would not be cross because he'd asked for him by name at the reception desk; he was so worried about everything and he needed to talk.

Jeremy tried to hush him but he was so agitated there was no hope of it. He kept mentioning the 'bad men' and confessing he too had been bad. His pimp (he used the word, much to Maria's amusement) was one of these 'bad men' and Jeremy must not have anything to do with him. There was danger.

Graham took him by the arm and led him away from a curious couple who were standing within earshot. He spoke to him in Arabic and was soon joined by Maria, who was anxious to be included. Jeremy was left to trail behind, not understanding but certain Khalid was spilling the beans about what had happened at his house.

It couldn't be helped. At least Graham and Maria were sensible enough not to panic in the way Percy had done. Graham shot Jeremy the occasional glance. By all accounts, he was not fazed by what he was being told. Maria was lapping it up.

'You appear to have involved yourself with gunrunners,' she said, clearly impressed. 'You're probably already a wanted man. I think this is fabulous.'

'It's not so fabulous when you're in the middle of it,' Jeremy complained. 'Anyway, nothing happened and it's not going to.'

The driver allowed Khalid into the calash under the impression he was their guide. They drove off with Graham and Maria still asking questions, Khalid anxious to supply any information and Jeremy wondering what on earth was going to happen next.

He hardly noticed the Colossi: two enormous seated statues which are all that is left of an ancient burial temple. They were both as tall as houses and breathtaking, if, as Jeremy said later, 'one was in the mood for that sort of thing'.

At least they had the effect of changing the subject of their conversation.

Maria and Graham wandered around them and took photographs. Khalid stayed by Jeremy's side, not sure whether he was in disgrace or not. Jeremy wasn't entirely sure himself. He felt as though he were being denied his right to any sort of private life and the other two were patronising him: Graham by assuming his usual air of control and Maria by poking gentle fun at him all the time.

Also, he was faced with the two men he felt most about – and together. Here was his dilemma. He knew he couldn't cope with Khalid on any permanent basis: apart from the impracticality of maintaining such an affair, there was all this danger surrounding him. Graham was clearly devoted to Maria so this too was a no-hoper. Jeremy was alone. His love life seemed to him to be juvenile and stupid.

'I love you,' Khalid said, not helping the situation one bit. 'You are my best friend.'

'We must deal with the pimp,' Jeremy replied.

Ahmed was not at all pleased Percy had offered Mrs Dryden a lift. He reacted by treating Percy as though he was no more than an ordinary passenger. Percy wanted to show off his friendship with Ahmed, for the best of reasons: to demonstrate that Mrs Dryden needn't be so confoundedly English when in the company of foreigners. This good intention was thwarted by Ahmed's silly mood.

Ahmed made a great show of bowing and scraping. He drove too quickly and he made no concessions to Percy on the ferry. He also pretended to misunderstand everything Mrs Dryden said to him.

Neither of the older people had the least interest in Egyptology. Mrs Dryden dared to suggest that the treasures, pictures of which she'd seen, were vulgar. Percy suggested the curse that descended on those who broke the seal on a Pharaoh's tomb extended to those who took very much notice of them or their work.

They visited the Valley of the Kings only briefly. One tomb was enough for them. Mrs Dryden thought the walls 'most interesting' and was disappointed Mr Carter wasn't there. Percy wanted to get out of the place as soon as possible. The two enjoyed a ride around the charming villages, took in the Colossi, eschewed the Valley of the Queens and decided to return to base.

Percy would rather have waited for the steamer than go on the ferry again but, as Mrs Dryden pointed out, it would be hours before it left. She again offered him her sleep mask. Percy had worn it on the outward crossing: she had brought it with her for that very purpose. The amusement this provoked was enormous, but at least Percy could pretend he was not on water. If he was to be mocked, he would hear only a lot of jabbering in Arabic. Mrs Dryden was made of sterner stuff and flicked her scarf at their tormentors. So they passed the quarter of an hour it took for them to get back.

'We're not really tourists,' Mrs Dryden concluded. 'We are simply visitors to the country. I like the sunshine but not the heat. I think the people are quite charming but I do not like their habits. I think I am much happier in the hotel.'

Percy seized on this opportunity and rid himself of her in the lobby of the Winter Palace.

Ahmed was not about to abandon his moody silence without a fight. Percy wondered how René was now; Ahmed didn't know. Percy suggested they go to the rooming house they used and have an hour or so together; Ahmed thought it was too early. Percy asked Ahmed what he *would* like to do; Ahmed asked him which of them was supposed to be the boss. Percy told him to drive wherever he pleased and himself fell into silence.

They rode around the bazaar. Percy bought one or two presents. Ahmed condescended to help him with these purchases. Prices had to be agreed by barter and this was something Percy had never been good at. Ahmed thought it too much of a disgrace to have a passenger who would accept the first, inflated price asked of him. He did what was required and, in so doing, began to enjoy himself.

Within an hour he was back to his normal self. He decided that, after all, they would have some time in the hotel. Percy breathed a sigh of relief.

He hoped Ahmed hadn't inadvertently spoken the truth when sex had first been suggested: he hoped it wasn't too early. He concentrated his mind on Ahmed's body, solid and powerful beneath the cotton of his jellaba. He remembered it naked and told himself he was about to see that sight once more and very soon. His cock began to respond: it wasn't too early.

Ahmed lay on the bed in his pristine underpants. He was stroking the front of them, encouraging the bulge which held Percy's attention. His free hand idly circled his nipples. He was posing and enjoying himself.

'I stole something,' he said.

Percy sat up in his chair. He knew from Ahmed's tone that, whatever this crime was, it wasn't serious. Even so, he wasn't going to condone petty theft. He demanded to know more.

Ahmed was bashful. He put his hand over his mouth as though he might give himself away if he didn't stop himself. His other hand left off stroking his underpants and slid inside. His penis was straining to get out. As he pulled at it, Percy saw the head poking out over the waistband. The cloth moulded to the shape of Ahmed's knuckles and, lower down, to the shape of his balls. Percy felt his own member growing.

'You not be angry?' Ahmed asked.

Percy said he didn't know; he wasn't going to promise. Ahmed must tell him what he had done.

'It is little thing. It won't be noticed.'

He dived off the bed and picked up his jellaba from the floor. He removed a small item from its pocket and held it in his fist. All this time, he continued to feel himself inside his underwear. He lay back again. Percy crossed the room to see what he held. Ahmed kept his fist closed and playfully pulled it away from Percy's grasp.

'It is surprise for me. Last time was your surprise. Now mine, yes?'

Percy sat down again. He nodded slowly. This flirtatious manner was most unlike Ahmed. Percy had really very little idea of what aroused him, but he was quite willing to find out.

Ahmed opened his hand and showed Percy what he had stolen. It was a tube of bright-red lipstick.

Ahmed started to apply the stuff clumsily to Percy's lips. Percy would have preferred to do it himself. He would have taken more care; done it properly. But he was no expert and Ahmed said it was important he took no part in 'preparing'.

When Ahmed was satisfied with his efforts and Percy had made himself more comfortable by removing his jacket and undoing his trousers, they lay together on the bed. Percy had imagined he would feel silly but, apart from the familiar taste of Mrs Dryden's pecklike kisses about his lips, he was not really aware of the paint.

'Naughty man,' Percy said. 'She's certain to miss it.'

Ahmed shrugged and declared Mrs Dryden could afford it. He thought it good payment from her for having spent the morning with them and not having offered any money. Percy considered this and, in a strange way, thought it fair.

Ahmed returned his hand to the inside of his underpants. His cock had remained rigid throughout the preparations. It was now oozing fluid, forming a patch of damp on the cotton. Percy stroked the insides of Ahmed's legs and felt that strong, workman's body go limp.

Ahmed went on looking up at him. His mouth was open

slightly, showing the gap in his teeth. He was totally engrossed in what Percy was doing. His whole body responded to each touch. He reached up and traced Percy's lips with his finger; the tip of it was red when he brought it away. He rubbed this colour on to his own nipples and examined the effect. Then he raised his hips and pulled his underpants down to his knees.

Percy removed them completely. This done, he found himself kneeling at Ahmed's feet. He pulled off his own shirt and wished he'd also had the sense to remove his pants and braces: they were in the way.

'Take time,' Ahmed said. 'I like to see you like this. It is Englishman with lady's lips. This is what my surprise is.'

Percy kissed Ahmed's feet, leaving more red on his toes and instep. Then he proceeded up his legs; his knees; his thighs and on to his genitals.

The lipstick left its trail of colour along Ahmed's erection. He was leaning up all the while, studying its effect and making satisfied noises in his throat. He pulled his cock from Percy's mouth and offered him his balls instead. Percy took them each in turn and then both together.

This action gave him a wonderful view of Ahmed's body: the bobbing erection in the front of his vision and, beyond it, the rounded form of his chest, horizontal to the eye.

Ahmed eased Percy off temporarily to apply more of the lipstick. This was done even more hastily than the last time. He drew circles around his nipples with it and, laughing with delight, painted an arrow down the centre of his chest, pointing to his dick.

'You suck again, ladyman.'

Percy returned to Ahmed's balls and took care to deposit on his skin as much of the colour as he could. It was not something he had ever thought of doing and he did think it a strange desire, but the bizarre nature of what they were doing was exciting him. He came up for air and lay next to Ahmed getting his breath back.

'You like my surprises?' Ahmed said.

Percy tried to answer but was stopped by Ahmed throwing himself full length on top of him and planting a hard, purposeful kiss upon his lips. Percy brought his arms around his friend and held him tightly.

Gradually the embrace slackened and Percy was able to explore Ahmed's back and buttocks: the rock-hard shoulder muscles, the prominent spine, the softer area below his ribs, the rise of his cheeks and the sweat-lined crack between them. He rested there, pushing with his fingers, asking permission to enter. Ahmed continued to kiss him over and over. Their mouths were hurting with the pressure of it but neither wanted to stop.

It must have been some five minutes later when Ahmed disengaged himself and bounded off the bed. He knelt on the floor, facing the chair, and leant his torso over the seat. Both his hands went to his arse. He parted the cheeks, displaying the wet hair and the darker skin around his sphincter. He kept his head turned towards Percy, his upper body curved upward like a ship's figurehead but with its face looking backward. Percy let him display himself thus for a short time while he disrobed.

He had to position Ahmed differently. The chair was discarded and Ahmed went on all fours with his arse up towards Percy's cock. His arse was also covered in lipstick by now. Percy paused for a moment and reached for the tube. He drew a circle of scarlet around Ahmed's sphincter and pressed more inside him. Ahmed tensed beautifully, craning his neck upward and quickening the rhythm of the guttural noises he was still making.

Percy's curved erection slid in and pushed upward. He watched himself being swallowed by the lovely brown body. He saw the warpaint mingle with his pubic hair and smear it with colour. He gripped Ahmed under his stomach and panted as he experienced the warm, tight grip of Ahmed's back passage round his determined thrusts.

Ahmed reached for his own cock and rubbed it briskly between two fingers. His back swayed from left to right and his head rolled slowly from side to side. Percy felt himself coming and gasped out a warning.

Too late.

He stayed inside until Ahmed had come as well. It didn't take very long. His spunk hit Percy's arm and splashed over Ahmed's chest; it dripped on to the floor, thick, creamy gobs of it. Percy still kept his soft penis where it was. He was enjoying just being joined to this man. There was more than sex here, he realised: what he was feeling was love.

Eleven

Graham Etherington prided himself on being a person who could take on anything and anybody and win. He knew Maria was the female equivalent of himself and in many ways they saw themselves as a team against the world. They often came across people who were less capable of dealing with life's vicissitudes and they enjoyed taking such people under their joint wing.

They had a great sense of justice. It was, to a large extent, their driving force. It was this sense which haunted them throughout the rest of the day. What they had learnt from Khalid would 'just not do'. It was going to be remedied and they were the people to remedy it. They were not the sort of people to walk away from that kind of challenge.

'How much does Percy know about all this?' Maria asked Graham.

Graham had no idea, but he suspected Jeremy had told him little more than they themselves had known. She had her 'I have an idea' face on: he knew better than to press her until she was ready.

He paced the room and smoked far too many cigarettes. She

sat on the floor with her fingertips lightly touching. She looked like a Western female version of the Buddha.

At last she came out of her reverie and announced, 'I think I've got it! Are you game for a bit of danger?'

Of course he was. Though he would rather her solution were more conventional than dangerous. He had still not said anything about the 'danger' to which he'd already subjected himself. Still, there was no reason why that should come out. The two incidents were entirely separate.

'The trouble is,' she continued, 'we're going to need Percy's help. Do you think Jeremy is going to allow him into all this?'

Jeremy was dead against any such notion. He was overdrawn on his account as far as Percy's generous spirit was concerned. In any case, he reasoned, it was nothing to do with Graham and Maria. Khalid's problems had precious little to do even with himself. Why should they bring anybody else into the equation?

'So what are you going to do about Khalid?' Maria asked. 'Leave him prey to that awful man he told us about? I don't believe you could be such a ghastly cad.'

Jeremy turned on her and was checked by Graham, who was standing directly behind his fiancée. Maria waited for the tirade but it never came. Jeremy turned away and stuck his hands in his pockets, trying to appear nonchalant but managing it not at all.

'It goes beyond your responsibility to Khalid,' Maria continued. 'What about your responsibility to your country?'

This hadn't occurred to Jeremy. It was true, of course. The man was running guns to aid some sort of coup against the Egyptian Government. British interests would certainly be affected. He seized on the idea.

'We can go to the High Commission and report what we know. Welch will be arrested and probably taken back to Britain, where he can do Khalid no harm at all.'

Graham interrupted here: 'And Khalid will be arrested for

living off immoral earnings. He will probably ask you to support his innocence and they'll find out none of you are free from blame. Welch isn't going to go calmly off to jail with his hands in the air and his tail between his legs. He'll bring everybody he can along with him.'

'What can Percy do about it?' Jeremy asked. 'I can't ask him to support me in this. He wouldn't do it anyway. He's said so.'

Maria remained patient. 'He might if I asked him. Despite being an adorable old thing, he does rather like the company of females. I think he's rather taken to me.'

Jeremy was about to say something but she held up her hand and stopped him. 'No, don't thank me,' she said. She turned to Graham and slid her hand round his waist. 'To tell you the truth, I think I'm going to rather enjoy all this.'

Khalid was the next person who had to be persuaded. Until he agreed, there was little point in worrying Percy. Jeremy had no wish to go back to the house: there was too much chance of meeting up with Welch. Maria thought him a coward, but did not say so. She was ever practical.

'Graham,' she declared. 'You'll have to do it.'

'Now hang on, old girl!'

'Don't you "old girl" me. I'm twenty-seven, not seventy-two. Don't worry, Jeremy, Graham knows exactly what sort of establishment he's going into. He might even be able to have a little bit of fun in the process.' She turned to Graham and gave him a light kiss on the cheek before saying brightly, 'Won't you, darling?'

Jeremy didn't know Khalid's address, but Graham's calash driver did – eventually.

'House near bazaar? Many houses. Many people live near bazaar.'

'A man called Khalid. He was our guide earlier today. He lives with another man, Mustapha.'

'Not live with family?' The driver thought this puzzling at

first. Everybody in Luxor lived with their family. Then the light began to dawn. 'You like to have company with men friends? This man Khalid, is he *habibi*?'

'Very good friend, yes,' Graham agreed. He was not going to confide in the driver but he was sure the man had taken hold of the general idea.

'Homosex?' the driver asked. He had more than a general idea.

'I'll pay you double,' Graham said.

He spoke in Arabic to let it be known that he wasn't the sort to be cheated. The driver laughed at his accent and came out with a stream of vernacular which Graham only partly understood. The gist of it was that English people could do what they wanted as long as they paid their way. The calash moved off.

At the first two houses they visited, Graham was asked to come in, asked to take tea and, insistent he was there only to deliver a message, reluctantly allowed to depart. He had had no idea such men were available. Jeremy must have been having a whale of a time on the sly. Why on earth had he chosen to fuck somebody in the open air when there were so many safer places to do it?

They drove down a narrow street that the calash could barely fit into. Children, as ever, flocked around it, but they were soon dismissed. The driver pointed with his whip to a blue-painted door which stood ajar. People were coming out of their houses to see who was visiting them in such style. Once they guessed which house the dark-haired Englishman wanted, they either retreated indoors or squatted on the ground, watching.

Graham tapped at the door. A slender, pretty youth opened it wide. He was not wearing a shirt, just a pair of loose trousers. Graham thought him very handsome in a girlish sort of way.

'I am Mustapha,' he said. 'You have come to see me? Yes?'

Graham explained he was looking for a man named Khalid. Mustapha nodded and gestured for him to enter. Having excused himself just long enough to pay the calash driver, Graham followed him into the lamplit room.

'Khalid has many visitors these days. He will be back in one hour. I too am with my friend. Do you wish to meet him?'

His manner was solicitous. He was extremely tactile: already he had linked arms with Graham as if they had known each other for years. Graham liked him well enough, but he thought him a little presumptuous. He resolved to leave and return when Khalid would be at home.

'I haven't time,' Graham said. 'I'll be back later.' Mustapha stroked his hair and Graham eased himself apart from him. 'Later,' he repeated.

Footsteps approached from the back room. Graham hoped the other person wouldn't turn out to be Welch. It wasn't likely. Mustapha wouldn't be so relaxed if it was.

'You have come for the other part of your lesson,' said a voice from within. It was familiar. Graham tried to think whose it was, but couldn't. The figure hovering in the darkness beyond the doorway emerged into the light.

It was Ali.

Graham had a growing feeling of paranoia. He also detected that the atmosphere was charged. Without knowing why, he stuck his hands in his pockets. Mustapha patted him on his backside.

'You have met my friend already?' Mustapha asked.

Ali came boldly forward and kissed Graham on the lips. Graham took it passively. He knew there was no chance of his leaving now.

'Don't tell me,' he said at last. 'You two are cousins.'

Ali laughed. He took hold of Mustapha's hand and squeezed it. Mustapha drew close to him and nibbled his ear.

'As you see, that is not the case,' Ali answered. 'Mustapha is my lover.'

Graham looked around for somewhere to sit. Not seeing any

162

obvious place, he eventually settled himself on the floor. The other two remained standing, Mustapha still petting with Ali.

'Did you know I was coming here by any chance? Did you follow me?' Graham asked Ali.

'It is hard to follow somebody and arrive at their destination before them. No, I did not know you were coming here. Though I am not at all surprised to see you.'

He sat down next to Graham. Mustapha came and sat on his other side. The two of them eased Graham's blazer off his back. Mustapha was massaging his shoulders; Ali unbuttoning his shirt.

'Hey! Hey!' Graham said. 'I've already explained. I've just come here with a message. I didn't mean to –'

Ali stopped him with another kiss. Mustapha's hands were inside his shirt, probing his spine. It felt wonderful, but Graham resented being taken for granted in this manner.

'Are all you people sex mad?' he said. He pulled away.

The insistent hands followed him and began their work afresh. He gave in and leant over his hunched knees, allowing his body to go loose. Mustapha smelt of some heady perfume and his hands were oiled. Graham allowed him to remove his shirt.

'We like to share our love,' Ali said. 'You are very handsome. Will you deny us your body?'

'I'll let you have my body if you lick my arse.'

Graham didn't know what made him say it. The words came out of his mouth unbidden. Perhaps he was susceptible to the erotic atmosphere. It didn't matter: they were not going to be prudish.

Ali gave Mustapha a look. They agreed.

Mustapha left off rubbing Graham's back and came round to undo his trousers. He did it carefully, as though it were part of a ceremony. Graham watched him, feeling all this to be unreal. It was as though they were doing it to somebody else.

His shoes and socks were removed and then his trousers were gradually pulled down. He lay there in his underpants, feeling his penis uncurl and stiffen. Ali joined Mustapha, each kneeling at one side of his legs. They kissed each other again, over him, and then the massaging recommenced. This time at his feet.

They mirrored each other's actions. When one pushed into his right heel, the other did the same with his left. Graham had never before known his feet could be sensitive in this way. He was usually ticklish, but this attention was not irritating him. He felt the pressure of fingers around his toes and in the soft part of his sole; it seemed to have a corresponding glow in various parts of his chest and stomach. He closed his eyes.

Wet lips took his toes and licked around them. He suddenly wanted to be naked, but, when he made as if to pull down his underpants, Ali stopped him.

'In time,' he said. 'Enjoy this first.'

His feet were now being lapped all around. Hands stretched out, symmetrically. They squeezed and prodded his calves. The tension left his legs and the muscles unknotted, making him feel supple and energised.

Further up: his thighs. The two youths brought their mouths into play once more. He was aching for them to deal with his cock, but he resisted asking for it. His underpants were gradually discarded. It was not a hurried thing; not the usual frantic scurry to be naked. It was reverent and erotic in itself. He could feel the air around his cock. He was properly naked. He had been slowly stripped: it meant something.

They kissed each other over his shaft, and then again, including his penis in their union, the slippery wetness of their mouths on his cock.

'Now it is time. Which of us would you like to do it?'

Ali's question was matter of fact. Graham might have felt awkward but there was no need of it. He nodded at Ali.

'Will you? Will you lick my arse?'

It was something he'd often wanted done to him, but he'd never dared ask anyone before. Maybe Ali was a mind-reader; maybe Graham had been put under some sort of spell. He didn't care. He sighed and rolled his legs into the air. Mustapha held them so he didn't have to make any effort. He gradually pressed Graham's legs down so they were bent back over his chest. Ali bent his head and kissed Graham's buttocks.

Ali prised the firm cheeks apart and, with swooping licks, covered the crack with his saliva. Each time Ali's tongue passed over Graham's hole, he experienced a thrill. He'd always had hard things in contact with that private area: penetrating cocks, a man's finger, a phallus. Ali's tongue, this live, soft thing, was unlike any other sensation.

Mustapha was slowly creeping his hand towards Graham's shaft. He took it carefully, his fingers moving around the head. Ali jabbed into Graham's arsehole and he cried out, 'Yes, yes. Lick my hole, please, lick my hole.'

The tongue pushed into him and moved around, moistening his sphincter and sliding easily across his hot skin.

'Are you going to fuck me?' Graham gasped. 'I would like you to.'

Mustapha strengthed the grip he had on Graham's cock. 'You should not be so much hurry,' he said. 'There is time for all things.'

Still the tongue in his backside. Now the familiar feeling of pleasure around the end of his penis. Graham stiffened his body and was gently reminded to relax by Mustapha smoothing his hand against his shoulders.

The licking stopped at last. Graham was held in position by Mustapha while Ali stripped himself.

Ali's body was perfect. He had shaved himself around his pubic area and, apart from under his arms, he was hairless. His nipples were almost black, large mounds on his young chest. He had strong, shapely legs and his cock, which Graham remembered from the hotel, was long and thick.

He fucked Graham very slowly. He was expert at it, not allowing himself to speed towards coming but enjoying their lovemaking for its own sake. Graham found himself breathing deeply. For once he was not concerned with his own orgasm. It swelled up as though from nowhere, all the physical warmth around him uniting in one spot and spurting out of his body. Ali took a few more moments and then his body went limp. They lay together and kissed. Mustapha lay beside them and masturbated over their skin. The three rolled together and shared each others' mouths.

'We don't often bring people back here,' Ali said at last. 'This is our private space where we live.'

'You didn't bring me back,' Graham answered. 'I came here all by myself.'

'Is my English good?' Mustapha asked.

Graham had not really noticed. 'It's better than my Arabic,' he said. He used the conventional phrase from the book: '*Ma etekellem Areby killish zain.*'

'You wrong. Your Arabic is very good,' Mustapha replied. 'Ali speaks very good English and you good Arabic.'

'My girlfriend is a linguist,' Graham explained. 'She speaks eight languages. She made me learn.'

'You have girlfriend?' Mustapha was surprised by this.

Graham didn't want to have to explain. 'I can't believe you two are lovers,' he said, changing the subject. 'I mean, is all of Luxor involved in this sort of thing?'

'There are circles and circles,' Ali answered. 'It depends where you come in. Believe it or not, many of my countrymen, like many of yours, are respectable. If you like, I will show you where you can sit and discuss religion, politics, the weather. No mention of the male body all night long.'

'That's not my kind of circle,' Graham said.

'You have come for Khalid, with a message?' Ali's tone had changed. They were getting down to business.

Graham didn't want to discuss the problems they were having with Welch. 'It's a private matter. I can't really tell anyone apart from Khalid himself. Will he be back soon?'

Mustapha sighed. 'Khalid can be most bad. I do not judge him. Mr Welch was supposed to deal with me. I am head of house: Khalid should not be part of his business. But Mr Welch do not really like me. I am too much like woman.'

Ali held his hand. 'You are not like a woman. Stop saying this.' He turned to Graham. 'My friend thinks he looks too young. He thinks men don't want such looks. Mr Welch likes Khalid best, but Mustapha wants to protect Khalid by dealing with Welch himself. He is very brave.'

Graham decided it would not be prudent to let too much information slip out, but he wanted to give them some indication of his trust in them. 'We are trying to deal with Mr Welch. I think he should be made to pay for the bad things he has done. We are going to help you.'

This provoked a violent reaction in Mustapha. He took hold of Graham by both arms and looked him straight in the eye. His expression was intense. 'No! You leave Mr Welch! You must do nothing. It would be most big mistake! You must promise me!'

Graham was touched by his concern. Really, Welch should not be allowed to have this sort of influence over people. He obviously terrified everyone he dealt with. His own fears of the man paled into insignificance. This was a just cause and he would see it through. 'It's all right,' he said. 'We know what we're doing.'

'I don't think you do,' Ali said quietly. 'What Mustapha speaks is the truth. You would be better to leave Welch to others. There *are* others who watch him. Believe it.'

'I hear you,' Graham said. 'But you mustn't worry. I tell you, we know what we're doing. Soon, Welch won't be able to harm anyone any more.'

Khalid arrived before they could continue the discussion. Graham, still naked and wishing he'd dressed himself, caught Khalid's approving eyes roving over his body. He decided to give him the message but not to refer to what had been said about Welch.

'Jeremy needs to talk with you, Khalid. He didn't want to come here himself in case that man was still here.'

With the man in question safely at home, Khalid was bravery itself: 'Mr Welch no frighten me! I will protect everybody.'

Mustapha held his head in his hands and groaned. He said, in Arabic, that he wished Khalid would learn some sense. Things were difficult enough and they should let him, Mustapha, be in charge.

Khalid repeated that he didn't fear anyone. He sat down next to Graham and slyly took hold of his penis. Graham had just been about to get dressed. He took Khalid's hand and laid it aside.

'You are not for me,' he said. 'Jeremy would be angry.'

'Jeremy is not here,' Khalid replied. 'You no tell him and he is no angry.'

The hand returned. It was laid aside again.

'I must be getting back,' Graham explained. 'I can't help you in that way. I'm sorry.'

His cock had responded and Khalid pointed this out. Graham put on his underpants and began to gather his clothing. Maria had given him licence to have a little fun, but she would think it a bit off if he proceeded to allow every man in the house to fuck him. He asked Khalid if he would come back with him and Khalid agreed.

Ali showed them to the door. He repeated Mustapha's advice. Khalid pricked up his ears. This was the first he'd heard of the plot.

'Jeremy will tell you all about it,' Graham said. 'We must go.'

They walked down the pitch-black road together, Khalid asking questions all the way. Graham told him little: just that they needed his help and all would be explained later. This eventually prompted a sulk. Eventually they found a calash and drove back to the Winter Palace in silence.

'I am not allowed,' Khalid said when Graham invited him to

enter the lobby. 'I am too much like whore. They not let me inside.'

'I'll say you're my guide,' Graham reasoned. 'I'll pretend I owe you some money and it's in my room. You're with me.'

Khalid wouldn't be persuaded. In the end, Graham had to go in alone and find the others.

Twelve

Percy was over fifty. His life as a homosexual in British society had always contained risks: the risk of ostracism, the risk of blackmail and violence, even the risk of prison. Somehow he had never thought of himself as a brave individual. He still blanched at the thought of passing through rough areas of London; he still edited his conversation so as not to cause offence; he still avoided policemen.

Prior to Jeremy's escapade he'd thought Luxor was a safe place for him to be. He could keep his British friends entirely separate from his Arab lover. He knew he was not alone and was accepted for what he was. If he came across in the hotel as a bit of an old queen, at least it wasn't the same as being similarly marked out in Chelsea or Kensington.

As these comfortable thoughts began to present themselves to him, he started to think about the possibility of becoming an old colonial. There was little to attract him in London or Brighton, but here, where the cost of living was so cheap, he had enough private income to live the life of a millionaire.

Percy was a fatalist, or at least he attempted to be. He tried never to regret anything in his life. He found 'ifs' and 'maybes' to be useless. His assessment of Jeremy, for instance, was never tinged with bitterness. He had always been aware of that particular young man's motives. He did not judge him for what he was. Had Percy been born into a life without a comfortable income always behind him and had he been blessed with Jeremy's looks, he might well have done the same.

But such relationships can sometimes cost more than money. When he and Jeremy had been frivolous, when both parties had understood their obligations to each other, it had been vapid but fun. Percy had enjoyed being seen in the company of a blond beauty half his age. When Jeremy had embarrassed him by being drunk or petulant, he had dismissed it as an excusable folly of youth. He was older and wiser and Jeremy's flaws made him feel stronger.

Now Jeremy was about to cross the line between the carefree attitudes of his early adulthood and the responsibilities that came with maturity. Percy was being asked to continue to support him, but Jeremy's responsibilities were not his and Percy wondered if he should not divorce himself from his charming friend.

He was being asked to do something that was so totally against his nature as to be ludicrous. His first reaction was a resounding no. Indeed, had it not been for the presence of Graham and Maria, he would have walked away there and then. He hadn't done so. Here he was faced with two young people with no axe to grind, a couple who had willingly involved themselves in Jeremy's problems and those of his friend.

'What you are asking is ridiculous and quite out of the question,' he said. 'I am not the person you take me for. Call me a coward. Yes, I probably am. I like being a coward – it suits me.'

'We can't do it without you,' Maria reminded him.

'That fact is something for which you will come to thank me. I cannot dictate to you what you should, or should not, do, but I can't help thinking your idea is very foolish. Forgive my presumption: I think you see yourselves as characters from some schoolboy romance. Life does not always support the avenging hero. Quite the reverse, in fact.'

They had walked some way up the road. Now they turned to walk back. Khalid was in front. He was gloomy and apprehensive. This may have been in part because he sensed Percy did not like him. The agitated conversation which was now taking place was upsetting him. The angry little man who had shouted at his Jeremy was going to stop them getting even with Welch. Khalid was naive enough to believe in the potential success of their plan without even questioning it.

They passed people he knew. Some of them shouted out greetings but he did not respond. He was aware he would be quizzed about this when next he saw them. He had already resolved to offer a complicated excuse: he was a guide for these people and they were refusing to pay him the proper rate. He'd embellished this premise in his mind. By the time it reached the ears of his friends it would be an obvious lie, but it would make Khalid feel better.

He was also cross with Mustapha. Mustapha had been overbearing, as usual. He was just a pretty youth and he should stick to selling his body. It was he, Khalid, who had taken all the risks with Welch. He had appeased him by finding clients who were willing to buy his goods. Guns, drugs or young men: it hadn't mattered at the time. The Englishman was their lifeline and had to be kept happy. Had it not been for Khalid's cleverness, they would not have a place to live and money enough to buy clothes and food.

His means of obtaining an income had meant being cold-shouldered by his family and some, though not all, of his friends. He had made sacrifices. Mustapha had to cope only with Welch's filthy temper when Khalid was not available and Welch's need for sex was urgent. Just because he was younger by two years did not mean Khalid wasn't the real breadwinner of the two of them.

Jeremy had told him not to worry about the future. Even so, he had some misgivings: with Welch out of the way, they would have to find money for their rent. It was a big step: Welch's presence meant they never had to worry financially. It had not occurred to Khalid that he actually paid Welch far more than Welch paid him. Jeremy had pointed this out to him:

'He wouldn't be doing it otherwise. Anyway, don't you think it's time you stopped selling your body and found a proper job?'

Jeremy couldn't be expected to understand. Khalid could try all he might to find employment in a shop or as a guide, but, though the Egyptians tolerated sex between males (they saw it as something that had to be done), they were not so approving of men who would never marry. The small band of homosexuals in Luxor was not accepted. Khalid had twice been beaten up. He had not forgotten the experiences.

Still, he was happy to put his trust in his English friend. Perhaps the fat man – not a nice person, but better than Welch – perhaps he would help them with their financial difficulties. English people had power: they could solve any problem.

Though he didn't know what was being said, Khalid gathered all was not going well. Maria's plan had not yet been revealed to him, but he had been told it hinged on Percy's acceptance. He was apprehensive about his own part in it, but had been assured he would not have to do anything that would be difficult or dangerous. Now the fat man was not going to join with them, Khalid had a growing feeling of relief tinged with regret. Life would presumably go on as before. He thought more and more of running away. Cairo had lots of opportunities and he was not known there. It was possible.

'Why does it have to be me?' Percy asked for the third time. 'Just because I'm the age I am does not mean this horrid man is going to trust me. Do I look like a government official? I don't think I'd be let through the door of the Foreign Office.'

Graham remarked that, with a little rehearsal, he would pass it off superbly. All Percy had to do was meet Welch and warn him Khalid was under surveillance and, in return for Welch's immunity, the British authorities wanted names, dates and other details. They had Khalid's information: all they needed was for the police to witness Welch confessing all. Before he knew where he was, Welch would be clapped in irons and marched away. Percy would be quite safe.

'It would make a good story,' Percy remarked. 'But I don't think I see myself doing any such thing. Besides which, your friend, Khalid, would still be implicated. It doesn't let him off the hook. Not at all.'

Maria smiled and dug Jeremy in the back. 'Shall I tell him?' she asked.

Jeremy didn't care. He wasn't sure about all this either. He had let himself be talked into it; now he was happy to let himself be talked out of it.

'Mrs Dryden told me something about what happened at the police station,' Maria explained.

Percy was stunned. 'How on earth does she know about that?'

'From the man who took the phone message about Jeremy's arrest,' Maria replied. 'He asked her how her friend was and said he hoped very much he was out of trouble. She managed to get most of the story out of him, and what little else she knew she'd got from Graham.'

Graham was shamefaced. When Mrs Dryden had asked, he'd tried to be diplomatic, but the old lady was not having any of it. After speaking to Graham, she had relayed the whole of her scant information to Maria. Maria had, in turn, secured the finer details from him. She, being the sort of person she was, had decided the incident was serendipitous: they would be able to bargain with the policemen and, with Graham and Jeremy there to hold a gun to their heads, they would be sure to keep Khalid out of it.

'It's perfect. We have two corrupt policemen who should be

easy enough to turn into tame corrupt policemen. They are bound to want the glory of arresting Mr Welch and, if it means letting Khalid off the hook and being sure their own mis-demeanours are kept under wraps, why should they worry?'

Percy was even more doubtful now. He thought it foolhardy to involve two such disreputable characters. It was his final word on the matter. He was hungry and he'd had quite enough of promenading up and down. They wouldn't mind, he ventured, if he dined alone?

In the event, this was not to be. Mrs Dryden joined him at his table. She was brimming with scandal but far too diffident to speak of it unless so invited. She had forgotten her previous opinions of Jeremy. He was now 'that poor boy'. She couldn't imagine what he must have gone through. She was reckless enough to refer, in coded sentences, to his sexuality – and to Percy's.

'There are certain things which I cannot condone, of course. But I always say live and let live. I know dear Reverend Mr Downing would think me foolish – he's our local vicar in Surrey – but "there are more things in heaven and earth" and all that nonsense. I think I've misjudged dear Jeremy. After all, he has been bereaved quite recently and that must give rise to all sorts of emotional turmoil. Then, there's your good self. You are not a wicked person and yet, forgive me, you are not the marrying kind. Maybe my life in England has been altogether too narrow.'

Percy did not speak. He was wondering how Mrs Dryden would react to what Jeremy was now planning. She would probably think it all terribly exciting and not have the least idea of how dangerous it really was.

He thought back to what he had said himself: that he was a coward and proud of it. Was it a thing to be proud of? Just supposing they could carry the whole thing off? Would his life not have more meaning? Would he not be a better person?

'By the way,' Mrs Dryden said, 'I wouldn't use that driver any more, the one who took us to the west bank. I know this sounds very strange and I can't think why he should have done it but, when I came back for my handbag after visiting the tombs, my lipstick was missing. There was no one else who could possibly have taken it. I suppose he thought he could sell it, stupid man. It was not an expensive one.'

Percy choked on a mouthful of potato.

Jeremy joined him later. He was calm and appeared to have accepted Percy's earlier decision. He said it had all been Maria's stupid idea. She had nothing to lose: she could enjoy the adventure without having any of the actual danger. Yes, she had volunteered to approach the police, but she was not the one who had to face Welch or take the blame if the whole thing backfired. Jeremy was pleased Percy had talked sense. They would go back to England and forget about the whole thing. After all, it wasn't their problem. Why should they bother about it?

Caprice was not normally a trait Percy was fond of. He liked to decide and stick by his decision. But maybe he saw something of himself in Jeremy. Here was a young man who always avoided things. He lived off his looks and a few white lies.

Jeremy was at a crossroads and Percy was leading him down the wide and easy path. He knew full well that the end of the journey would not be as inviting as the beginning of it. What would Jeremy be like when he reached Percy's age? He would be a no-good who cared only for himself. Graham and Maria might be foolhardy, but they were good people and they cared. If Percy allowed Jeremy to walk away this time, he would be as good as ruining him for life.

'You mistake what I said,' Percy declared. 'I have decided to help your friends as much as I am able.'

The next day, after Percy had nervously agreed to his role, Maria and Graham set off for the police station.

The officers Graham knew were not on duty. Graham insisted they needed to talk to them privately and would not divulge anything further. Maria's presence at least provoked a degree of politeness from the man on the desk. He told them to come back in the evening. The men they wanted would be on duty then and he would give them a message telling them to expect a visit.

When they returned, they were shown into an empty office. Presently two of the guards appeared. The youngest one was not with them.

'These things should not be spoken of when woman is here,' the superior guard declared.

Maria set her face into its most stony expression and asked if women frightened him.

He avoided her eyes and addressed himself solely to Graham. 'I have had man read your confession . . .'

'Which I was told would be returned to me,' Graham reminded him.

'You very clever individual. I give it back to you. Our business is finished.'

He handed the paper over to Graham, who tore it in half.

'Do you not want to have the honour of arresting a criminal – a real criminal?' Maria asked.

Her Arabic was flawless. It was the first time she had spoken in their language and it certainly gained the man's attention. The guard's subordinate stood behind him and swallowed hard. Neither of them liked the idea of strong women: it wasn't something they were used to dealing with. Maria was a huge threat to them, especially as she went on to make it clear that she knew about their sexual tastes.

Graham then outlined their plan.

'This man you say. He has guns?' asked the senior guard.

Graham went over their tale yet again. All the officers had to do was to be within earshot when Percy talked with Welch. They would hear everything they needed to make an arrest. They could have all the glory – all that was asked in return was for Khalid to be kept safely out of it.

'This meeting is to take place in hotel? With others around? We would not be thanked for it. The Winter Palace is very respectable place,' the guard said.

Maria stuck to her plan. They had to be sure Welch wouldn't try anything if he began to suspect. It was to be the hotel or nowhere. If the officers did not agree, she was prepared to make an official complaint about Jeremy's arrest and what had happened to Graham.

Graham marvelled at her directness. She really a little gem, he thought. When all this was over, she would probably go on to become a most accomplished blackmailer – or maybe a spy.

The police officers drew close together and discussed. Afterwards, Graham said there had been something unnerving in their attitude: they seemed to be too confident and too willing. Maria thought he was being silly.

The main thing was they had agreed. 'The Welch Plot', as she had dubbed it, was on.

Thirteen

Welch had had as many male prostitutes as any of them had had clients. This one was special. Welch was even wondering whether he might be in love.

He crashed his belt against Abdul's quivering backside and waited for the mark to flare up: angry purple across the brown skin. It crossed four other such marks.

Abdul didn't make much more than a very low groan. His eyes were closed and the weight of his body was completely taken by the ropes which bound his wrists together, suspending his body from a ceiling support.

Welch experimented by whipping the leather across Abdul's back. The skin there was nearer the bone: it should hurt him more.

It did. Abdul, who had been taking all that was meted out to him, screamed loudly. He followed his cry by groaning in a resigned, hopeless way. His body became rigid and arched away from the assault; his eyes opened wide. When the first effect of the belt had died, it left him shaking visibly.

Welch ran his finger along the mark he'd created before standing back. He let the belt swish through the air a couple of times, noting with great pleasure how Abdul was now unable to prepare himself as he had before: he didn't know where the next blow would fall.

Abdul was still arching his back away from the belt, but this had the effect of making his unmarked shoulders more vulnerable. It was on this virgin skin Welch brought the next bruising crack of leather. Abdul screamed again.

Abdul was, for the first time since he had been tied there, trying to get free. He pulled at his bonds and wriggled about like a fish on a hook. Welch felt satisfaction: he knew how to tie the bastard up; Abdul had no chance of loosening the knots.

Welch watched his efforts while he stroked his cock. He was shirtless, but he'd retained his trousers for now. He drew close to Abdul and whispered soothing words in his ear. Abdul didn't understand what was being said, but the tone calmed him somewhat. He became still, but his breathing was sharp and irregular. Welch laid kind hands upon him: the light touch soothing the hurt he had inflicted.

He brought cold water and a sponge and squeezed the liquid over the burning wounds. Abdul relaxed properly. He must have thought it was finished. He must have thought he was going to have his own pleasure now. These natives had no idea at all.

He was a fine beast though. Welch liked the muscled ones and this one had muscles aplenty. He was in his mid-twenties and yet his square jaw and rugged face made him look about five years older. This did not mean he wasn't good-looking. In fact his looks were absolutely symmetrical and really very beautiful. It was his bone-structure that gave his face its male strength. His skin was silky, feminine. Like lots of lads his age, he had an excuse for hair on his upper lip. Many of these people found it incumbent upon them to grow a moustache long before they were capable of doing it properly.

Welch kissed it and then placed a kiss on Abdul's lips also.

Abdul tried to smile. He was still nervous, but he was falling for Welch's ploy.

Welch squeezed cooling water down the front of Abdul's chest. It ran down to his shaved groin. His cock, which had softened during the beating, was rising again. Its head – dark, almost black – emerged from the folds of his foreskin. His balls tightened into a small sac. He tried to indicate he wanted to be kissed once more. He thrust his chin forward to Welch and pursed his lips ridiculously. Welch scoffed.

He stood back and enjoyed the sight of Abdul twisting around as best he could, to see what was happening behind him. He was unable to see anything and eventually gave up. Welch was content to let him hang there for a while.

He left the room and went to lie down on his bed.

On the floor, where he'd thrown it, was a piece of crumpled paper. It was, in fact, a letter, written on hotel notepaper and purporting to be from a minor official at the British High Commission.

Welch sneered to himself. They must think he was stupid. Anthony Welch did not fear anybody. This was the code by which he lived his life and it was not a code he would renounce easily. So far, his dealings had been free of trouble. He had never had to defend himself. He had never had to answer for any of his many dubious activities. Now somebody was making trouble for him and that very fact enraged him beyond measure.

Of course it wouldn't be a problem, but it was irritating to think that somebody, somewhere, thought they could get the better of him. They certainly weren't going to succeed, but the very existence of such a person was galling.

He would meet them, as they had asked him to. He would listen to what they had to say and he would decide how to set about the task of crushing them into the ground. For this activity, he had set aside his plans for the day and, instead of screwing Abdul (definitely a more enjoyable use of his time), he lay brooding and building up a reservoir of resentment.

He released his prisoner an hour later: his sex drive had been ruined. By the time eight o'clock came, he was livid.

He splashed his face with cold water, changed into a tuxedo and neat bow tie, had a double whisky and ordered a carriage to take him to the Winter Palace Hotel. His face was set without expression. His lips were dry and, had it not been for telltale beads of sweat on his forehead, he would have shown no outward signs of his inner turmoil. His driver turned to him to ask a question and found his customer smiling to himself. The question went unheard. The driver cracked his whip and they sped on their way.

Welch hated hotels. He also hated the kind of person who frequented hotels. Most of them were stupid and all of them were hateful. They were people who supposed two or three weeks gave them an insight into a country. Even the ones who stayed for a length of time were no better: they never got their hands dirty as he had had to. He was worth ten of every one of them.

He dismissed his carriage and walked swiftly through the doors, across the lobby and into the main bar. His eyes took in every person in the room.

A couple in the corner glanced at him and turned their heads away. A young woman half smiled invitingly and then changed her mind. Two Arab men in the corner went on with their conversation. The man he had to meet was not yet present.

The waiter ushered him to a table and brought him a drink. His eyes followed the man's tightly clad behind. Black trousers and a pert arse: it was pleasing.

Percy mopped his wet brow once more. Jeremy gripped his shoulder in the manner of a second giving the boxer moral support before a fight. Percy grasped the younger man's hand and held it.

All his old misgivings had come back to him. What on earth had he agreed to? He had hinted more than once in an attempt to get out of it. After all, he'd reasoned, if he couldn't go through with it, the man would simply stay for one or two drinks and leave. He would think it a bluff, or a mistake. He would be none the wiser.

They had all assured him this was indeed the case. So why, now he wanted to avail himself of this escape route, did they not seem to be listening? Jeremy was a tower of strength. He could afford to be: he didn't have to go in there and face the man.

'I will probably blow the whole thing,' Percy said for the hundredth time. 'I am no actor. I have no idea what I'm supposed to say if he asks me for identification or traps me in some conversational way. He's not a shop assistant who's been caught with his fingers in the till.'

Jeremy sat down next to him and put an arm around his shoulder.

Percy was still not quite sure what to wear: he'd got no further than putting on his shirt and trousers. Would an official go about in a tie? Or maybe a bow tie? Would he wear a dark jacket or lighter one? Maybe if he wore his spectacles he wouldn't be so easily recognised if things went wrong. He wouldn't want to bump into Welch again.

Jeremy said yes to each of his sartorial suggestions, which didn't help in the slightest. Jeremy thought the spectacles were an excellent idea, but only if Percy felt comfortable with them. He was, in short, patronising him.

'I'm trembling from head to foot. A man from the High Commission is hardly likely to be a nervous wreck,' Percy complained. 'Give me a drink.'

The spirits didn't help to steady him, but their intoxicating effect gave him a little more courage than he'd had.

'It's time for you to go down,' Jeremy said. 'We can't leave him waiting for too long in case he gives up and leaves.'

'As I keep saying, that might be the very best thing. This sort of bravado is terribly foolhardy. What if one of the other guests says hello to me? It would be disaster.'

'Nobody knows what you do for a living. Stick to what we said: you're here in Luxor unofficially. You are posing as a tourist, but you are shortly to return to Cairo. The Governor General was shot last year; the Egyptian Prime Minister nearly assassinated. You are worried the insurrection is spreading from the capital. You have permission from your people to offer immunity to anyone who is prepared to help. It all sounds absolutely plausible. And, remember, the police are in the bar – Maria checked. They are there, in plain clothes.'

Percy nodded his head rapidly. 'Yes, yes, yes, but . . .'

Jeremy didn't give him chance to put any other objections forward. 'Just remember how proud we all are of what you're doing. You're absolutely safe. Nothing can happen in the hotel bar. When it's all over, we'll get you disgracefully drunk.'

Percy opted for a dark tie and a dark-blue blazer. He put on his spectacles, took them off again, replaced them and, gripping Jeremy's hand one last time, left the room.

'Mr Welch?'

The man who had spoken blinked at Welch. He was portly and effeminate; he was also a bag of nerves. Welch decided to have some fun. He affected what he thought was a disarming smile: he looked like a predator that has just spotted dinner.

'I must have been early,' he said. 'You people are always punctual and I've been waiting for a full ten minutes.'

'No, I'm late – telephone call,' the man gabbled. 'Very important telephone call. I had to attend to it immediately. London, you know.'

'Ah yes, London. You must miss it, posted out here in the middle of nowhere.'

'Might I order myself a drink?' the fat man said. 'I think we may as well do these things in a civilised way.'

★

Percy looked wildly around the room for a waiter. The two policemen were at the next table and they caught his eye. He inclined his head towards them in greeting. Welch noticed.

'Friends of yours?' he asked. He sounded as though he didn't believe this was entirely possible. Percy managed to order a gin and tonic. He offered the services of the waiter to his guest.

Welch ordered a whisky. 'I expect you're always having to deal with the wogs.'

'We prefer not to use that word,' Percy said primly. 'Of course one has to rub shoulders with all sorts in my job – High Commission in Cairo, don't you know? Very, very good job to have, believe me.'

The young couple across the room were evidently listening to their conversation. Welch wondered if they were in on this charade as well. He had better be slightly on his guard. The man opposite him was an idiot, but others might be present. The idiot might have been chosen to lull him into a false sense of security. Never underestimate the enemy.

'It has come to the attention of my people,' that same idiot was saying, 'that certain groups who have been active in Cairo over the past few years are planning to cause trouble elsewhere in Egypt. You understand what I mean by "certain groups", do you?'

Welch adopted a more comfortable position in his chair. 'Students, nationalists – it happens everywhere,' he replied. 'What are they about to do? Steal King Tut's treasures and hold us all to ransom?'

'Very possibly,' the fat man agreed. 'Yes, good point. The thing is, we have information which leads us to believe you may have had dealings with these people. Forgive me, I don't for one moment mean to imply –'

'But you are implying,' Welch snarled. 'You're saying I have dealings with people who want to steal the results of Mr Carter's splendid efforts. I think you ought to get your facts right.'

185

'I didn't say that. I mean . . . you know, you're quite safe. I have it from my people that anybody who is willing to help us will be sure to have any little misdemeanours of their own entirely overlooked. You see . . . I mean . . . This is very difficult. I'm very new at this job, you see. In fact, this is my first assignment. I do hope you'll forgive my inexpert approach.'

'Let me make it easy for you,' Welch said.

Their drinks had arrived. Welch sipped his and the fat man downed the gin as though it were water. His face flushed bright red. He was sweating profusely. His eyes were beginning to water. Welch thought of getting him drunk: it might be amusing. He ordered another 'for my friend'.

'That is most kind, and really quite unnecessary. I don't drink very much. Thank you.'

The alcohol was getting to Percy's head and confusing him. He appeared to be making some sort of headway, but he had no idea what to say now. He had proposed what he was supposed to, hadn't he? Wasn't the man now meant to confess everything? Weren't the police meant to sweep into action and it all be over? He tried to light a cigarette but the matches kept breaking. Welch leant over and offered his lighter.

'Thank you. I don't smoke very much. Just the odd one. I'm terribly sorry, would you like . . .?' Percy gabbled.

Welch laughed. Percy froze. Welch was supposed to be nervous. He was supposed to be threatened. He shouldn't be laughing. Maybe it would be better to call it quits.

'Evidently you cannot help us,' Percy began. 'I'm sorry to have wasted your time. I won't repeat any of our conversation to anybody. I will be discreet. You can count on that. Thank you.'

The 'thank you' was to the waiter who had given him another double gin. Percy reminded himself he must sip this one. He didn't want to blow everything. Then again, perhaps he had already done so.

'You want these,' Welch said. Incredibly, he reached inside his jacket and produced a piece of paper. 'These are all the names your people require. What are your terms for my handing them over?'

This was it. Percy turned to the two policemen who had been following what they said. They smiled at him. It was strange. Percy sensed all was not well. It couldn't be this easy.

'You will have full immunity. I just want the names and for you to . . . Well, to let us know all you have done which isn't – shall we say? – which isn't . . .'

'Lawful?' Welch suggested.

'Precisely.'

Percy leant back and took a mouthful of gin. If he had just sung *Don Giovanni* to a crowded La Scala, he couldn't have been more exhausted. Surely it was time for the others to finish this now?

Welch stood. Percy, not expecting this, scrabbled about and almost knocked his chair over as he also rose to his feet. They faced each other across the table. Welch was still relaxed; still smiling.

'Officers,' Welch said.

The two policemen responded immediately. Percy's heart missed a beat.

'Arrest this man,' Welch ordered. 'He is an impostor who is trying to blackmail me. You've heard his conversation. Now do your duty.'

The policemen were at Percy's side in seconds. They held on to his arms and began to pull him away. Maria and Graham, who had been sitting across the room, joined them and tried to get the officers off him. Welch stood motionless, totally sure of himself. The other guests stopped their conversations to watch this unexpected show.

'You won't get away with this,' Maria shouted to Welch.

He turned to her. Graham interposed himself between them and glared. Welch was supremely cool. The officers had the loudly protesting Percy at the door. He was hustled out of the room.

In the corridor, they ran into the middle of a group of uniformed, armed men. At their head was somebody Graham knew.

'My God!' he said. 'Ali! What are you doing here?'

Ali gave an order and several men rushed into the bar. Seconds later, Welch was being marched out, Percy was freed and the two policemen put safely under escort.

Percy was almost in tears. Maria hugged him and he all but collapsed. By now, Jeremy was hurrying down the corridor with total amazement written all over his face. Ali, no longer the bartender, but dressed in an expensive suit, turned to Graham.

'I did warn you, my friend,' he said. 'These things are not to be done by amateurs. I hope that, in saving this gentleman from his folly, we have not ruined our many months of work.'

'I don't believe this,' Graham said. 'You're . . .'

'Did you really think somebody with my qualifications would be working as a room waiter in a hotel?'

Maria came forward, demanding to know what was going on. Jeremy and Percy joined her. Other guests were emerging from the bar. Graham found himself to be the centre of attention.

Ali took his hand. 'I have no criticism of your courage,' he said. Then he added slyly, 'I just wish you would take everything in life more slowly.'

Graham blushed. Maria knew exactly what that meant. She took him by the arm and marched him off down the corridor.

Percy turned to Jeremy. 'I think something was said about getting me disgracefully drunk,' he said.

Jeremy linked his arm in Percy's. They pushed through the whispering group who blocked their way and went back into the bar.

Fourteen

Their time in Luxor was nearly at an end. Soon, the *Jewel of the Nile* would reappear like an old friend come to see them safely home. Graham, Maria and Jeremy had decided to spend the evening indulging in innocent fun.

'No, not like that, stupid! Like this.'

Maria demonstrated the steps once more and Graham clumsily tried to copy her. He tripped over and nearly fell. Maria stopped her own expert steps. The music continued for an elderly couple who were attempting a more sedate interpretation of the lively tune.

'I suppose I'll just have to find somebody else to dance with,' Maria said complainingly. 'Don't you even like the charleston? It's going to be the hottest dance of next season. I guarantee it.'

'Of course I like it,' Graham said, sounding very unconvincing. 'You know I can't dance. I never could.'

Freed from the dance floor, he joined Jeremy, who had been sitting watching. Percy was due to meet them, but he hadn't showed yet.

A familiar figure bustled into the room. The young men rose to their feet.

'Hello, Mrs Dryden. Do you fancy a drink?'

Mrs Dryden did not fancy a drink. She was still cross with them for not having included her in their thrilling adventure. This was something she had mentioned at least three times that day.

Mrs Dryden now regarded Percy as something of a hero. Apparently, so did every other guest in the entire hotel. Mrs Dryden had told them they must.

'That horrid man will be well out of harm's way now, and it's all thanks to Mr Gilbert. I think he's quite something.'

Graham and Jeremy refrained from defending their part in the proceedings. They were still ashamed of having botched things for Ali. He had been forgiving: they couldn't have known what his real purpose was. Even so, in the light of day, Maria's great idea seemed like it had never had the vaguest chance of success.

Maria had been joined on the dance floor by a tall, elegant female who was wearing trousers and a tie. She had her hair slicked back and wore stark, harsh make-up. She was extremely competent at the charleston.

'The way some of these women will dress!' Mrs Dryden said huffily. 'Really, I can scarcely tell she's female. I hope your dear fiancée would never take to those dreadful fashions, Graham. And this music! It has no real tune and it's so *insistent*!'

Jeremy grinned at Graham, who managed to keep a straight face.

'It looks like Percy has stood us up,' Graham said. 'And it looks like my little girl is going to be busy for the rest of the evening. Do you fancy a stroll, Oakland?'

Mrs Dryden extracted herself from their company. She was not one to stand in the way of young people having a good time, but the music was really *not* to her taste and she had better find somewhere a little quieter. She was stopped at the door by the arrival of a tall, military type of man in his early sixties. He bowed to her most charmingly and she preened. After a brief conversation, she was escorted back into the room.

'Well, what do you know?' Graham said. 'It looks like Mrs D has found herself a chap!'

The two young men stayed only a few moments longer.

The night air was fresh and there was a hint of a breeze. The river was a ribbon of ink with the mountains of the desert silhouetted behind it. The moon was perfect. They were alone on the road, just outside the town. Graham reached over and grasped Jeremy's hand.

'I'm going to miss you, Oakland,' he said. 'I expect we'll remember this week for the rest of our lives.'

'Ali says he doesn't know whether they'll be able to do much as far as Welch is concerned,' Jeremy said. 'They have no real evidence. Anyway, at least the two police officers have been dismissed. Welch won't be able to pay off the forces of law and order any more.'

'And he won't be able to operate so freely. He's going to know that his every step is being watched.'

They fell into silence for while; Graham broke it.

'I suppose Khalid is going to have to find somewhere else to live.'

Khalid had escaped any sort of punishment for his part in Welch's activities. When Welch had brought his name up, Ali had ignored it. His officers were told to do the same.

The mention of his name gave Jeremy a feeling of warmth tinged with melancholy. He had long since realised their love affair had really been a holiday romance. It couldn't last: Jeremy didn't really love Khalid; he desired him. It wasn't enough. Besides, he was English and Khalid was Egyptian. Where could they possibly build a life together?

'He's going to Cairo with the other two,' he explained to Graham. 'He reckons he can find a good job there. Mustapha and Ali are going to help him.'

'He'll be all right,' Graham said. He kissed Jeremy on the cheek.

Jeremy turned to him in the darkness and held him. They stayed in the embrace for a long time. Eventually, Jeremy pulled away. There were tears in his eyes.

'Khalid's off to the big city; you're going to be married; Ali and Mustapha are together; Percy's thinking of staying here with Ahmed. I'm the only one who's come out of this with nothing at all.'

Graham kissed him again. Pain swelled up inside Jeremy's heart. He knew who it was he really loved.

It wasn't going to help to say anything about it. Graham would go back to England and become a married man with a family. He would lose his good looks as home cooking and warm English beer took their toll on his body. They would meet in years to come and the attraction they'd held for one another would not be mentioned. Jeremy would be alone, or maybe he would be like Percy with some young wastrel in tow. It was all too horrible to think about.

Graham spoke: 'Should we go back to my room? Maria's going to be out of the way for ages. We could put the DO NOT DISTURB on the door!'

Jeremy agreed readily, but he wasn't sure it was a good idea. He thought it was time he started to harden himself to the inevitable.

Even Percy had advised him to find someone else. It was good advice, but where was he going to find another man? Nobody, but nobody, could take Graham's place.

They each stripped. The blinds were drawn and the room was too hot to bother with rolling about as they undressed each other. They folded their clothes neatly and put them in separate piles. Graham commented upon this: it was as though they were a couple who undressed in front of each other every night.

The solid bulk of his body was just perceptible in the darkness. Jeremy put his hand out to feel the hair on his chest. It was damp with sweat. Graham took Jeremy's hand and pressed it to himself. He reached around Jeremy's back and drew him close as he had done on the road. Now, without clothing, Jeremy could feel the maleness of him; he could smell the clean sweat. He pressed his groin against Graham's.

'Lie down,' he said at last.

Graham lay on the bed with Jeremy beside him. They cuddled for a while. Jeremy would have liked to have fallen asleep next to him but he didn't want to waste this opportunity of having sex. His dick was not going to grow soft by itself.

'My nipples are very sensitive,' Graham said suggestively.

Jeremy nibbled at his breast: sharp nips followed by careful, light bites. His tongue flicked over the one tip of flesh as he kept his fingers working on the opposite side.

'Oh, God! Yes, do that again. It's really beautiful.'

Graham's nipples were circled with light hair. Jeremy let it graze his tongue before licking it down, flat to the skin. He let his hand wander away from Graham's upper chest and down towards his penis. It was burning hot and massive. Beneath it, Graham's tight balls bristled with his pubic growth. Jeremy ran his fingers lightly through it, tickling, without touching the skin.

His fingers wandered further downward. Now, he had to leave off suckling Graham's nipple and, instead, he let his tongue form a trail of dampness down Graham's hard body.

Soon Jeremy smelt the erotic aroma of Graham's sex. He buried his face in his friend's pubic hair and licked. Graham's cock slapped against his face; he took the base of it in his mouth and massaged it with his lips.

'I'd rather you did something else –' Graham began.

Jeremy stopped him. 'I know Maria is able to suck you just as well as I can, but tonight I want to. Don't worry. You'll have me up your backside before the evening is out.'

He took the penis into his mouth in full. It made him choke, but he was determined. He sucked like he had never sucked before: as though he might drag the spunk from Graham's balls with effort. The sides of his mouth were hurting, but he was not going to let go until he absolutely had to.

When that time came, he brought his mouth up to the bulb of Graham's shaft and lapped around it.

He found Graham's piss hole with the tip of his tongue. It tasted salty, more pungent than the rest of his dick. Jeremy parted the tiny opening and pushed inside.

Graham was making satisfied movements with the rest of his body: rising up and down slowly.

'I want to piss,' Graham said suddenly. 'I want to piss.'

Jeremy felt his emotions surge. Graham knew about what had happened to him at the police station: he knew Jeremy had taken piss in his mouth before. Was he hinting? Would he be disgusted? Jeremy decided to risk it.

'Do it,' he said. 'Do it inside me. I want to drink it.'

Graham relaxed for a second or two. He brought his hand to the base of his cock and rubbed it briefly. There was a pause; it felt like ages but it couldn't have been more than a few seconds.

Then the hot spring of liquid gushed into Jeremy's mouth. He was drinking from Graham: he was actually drinking his piss! He swallowed it down: more and more of it. This was the most private thing they could ever do together. It was like a pact drawn in blood. It united them for ever.

The gush of urine subsided and eventually died. Jeremy licked the hole that had given it to him. He cleaned the throbbing shaft with his tongue. He laid his head against Graham's stomach and gripped his body tightly.

'Thank you,' he said.

'It was wonderful,' Graham replied. 'I wish I could do it again.'

They lay there, savouring the experience they had shared. Eventually Graham started to finger his cock again.

It had grown soft for a while. Now it was rising again. He raised his hips and carefully guided Jeremy's head downward.

Jeremy took his cock into his mouth once more, but Graham kept on pressing him further. He went to Graham's balls – further still. Eventually Jeremy's mouth was where Graham wanted it to be.

'You've drunk my piss,' he said. 'Now lick my arse.'

Jeremy did as he was told. He would have done anything that was asked of him. The hole was fiery and smelt vaguely of soap. Jeremy licked the hairs around it and then, as he had done with Graham's penis, he pushed his tongue inside.

Graham moaned softly. He reached down and lovingly stroked Jeremy's head. His legs were bent back over his body. Jeremy remembered seeing him clothed at the time of their first meeting. He had seemed so unobtainable then. Now, that same athletic, handsome male was naked, his arsehole absolutely available. His dick was right there where Jeremy could touch it. All that power, all that superb, rippling manliness, was his.

He had wetted the hole thoroughly and licked inside. Now he would fuck it.

Jeremy told Graham to turn over on the bed. He put cushions underneath his belly to raise him up. Graham was totally passive. He continued to moan softly, but he said nothing. Jeremy was soon poised to take him.

His dick speared the opening and then sank into Graham's anus. He pushed still further, feeling the familiar gripping and throbbing of soft muscle. He pulled out a little before shoving back again. Graham let out an involuntary cry.

'Fuck me! Please, fuck me!'

Jeremy was kneeling in between Graham's legs, which were spread apart for him. He placed his hands on each of Graham's hard buttocks, pushing with his fingers into the flesh. Then he felt his way up Graham's back, his own body folding over until he was lying fully on top of his lovely man.

Jeremy made short bucking movements with his hips. He was almost sadistic in his desire to take Graham's arse. He grunted as he fucked him, enjoying the yelps and groans coming from beneath him.

The vulnerable state Graham had placed himself in was akin to Jeremy's dreams of slavery. It was that other side of being male: the aching loveliness of the youth in chains; the pathos of captive manhood. Jeremy's movements quickened and became even more aggressive. He leant upward, away from Graham's back. He wondered, fleetingly, what that back would look like if it were striped with a lash.

It was this last thought that brought him through. Jeremy wished it could have lasted longer, but it was as forceful as he'd ever experienced. He pulled out as it splashed from his dick: shooting streams of semen, splashing over Graham's body.

When Jeremy was done, Graham rolled over. Jeremy took Graham's penis in his fist and wanked him violently. Graham lay there, biting his lip and concentrating, his eyes tightly closed. They opened all of a sudden and, with a look of complete wonder on his face, Graham half raised himself as his own come shot out of him.

His dick softened and he lay back again. Jeremy put his arms around him happily. They lay there in the dark together.

Percy was in the bar. There, Maria had informed him the chaps had gone off somewhere together. Percy had no wish to stay. He was still very aware of the looks the other guests gave him.

He didn't know whether he regretted what had happened or not. He was afraid of reprisals from Welch. This concern forced him to reconsider his previous ideas. He couldn't stay in Luxor if Welch was going to be living here.

The nice man, Ali (to whom Percy had declared undying gratitude), had told him he would be quite safe. In any case, Welch didn't blame Percy for what had happened. He thought him too nervous to have been acting for himself. Welch's real hatred was for Jeremy, whom he supposed to have masterminded the whole thing. This mattered very little: by the time the case was sorted, Jeremy would be safely back in London.

Percy found Ahmed at the calash rank and suggested they go for a drive.

'What would you most like to do with your life if you had the money?' Percy asked his friend.

Ahmed didn't have any idea.

'There must be something. Think. It's important.'

'I never have money,' Ahmed replied philosophically. 'What good of thinking?'

'I have money,' Percy said. He was about to seize the moment and he felt curiously excited. He was going to do something that was totally spontaneous. He refused to think it through. It had to be now or never.

'I would like house in Alexandria,' Ahmed said. 'Is where I came from. I would like to go back there. But I do not think this happens.'

It seemed the perfect solution. Percy told him to stop the calash. Once the vehicle was steady, with some difficulty, he climbed up beside Ahmed on the driver's seat.

'This not place for you,' Ahmed said. 'This is where Arab people sit.'

Percy patted his knee. 'From now on,' he said, 'I intend to be Arab person myself. We will go to Alexandria before the week is out and look at some places. I will buy you your house and, if you'll have me, I will live there with you.'

He wasn't sure of Ahmed's reaction for there had been no change in his facial expression.

'I hope you like the idea,' Percy said. 'I quite understand if you would rather not. I know I am an elderly man and you have all your life before you. I know –'

Ahmed's face broke into a wide grin. He hollered long and loud. Even the horse whinnied as though she too was overjoyed. 'I like this very much,' he said at last. 'I will love you for always. You are my man and I am yours. Yes?'

'Yes,' Percy agreed. He linked his arm in Ahmed's and, with a crack of the whip, the calash sped off.

Ali was removing his things from the locker below stairs that had been his during his period of employment. One of the hotel's managers was standing nearby.

The manager was grim faced. Their establishment was a respectable one: they did not take kindly to being subjected to the kind of scene they had witnessed the previous evening.

Ali had apologised of course, but he cared little for what they thought of him. He was going back to Cairo and Mustapha was going with him. That was all that mattered.

The two of them would have to look after Khalid. He was depressed because his English friend, Jeremy, had deserted him. Ali had tried to cheer him, but it hadn't worked. Such love was available at any time, he'd said, but it could not last. Young Englishmen did not tend to bind their lives with the likes of Khalid.

In Cairo, Khalid would have a job and opportunity enough to meet someone of his own kind. He would find his man, but his man was not to be Jeremy Oakland.

Ali had packed his bag. He extended his hand to the manager, who refused to take it.

'I am sorry this excellent hotel was the scene of such disturbance,' Ali said. 'I am sorry, too, I was unable to let any of you know the real reason for my work here. I am sure you will agree that your business depends on our government, who encourage the tourists. Our government depends on the British. We must all be vigilant or Egypt will not be a place for hotels.'

The manager spat on the floor. He glared at Ali and ushered him out.

Mrs Dryden was just leaving the bar as they passed. She was on the arm of a suave-looking gentleman in his sixties. She apprehended Ali immediately.

'Do allow me to introduce you. You're the gentleman from

Cairo, are you not? This is Colonel Dennis. He has just been telling me thrilling tales about the war. Now we're off to dinner.' She turned to her companion. 'This is the brave gentleman who arrested the gunrunner last night. He's been working undercover. It's so exciting.'

The colonel shook Ali's hand. He was good-looking in an old-fashioned sort of way. He seemed very protective of Mrs Dryden: he kept her close to him as though she might run away at any second.

'I am leaving,' Ali said. 'It has been a pleasure.'

Maria and her new friend appeared behind them. She winked at Ali and waved. Her friend was holding her by the hand: openly affectionate. This was a woman who was to be married to a man who bedded other men.

Ali sighed: these English people were so strange. He would never be able to make them out.

The *Jewel of the Nile* was once again moored near the Winter Palace. Percy excepted, the English friends were preparing to leave. It was early morning and they'd just breakfasted. The quartet in the lounge had played *Greensleeves* in their honour. Maria said they were off-key, but the gesture was sincere.

Jeremy still had the journey to look forward to: he still had some time during which he could share Graham's company. It wouldn't be the same: Maria would be always there. Her girlfriend was not travelling with them. She would be in Luxor for another week and then she was going home to New York.

Maria never mentioned the woman. When asked by Graham, she tapped him on the nose with her fan and told him to 'mind his own'. Mrs Dryden, on the other hand, was boasting of her newly found friendship with Colonel Dennis wherever and whenever she could.

'Who would have thought it?' Graham commented. 'Two of our group have found true love and both of them are oldies. What does that tell us, Oakland?'

He was being deliberately formal. It may have been he was afraid of his emotions; it may have been he was a practical sort who knew it would be useless to love a man when one is engaged to be married to a woman. Jeremy wondered if the two of them would continue to have extramarital affairs after they'd tied the knot. He had thought about suggesting a long-term arrangement: Maria and her girlfriend and Graham and himself. They wouldn't have to be jealous of each other and everybody would be happy.

It wasn't practical of course: Jeremy couldn't bear the thought of taking second place in Graham's affections. Besides, he didn't for a moment think Graham would want him around on a permanent basis.

Percy was tearful at the landing stage. He made each of them promise to come and visit him. Ahmed stood some little way apart, watching and smiling. Graham waved to him but he was not looking at them: his eyes were fixed on Percy.

'I'll put some money into your account,' Percy whispered to Jeremy. 'I know things must be difficult. Do try and do something with your life. When you get back to London, you must find yourself a job which you'll enjoy. You really can't continue to drift around the world as you have been doing.'

His tone changed; he gripped Jeremy's hand.

'I do so hope you find somebody to be close to,' he said. 'It's the most wonderful feeling in the world. Be happy, my dear fellow.'

Jeremy was as choked as Percy. He resolved to do everything in his power to make Percy proud of him. He would find a job and make good. In a few years, he would return to Egypt, or Percy would visit London, and Jeremy would have something to show for himself.

Later, in his cabin, Jeremy looked once more on the picture of Ramses. He closed his eyes and his thoughts drifted.

The slave market at Thebes: Jeremy was one of many near-naked men penned into a small courtyard. They were chained hand to hand and foot to foot: one man linked to another by heavy iron. Jeremy dared to look around him.

Percy was sitting on a throne some way off. He was dressed richly and was discussing with Ahmed, who stood beside him, which slave he might buy. Jeremy felt shame for his wretched position. He saw Maria there, fleetingly. She was now a wealthy Egyptian maiden and in the company of an androgynous person who doted upon her.

The other slaves, Jeremy thought. I must look at the other slaves.

In reality, he was still wearing his underpants, but was otherwise naked. He imagined himself in a loincloth and tried to achieve a real sense of iron fetters round his limbs. The faces of the men to be sold were blurry, apart from one: it was Graham.

Graham was right next to Jeremy now. His back was striped with the marks of a whip. His face was calm but sorrowful. He tried to hold Jeremy's hand but received a crack across his shoulders from the slavemaster for his trouble.

Welch entered the market. Jeremy didn't want to think about him and tried to blot him out of his mind, but he refused to go. He was splendidly arrayed and seemingly all-powerful. He came very close and barked an order to the slavemaster.

The man pushed Graham forward for Welch's inspection. Graham stood with his head bowed while Welch felt various parts of his body. After some moments, the slavemaster was told to remove Graham's loincloth. It was taken from him, leaving him naked before his enemy.

'Have that one fuck his arse,' Welch said. He was pointing at Jeremy.

The scene swam around Jeremy's head. Snatches of it focussed and then disappeared. He remembered details of his sex with Graham: the piss in his mouth; the wonderful satisfaction of being inside him, holding him, kissing him. He wanted it back.

He pulled down his underwear and tried his hardest to keep Graham's face in his mind as he tossed himself off. Welch faded into the background of his fantasy, but he didn't disappear completely. Jeremy thought of Graham's arse. He had been near to that arse; he had licked it. He tried to recollect the taste and the smell. He rolled over and rubbed his penis against the mattress. He wanted Graham to be underneath him. He hugged his pillow and tried to make his imagination stronger.

Maria came back into his mind. He didn't want her there, but she stayed. She was still with her lesbian friend and she now had Graham at her feet. Welch was no longer Graham's owner: Maria was.

Graham was naked, his hands bound behind him with rope, the end of which Maria held like a lead. He had a collar round his neck. He knelt with bowed head. He had been tamed: robbed of his masculinity. Jeremy saw his face and ached with emotion at the lost look it held. He wanted to protect his friend, but all he could do was watch as Graham was eventually led away.

He kept that picture in his head while he masturbated. He was trying to see what lay behind his own feelings. What was it about rippling virility that he always wanted to see conquered in some way? He remembered again fucking Graham; remembered the pleasing noises the man had made as his arse was taken by Jeremy's cock. Jeremy tightened his fist to make it feel similar to Graham's gut. The surge came and went.

Jeremy still felt empty.

Up on deck, the tourists were about to take their last look at Luxor. Percy and Ahmed were on the bank, waving. Jeremy joined Graham and Maria. It was Maria's turn to be tearful. Graham was patting her on the back and murmuring words of comfort.

'There, there, old girl. Soon have you settled.'

He winked at Jeremy, who was at a loss to equate this

strapping, confident young fellow with the naked slave he had just imagined. All Graham's heterosexual prowess was in force now. He was no longer Jeremy's lover: he was just a friend.

Jeremy felt his own tears falling. He pretended he'd got something in his eye, but Graham knew better. The steamer began to move out into the river. A cheer went up from the crowd. Luxor gradually disappeared from view.

Fifteen

It was 1927. London was impossibly dull. The drizzle swept down the streets, covering the bustling pedestrians with fine, wet, glistening rain. It formed a silver coating on the wool of Jeremy's sleeve. Winter was threatening to descend early upon the city.

Jeremy left his office and pulled his hat down over his brow. His overcoat was new, a present to himself. He was grateful for it.

He had three hours before he was due in St James's to meet some friends. He didn't have time to go all the way back to Bayswater and he had no desire to do anything very productive.

Several colleagues passed him. They wished him a good weekend. Though he tried to sound cheerful, Jeremy couldn't match their enthusiasm for five o'clock, Friday. He didn't know what to do with himself when he wasn't at work. From being an idler, he'd become an industrious employee. He enjoyed being with Mason and Shaw's. In another year or so he would be a manager. Property was a good enough line to be in. It payed a wage.

But he hated living alone; 'splendid isolation', his secretary called it. She was always attempting to play matchmaker for him. She said bachelors were never something she had been able to tolerate, not on any account. None of the young ladies she sent his way ever got more than a polite conversation out of Jeremy. His secretary had once asked him if he was queer and he had denied it.

Jeremy had not been abroad since Egypt. That seemed such a long time ago. The slow foxtrot had replaced the charleston as the fashionable dance. Jeremy still couldn't master the steps to either.

He was reading Hemingway. He thought the book on his desk would make him seem more masculine but it wasn't really to his taste. The latest novel at least had an ironic title: *Men Without Women.*

He turned a corner into the Charing Cross Road. Perhaps he would sit in a café for a while. None of them looked inviting and it was beginning to pour.

He raised his umbrella and wandered down to Tottenham Court Road, quickening his pace. It was too wet to walk the streets: that much was certain.

Percy wrote often. Jeremy had received a letter that very morning. Percy was well, pleased with Jeremy's progress in business. Ahmed sent his fondest regards. Would Jeremy visit soon?

Maybe he would. Now was the perfect time to escape Britain for the sun. Percy would make him welcome and he could find some relief from his loneliness in the arms of another Khalid.

It was this thought that subconsciously guided his steps towards the British Museum. He often went there to kill time. He would stand and stare at the Egyptian relics in their glass cabinets. He saw them as being rather forlorn: the mummies torn from their graves and shipped across the world to be exhibited as curiosities. Had he existed, this would have been the fate of Jeremy's imaginary Pharaoh. It was sad, but sadness was a state Jeremy identified with. It made unrequited love romantic rather than foolish.

He sat down opposite the exhibits and closed his eyes. He really had no wish to dine with the crowd that evening. They, too, always asked him about his love life. It was a subject that greatly amused them. They were always hinting about a girl he'd been seen with in the street, or the young woman who sat next to him on the underground most mornings, or even his secretary – all were suspect romances.

He'd often thought of telling them the truth, but such a revelation threatened his career. Besides which, homosexuality was illegal. If it got out and he was arrested, he couldn't expect the London bobbies to let him go after a good fuck and a backhander.

He might have been there half an hour or so. He wasn't sure. He felt parched and was about to go for a cup of coffee. He rose and, as he opened the door, nearly collided with someone who was entering.

'I'm so sorry,' Jeremy said. 'I didn't see you.'

Then he recognised the person. It was Maria's lesbian companion from all that time ago at the Winter Palace.

She was still dressed in masculine clothes, a trilby hat jauntily on top of her black hair. She was wearing a suit and tie and had patent-leather shoes. She could easily have passed for a young man.

'It's quite all right,' she said. She was American and evidently was not about to have any of the usual British thing about swapping profuse apologies. Normally, Jeremy would have thought her rude.

'I say,' he said. 'We've met before. A long time ago, in Luxor.'

'Yeah?' she said. She wasn't interested.

'I was friendly with Graham Etherington and his fiancée. I suppose she's his wife now. She was your friend, Maria.'

'She still is my friend,' the woman said. 'I'm Vanessa. I'm Maria's partner and we're supposed to be meeting here. She's late.'

Partner? Did that mean what Jeremy thought it meant? He ventured further, despite the woman's obvious reluctance to talk.

'Did Maria and Graham get married? I would so much like to see them again. Perhaps I could wait with you.'

The woman turned to him with a look of contempt. 'You British are so goddamn polite all the time,' she said. 'No, they did not get married. Maria is with me. It's all blown over with Mr Etherington. I presume it's him you really want to see, so, no – don't wait with me. But I will give you his address.'

He was living in Bloomsbury, not very far away.

Jeremy was reeling from his encounter in the museum. What Maria saw in that woman he had no idea, but that was scarcely important. He hoped again and again Graham would be at home. Jeremy was impossibly nervous. He was actually going to see Graham again.

He had realised Graham would eventually return to London, but he had never made any attempt to find him. He didn't think he could possibly cope with seeing him settled, maybe with a child. Now he knew that wasn't the case, he couldn't wait.

On the way, he thought of other nightmares. Graham might be with another woman, or even another man. Somebody as good-looking as he would not have been likely to stay single.

He might have forgotten Jeremy. No, that wasn't possible. Jeremy resolved to be cool headed and see how the land lay before he got his hopes up.

He had reached the street, counted the houses and eventually found himself standing on the step of a neat terrace with a green door and brass door knocker.

A maid answered. Mr Etherington was in his study and she would go and tell him. Jeremy sat where he had been told and took in the rich furnishings and the book-lined walls. Graham had done well for himself. That much, at least, was predictable.

'Jeremy. I don't believe it! Is it really you?'

Graham was standing inside the doorway. He was no different to look at: maybe his face was a tiny bit older, but he still had that floppy black hair and athletic frame. He was smoking a pipe and grinning foolishly. His pleasure at seeing his old friend was totally obvious.

'I ran into Maria's Vanessa at the British Museum,' Jeremy explained. 'She brought me up to date. Well, she did as far as she and Maria are concerned. I just had to come and see you.'

'I'm glad you did,' Graham said. He came and sat on the arm of Jeremy's chair. 'You look prosperous. Are things going well?'

Jeremy gave a hurried account of his career. Graham listened, smoking the pipe and giving encouraging little interjections. His hand drifted on to Jeremy's shoulder. It was like an electric charge going through him. Jeremy let it stay there, feeling the pressure of it intensify. They had both been silent for some minutes.

'It wasn't Maria who broke it off,' Graham said at last. 'It was me. I couldn't lie to myself any more. She wasn't at all upset. She said she'd known all along. What the hell! She's happy.'

'Are you happy?' Jeremy asked. 'I mean, are you . . .?' His voice trailed off.

'Am I with some other little woman? No, I'm certainly not. I told you. I couldn't lie to myself any longer. I have thought about seeking out a friend to share my days with, but . . .'

He went into his own thoughts for a while. Jeremy waited.

'Oh God! It is so good to see you!' Graham said. He rolled off the arm of the chair and embraced Jeremy properly. They held each other as they had before. Jeremy closed his eyes and breathed deeply.

'You will stay for the evening?' Graham said eventually.

Jeremy thought of his friends waiting at the restaurant. They would no doubt accuse him of having found a girl at last. They would know something of the sort had happened: he would never be able to disguise the fact. He didn't care. Let them think what they would. Let them wait all evening and tease him mercilessly for having stood them up. He was back with the man he loved.

'I'm free for the whole weekend,' he said.

Graham kissed him. Jeremy had no doubts any more. He was where he was meant to be. He remembered hot sun, the Nile, the tombs, the temples. Egypt had finally given him the man he had always dreamt of.

'Come along,' Graham said, rising and keeping hold of Jeremy's hand. 'It's way past our bedtime.'

IDOL NEW BOOKS

Also published:

THE KING'S MEN
Christian Fall

Ned Medcombe, spoilt son of an Oxfordshire landowner, has always remembered his first love: the beautiful, golden-haired Lewis. But seventeenth-century England forbids such a love and Ned is content to indulge his domineering passions with the willing members of the local community, including the submissive parish cleric. Until the Civil War changes his world, and he is forced to pursue his desires as a soldier in Cromwell's army – while his long-lost lover fights as one of the King's men.

ISBN 0 352 33207 7

THE VELVET WEB
Christopher Summerisle

The year is 1889. Daniel McGaw arrives at Calverdale, a centre of academic excellence buried deep in the English countryside. But this is like no other college. As Daniel explores, he discovers secret passages in the grounds and forbidden texts in the library. The young male students, isolated from the outside world, share a darkly bizarre brotherhood based on the most extreme forms of erotic expression. It isn't long before Daniel is initiated into the rites that bind together the youths of Calverdale in a web of desire.

ISBN 0 352 33208 5

CHAINS OF DECEIT
Paul C. Alexander

Journalist Nathan Dexter's life is turned around when he meets a young student called Scott – someone who offers him the relationship for which he's been searching. Then Nathan's best friend goes missing, and Nathan uncovers evidence that he has become the victim of a slavery ring which is rumoured to be operating out of London's leather scene. To rescue their friend and expose the perverted slave trade, Nathan and Scott must go undercover, risking detection and betrayal at every turn.

ISBN 0 352 33206 9

DARK RIDER
Jack Gordon

While the rulers of a remote Scottish island play bizarre games of sexual dominance with the Argentinian Angelo, his friend Robert – consumed with jealous longing for his coffee-skinned companion – assuages his desires with the willing locals.

ISBN 0 352 33243 3

CONQUISTADOR
Jeff Hunter

It is the dying days of the Aztec empire. Axaten and Quetzel are members of the Stable, servants of the Sun Prince chosen for their bravery and beauty. But it is not just an honour and a duty to join this society, it is also the ultimate sexual achievement. Until the arrival of Juan, a young Spanish conquistador, sets the men of the Stable on an adventure of bondage, lust and deception.

ISBN 0 352 33244 1

TO SERVE TWO MASTERS
Gordon Neale

In the isolated land of Ilyria men are bought and sold as slaves. Rock, brought up to expect to be treated as mere 'livestock', yearns to be sold to the beautiful youth Dorian. But Dorian's brother is as cruel as he is handsome, and if Rock is bought by one brother he will be owned by both.

ISBN 0 352 33245 X

CUSTOMS OF THE COUNTRY
Rupert Thomas

James Cardell has left school and is looking forward to going to Oxford. That summer of 1924, however, he will spend with his cousins in a tiny village in rural Kent. There he finds he can pursue his love of painting – and begin to explore his obsession with the male physique.

ISBN 0 352 33246 8

DOCTOR REYNARD'S EXPERIMENT
Robert Black

A dark world of secret brothels, dungeons and sexual cabarets exists behind the respectable facade of Victorian London. The degenerate Lord Spearman introduces Dr Richard Reynard, dashing bachelor, to this hidden world. And Walter Starling, the doctor's new footman, finds himself torn between affection for his master and the attractions of London's underworld.

ISBN 0 352 33252 2

CODE OF SUBMISSION
Paul C. Alexander

Having uncovered and defeated a slave ring operating in London's leather scene, journalist Nathan Dexter had hoped to enjoy a peaceful life with his boyfriend Scott. But when it becomes clear that the perverted slave trade has started again, Nathan has no choice but to travel across Europe and America in his bid to stop it.

ISBN 0 352 33272 7

SLAVES OF TARNE
Gordon Neale

Pascal willingly follows the mysterious and alluring Casper to Tarne, a community of men enslaved to men. Tarne is everything that Pascal has ever fantasised about, but he begins to sense a sinister aspect to Casper's magnetism. Pascal has to choose between the pleasures of submission and acting to save the people he loves.

ISBN 0 352 33273 5

ROUGH WITH THE SMOOTH
Dominic Arrow

Amid the crime, violence and unemployment of North London, the young men who attend Jonathan Carey's drop-in centre have few choices. One of the young men, Stewart, finds himself torn between the increasingly intimate horseplay of his fellows and the perverse allure of the criminal underworld. Can Jonathan save Stewart from the bullies on the streets and behind bars?

ISBN 0 352 33292 1

CONVICT CHAINS
Philip Markham

Peter Warren, printer's apprentice in the London of the 1830s, discovers his sexuality and taste for submission at the hands of Richard Barkworth. Thus begins a downward spiral of degradation, of which transportation to the Australian colonies is only the beginning.

ISBN 0 352 33300 6

SHAME
Raydon Pelham

On holiday in West Hollywood, Briton Martyn Townsend meets and falls in love with the daredevil Scott. When Scott is murdered, Martyn's hunt for the truth and for the mysterious Peter, Scott's ex-lover, leads him to the clubs of London and Ibiza.

ISBN 0 352 33302 2

HMS SUBMISSION
Jack Gordon

Under the command of Josiah Rock, a man of cruel passions, HMS *Impregnable* sails to the colonies. Christopher, Viscount Fitzgibbons, is a reluctant officer; Mick Savage part of the wretched cargo. They are on a voyage to a shared destiny.

ISBN 0 352 33301 4

THE FINAL RESTRAINT
Paul C. Alexander

The trilogy that began with *Chains of Deceit* and continued in *Code of Submission* concludes in this powerfully erotic novel. From the dungeons and saunas of London to the deepest jungles of South America, Nathan Dexter is forced to play the ultimate chess game with evil Adrian Delancey – with people as sexual pawns.

ISBN 0 352 33303 0

HARD TIME
Robert Black

HMP Cairncrow prison is a corrupt and cruel institution, but also a sexual minefield. Three new inmates must find their niche in this brutish environment – as sexual victims or lovers, predators or protectors. This is the story of how they find love, sex and redemption behind prison walls.

ISBN 0 352 33304 9

ROMAN GAMES
Tasker Dean

When Sam visits the island of Skate, he is taught how to submit to other men; acting out an elaborate fantasy in which young men become wrestling slaves – just as in ancient Rome. He must learn how to win and how to lose. Indeed, if he is to have his beautiful prize – the wrestler, Robert – he must learn how the romans played their games.

ISBN 0 352 33322 7

VENETIAN TRADE
Richard Davis

From the deck of the ship which carries him into Venice, Rob Weaver catches his frist glimpse of a beautiful but corrupt city where the dark alleys and misty canals hide debauchery and decadence. Here, he must learn to survive among men who would make him a plaything and a slave.

ISBN 0 352 33323 5

WE NEED YOUR HELP . . .

to plan the future of Idol books –

Yours are the only opinions that matter. Idol is a new and exciting venture: the first British series of books devoted to homoerotic fiction for men.

We're going to do our best to provide the sexiest, best–written books you can buy. And we'd like you to help in these early stages. Tell us what you want to read. There's a freepost address for your filled–in questionnaires, so you won't even need to buy a stamp.

THE IDOL QUESTIONNAIRE

SECTION ONE: ABOUT YOU

1.1   Sex (*we presume you are male, but just in case*)
      Are you?
      Male   ☐
      Female   ☐

1.2   Age
      under 21   ☐   21–30   ☐
      31–40   ☐   41–50   ☐
      51–60   ☐   over 60   ☐

1.3   At what age did you leave full-time education?
      still in education   ☐   16 or younger   ☐
      17–19   ☐   20 or older   ☐

1.4   Occupation _____

1.5   Annual household income _____

1.6　We are perfectly happy for you to remain anonymous; but if you would like us to send you a free booklist of Idol books, please insert your name and address

_____

_____

_____

_____

SECTION TWO: ABOUT BUYING IDOL BOOKS

2.1　Where did you get this copy of *The Love of Old Egypt*?
  Bought at chain book shop ☐
  Bought at independent book shop ☐
  Bought at supermarket ☐
  Bought at book exchange or used book shop ☐
  I borrowed it/found it ☐
  My partner bought it ☐

2.2　How did you find out about Idol books?
  I saw them in a shop ☐
  I saw them advertised in a magazine ☐
  I read about them in _____
  Other _____

2.3　Please tick the following statements you agree with:
  I would be less embarrassed about buying Idol
  books if the cover pictures were less explicit ☐
  I think that in general the pictures on Idol
  books are about right ☐
  I think Idol cover pictures should be as
  explicit as possible ☐

2.4　Would you read an Idol book in a public place – on a train for instance?
  Yes ☐　　　　No ☐

SECTION THREE: ABOUT THIS IDOL BOOK

3.1　Do you think the sex content in this book is:
  Too much ☐　　About right ☐
  Not enough ☐

3.2 Do you think the writing style in this book is:

      Too unreal/escapist ☐ About right ☐

      Too down to earth ☐

3.3 Do you think the story in this book is:

      Too complicated ☐ About right ☐

      Too boring/simple ☐

3.4 Do you think the cover of this book is:

      Too explicit ☐ About right ☐

      Not explicit enough ☐

Here's a space for any other comments:

SECTION FOUR: ABOUT OTHER IDOL BOOKS

4.1 How many Idol books have you read?

4.2 If more than one, which one did you prefer?

    _____

4.3 Why?

SECTION FIVE: ABOUT YOUR IDEAL EROTIC NOVEL

We want to publish the books you want to read – so this is your chance to tell us exactly what your ideal erotic novel would be like.

5.1 Using a scale of 1 to 5 (1 = no interest at all, 5 = your ideal), please rate the following possible settings for an erotic novel:

      Roman / Ancient World ☐

      Medieval / barbarian / sword 'n' sorcery ☐

      Renaissance / Elizabethan / Restoration ☐

      Victorian / Edwardian ☐

      1920s & 1930s ☐

      Present day ☐

      Future / Science Fiction ☐

5.2 Using the same scale of 1 to 5, please rate the following themes you may find in an erotic novel:

Bondage / fetishism ☐
Romantic love ☐
SM / corporal punishment ☐
Bisexuality ☐
Group sex ☐
Watersports ☐
Rent / sex for money ☐

5.3 Using the same scale of 1 to 5, please rate the following styles in which an erotic novel could be written:

Gritty realism, down to earth ☐
Set in real life but ignoring its more unpleasant aspects ☐
Escapist fantasy, but just about believable ☐
Complete escapism, totally unrealistic ☐

5.4 In a book that features power differentials or sexual initiation, would you prefer the writing to be from the viewpoint of the dominant / experienced or submissive / inexperienced characters:

Dominant / Experienced ☐
Submissive / Inexperienced ☐
Both ☐

5.5 We'd like to include characters close to your ideal lover. What characteristics would your ideal lover have? Tick as many as you want:

Dominant	☐	Caring	☐
Slim	☐	Rugged	☐
Extroverted	☐	Romantic	☐
Bisexual	☐	Old	☐
Working Class	☐	Intellectual	☐
Introverted	☐	Professional	☐
Submissive	☐	Pervy	☐
Cruel	☐	Ordinary	☐
Young	☐	Muscular	☐
Naïve	☐		

Anything else? _____

5.6 Is there one particular setting or subject matter that your ideal erotic novel would contain:

_____

5.7 As you'll have seen, we include safe-sex guidelines in every book. However, while our policy is always to show safe sex in stories with contemporary settings, we don't insist on safe-sex practices in stories with historical settings because it would be anachronistic. What, if anything, would you change about this policy?

_____

_____

SECTION SIX: LAST WORDS

6.1 What do you like best about Idol books?

_____

6.2 What do you most dislike about Idol books?

_____

6.3 In what way, if any, would you like to change Idol covers?

_____

6.4 Here's a space for any other comments:

_____

_____

_____

_____

Thanks for completing this questionnaire. Now either tear it out, or photocopy it, then put it in an envelope and send it to:

Idol
FREEPOST
London
W10 5BR

You don't need a stamp if you're in the UK, but you'll need one if you're posting from overseas.